Demon Memories

Pamela K. Kinney

This is a work of fiction.

Names, characters, businesses, places, events, or incidents are either the products of the author's imagination or used in a fictitious manner. Any resemblance to actual person, living or dead, or actual events is purely coincidental.

Demon Memories

No one who, like me, conjures up the most evil of those half-tamed demons that inhabit the human beast, and seeks to wrestle with them, can expect to come through the struggle unscathed.
~Sigmund Freud

Prologue-Harper

"Look, this will be fun. It'll just be like a ride at the amusement park."

I shook my head. "You think calling up a demon's exciting? We get caught inside this place, and you see how scary the inside of Juvie is. I heard Hell is kindergarten compared to that place."

Barbie juggled the black candle, the grill lighter she'd stolen from her dad's shed, and a box of sea salt, as she handed over a package of bloody chicken parts to another friend, Jazz. "Hey, it's not like summoning a demon hasn't happened in Moon Ridge before. Remember the town's legend about witches who settled here? And we know witches like to call up demons." Her eyes flashed with impatience as she called out behind us. "Joanie?"

I grumbled under my breath about stupid myths and those who believed in them.

A petite girl with a full figure wobbled out of the darkness, barely holding a big, fat book that blocked her face and the upper half of her body. She tripped over something, and Barbie dumped the stuff she held onto the drying grass and saved the book before it fell. She glared at Joanie, hissing, "Hey, this book is front and center to what we plan to do tonight!"

Joanie blushed and took it back. "Sorry, but the book's heavy."

Crack. Jazz used the baseball bat she held and slammed a home run with it against the window; glass shattered.

Jazz grinned and pumped her fist in the night air. "Yes! We have a way inside." She pulled her sleeve over her hand and brushed pieces of the glass into the abandoned house before she propped the baseball bat against the exterior of the building. "Careful now, there's glass on the floor inside." She crawled over the ledge and toppled inside. The crunch of glass beneath her combat boots came from inside.

I gave the book's title, *Demon Summoning for Dummies,* a cursory glance when my flashlight's beam hit the front cover. I still couldn't believe someone wrote it for the *Dummies* series of books. Like people needed a how-to book for summing demons like they needed how-to book to work a computer or build a shed.

Jazz and I helped Joanie and the hefty tome over the window ledge.

Joanie cried out. "Ouch. I think a splinter of wood jabbed my butt!"

"Shush," hissed Barbie. "You want to wake the neighbors?"

Barbie handed the objects she carried to Jazz, then proved why she excelled in gymnastics, using her arms to lift herself up and over the ledge, doing a flip over into the place.

I stared at the window and wondered for the umpteenth time why I'd agreed to do this. I've never done anything half-brained like this before. Guilt plagued me as the memory of my mother kissing me goodnight before I went upstairs to bed flashed in my mind. An hour later, after she fell asleep, I'd slipped out of the house to join my waiting friends.

Sensible Harper Doyle, who never went to the extreme, dull as oatmeal without sugar and milk. No doubt, tasteless, too. I'd agreed to Barbie's scheme a few days ago at lunchtime, to prove I could be wild as a half-tamed horse. Now that I was here, the thought had crossed my mind how stupid this harebrained scheme truly was. Me, too, for ever agreeing to do it.

Barbie had gotten some notion she was the descendant of one of the witches in the legend that was told about Moon Ridge's beginning. Using a necklace that she knew Joanie loved as bribery, she convinced the girl to steal a book of spells she'd discovered in the Moon Ridge Library. Joanie volunteered at the library after school, and Barbie felt assured the other girl could sneak it out past the sharp eyes of the librarian, Mrs. Potts.

"It's nothing but a legend," I whispered to myself.

Barbie, her arms crossed, flashed me an impatient look as she leaned out from the window. She'd heard me. "It has to be real. Otherwise, it would have ended up as a story in one of those ghost books by that Virginia author. What's his name? L. B. Tilyer? Naylor? Whatever. It did happen. Mother said one of the witches happened to be an ancestor, Abigail Proze."

As if her mother knew real history. Which she didn't.

"It's L. B Taylor," I said.

Barbie blinked. "What?"

"The author of those ghost books."

Amusement lit her eyes and she twisted her lips. "Whatever. Coming, Doyle?" She melted back into the darkness.

I pulled myself up and swung my legs over the sill. Odors of new wood and fresh paint assaulted my nose. This place was the last house built in a new subdivision.

Joanie kneeled and drew a large circle with black chalk. Jazz followed on her heels, pouring sea salt along the line. Barbie placed the black candle on the floor outside of the circle and lit it. The flame cast dancing shadows on the nearby wall. For a moment, they gave the appearance of demons. Another glimpse showed nothing but moving silhouettes from the candle flame.

Barbie handed me the book. "Soon as Joanie and Jazz finish, read this page here"—she pointed to a poem in Latin in chapter six—"while I sprinkle the chicken blood. You're the only one of us who took Latin."

Yeah, most take German or Spanish for their high school language. Me? I had to take a dead language.

Done with their part, Joanie and Jazz stepped away. I chanted the Latin words while Barb splashed, not sprinkled, the chicken blood. A chicken wing flew into the circle, barely landing on the salty line.

Barbie shrugged. "I doubt it'll matter. Keep reading, Harper."

A headache pounded behind my eyes. If I had any psychic abilities, I might have taken the pain as a sign to quit. Instead, I chanted louder.

Joanie called out. "Hey, I see smoke inside the circle."

I stopped. *Huh? Is the candle smoking?*

Barbie, Jazz, and I looked to see.

Sure enough, black smoke, or more accurately, black mist rose. It undulated, like a belly dancer performing for our amusement.

The book fell from my nerveless fingers, barely missing my shoes. The thing spun around and around, faster, and faster. It shot up until it towered over Jazz, the tallest of us.

All four of us gathered together like a herd of frightened deer. My palms moistened with sweat, and my stomach roiled. The black mist molded into something more substantial than spirit. It had red eyes and rope-like things whipped out from it.

The eyes looked angry. *"Can't a demon be left alone? Why teenagers? What are you asking for, a lack of acne and some rock star to fall for your pubescent selves?"*

The voice echoed in my head, and my headache worsened.

Barbie shook a finger at it. "Look, we sent for you. You're disappointing. After all, you don't look like much of anything." She sneered. "A loser demon."

Now the idiot gets stupidly brave. Aloud, I said, "Barbie, it's not your boyfriend you dumped, but a fiend from Hell."

She whirled around. "It looks more like an imp to me than a badass demon."

The demon left the circle. I saw it pass over the chicken wing.

Oh no! The wing had broken the line. Which of us did that?

"Barbie," I said, pushing the other two girls toward the window and gestured at her, still standing near the circle. "It's time to leave."

She crossed her arms. "I am not going anywhere. Pick up the book and send the demonic idiot back to Hell."

I hissed, "Ixnay on the smart mouthiness and get your butt over here!"

The demon rushed her with a roar.

Barbie squealed like a pig and knocked the candle over. Flames caught hold of the rug.

Jazz picked up the book and opened it.

Is she going to try and read from it? She never took Latin. Heck, she flunked German.

A gust of wind snatched the book out of her hands, and it slammed against my head. I cried out and turned to stare straight into the demon's eyes.

It had caused the wind.

Screams filled the place and I understood they came from us.

The room, growing flames, screaming girls, and the demon spun like a merry-go-round as I punched the floor with my face.

****

Burning heat was licking my skin, hungry for me.

God, it hurts!

I opened my eyes and saw the orange-red flowers of heat chewing at the wood inside the house. I sat up and skidded my butt away. Oh God, Oh God, Oh, God! Fire! I gotta get out!

I shot up and looked for a way out when it hit me. My friends! Where are they? Did they get out and forget about me?

Smoke blanketed my face, and I coughed, swallowing so much of it. Oh, God, people died from smoke inhalation! I covered my nose and mouth with my sleeve.

I stumbled. I couldn't see anything. I tripped over something, catching myself in time from falling. I looked down; the smoke cleared enough to reveal a body. Barbie! I checked for a pulse: none.

Oh no, Barbie's dead.

The others lay a few feet away. I saw Jazz's red hair. Both she and Joanie were positioned side-by-side like interlocking puzzle pieces. They might still be alive. I ran over, dodging flaring waves of fire. But neither girl appeared to show a sign of life. A quick check of their pulses revealed nothing.

A giant wave of flame arose with a boom, its intense heat forcing me back. I watched in horror as the fire consumed my friends.

Another flash of fire surged. Its heat grew unbearable. I'll burn alive, too. Just like my friends. God, how do I get out?

I spun around to find an exit and spied the window Jazz had shattered earlier. Glass glinted in the firelight, scattered like diamonds across the floor beneath it.

Lurching over to the ledge, I climbed out, landing on my bottom. The cold wet grass felt welcoming. I'd have loved to stay there and hug it all, but the heat burning my back told me otherwise. Not just the fire, but the demon, too. I hadn't seen it when I regained consciousness, but that didn't mean it wasn't somewhere around here.

I crawled across the lawn until I knelt at its edge by the street, then stumbled to my feet and tottered away. The sirens of fire engines sang in the night and I stopped far enough away to mingle into the crowd gathering to watch the burning frame. No one appeared to notice my singed clothing or smoky odor.

Something glimmered in the darkness before me. Blinking, I thought, is that a face? It leered at me, and then it rushed at me. I staggered back. My vision swam, and I rode a carousel out of control, fighting the urge to throw up. The noise all around me grew distant.

And I forgot everything. Even the—

Chapter One—Harper

Oh no, not again.

Did I sleepwalk? I looked up at the large hole in the roof and saw glittering stars and the full moon against the black velvet sky. Great, I'm back in the burned-out skeleton of the house I've woken up in for the past year.

I rubbed my forehead. *Really odd, Harper Doyle. What draws you back here only when you're asleep?*

I puzzled over that mystifying question. In a blinding flash, a pounding headache washed over me. Nausea curdled in my stomach, and I dropped to my knees, holding my head nearly to my thighs as tears flooded my eyes. Whatever this room meant to me was lost within my mind and trying to remember the secret always brought on this agony.

Every. Single. Time.

The pain subsided enough for me to find my feet. I scrubbed at tear-stained cheeks, no doubt making them dirtier. Looking down, I saw my pajamas were dirty, and further down, my bare and grimy feet peeped out from beneath the bottoms. The 'Hello Kitty' on the front of my top looked mostly black.

Under normal circumstances, I wouldn't leave home without shoes. I never went barefoot in the summertime like the other kids did. Even worse, I wouldn't be caught dead in my Hello Kitty jammies outside of my house. One hint of this and I would be a pariah at school. A flush of heat burned my cheeks.

I'd rather die. Just dig me a hole, let me jump in it, and bury me.

Wiping at drool at the edge of my mouth, I tasted ash. "Ewww," I spit, peering at the wet glob of soot on my hand.

I needed to get out of here. I hoped Mom hadn't woken up and found me gone. Luck only stretched so far.

I shoved my messy hair out of my face and really looked around. All I saw was a bad memory. Friends of mine died here in a fire; I hadn't. Mom taking me to a shrink hadn't helped; I was still sleepwalking.

Why do I keep coming back? Guilt...or something else?

Dr. Thompson said to fight to remember to get to the truth of what happened that night. To stop being a headcase and search within my psyche. Another flash of pain rolled over me and I dug nails into the palms of my hands. More tears.

"That shrink's a stupid jerk, Harper. He thinks he knows what's good for you. I'd like to show him what's good for him."

Whoa! Where did that voice come from? My head? Sounded spiteful and, honestly, it didn't sound like my voice at all. This hasn't ever happened to me before. Never.

It's like someone else besides me existed in my head.

Can't be. Yeah, I'm going schizo.

I clenched my jaw and closed my eyes as the pain returned. The agony became full blown torture. I fell uncaring to the grimy floor and lay there, crying.

That was when a floodgate opened, and I remembered everything.

One of my friends, Joanie, snatched a book from the library, *Demon Summoning for Dummies*, on another friend's, Barbie, lark to see if the ritual in the book would actually work. How four of us had gotten together the stuff we needed and headed over to this empty house to perform the summoning.

It worked all right.

A shadow with red eyes had appeared out of nowhere inside the circle we'd made with blood from a package of frozen chicken parts. The thing charged us with a chilling scream. The panic. The stink of our fear. The musk of something unholy. The all-consuming fire. The heavy smoke we choked on and blinded us. The dying.

I screamed. "Oh, God, my friends!"

Like I was watching a movie, I saw the giant wave of flame again as it boomed, its intense heat forcing me back. I watched in horror as the roaring fire consumed their bodies.

Another roar of fire swept through the room, bearing fat-popping heat upon me. I spun around and looked for an exit. That was when I spied the window we'd shattered earlier to break into the place. Glass lay glinting in the firelight like diamonds scattered across the floor beneath it.

Another roar from the fire and I kicked the shards aside, and safely climbed up on the ledge. I stumbled over to its ledge and dropped down onto the welcoming cool, wet grass. A growing crowd of people stood on the street, watching the firefighters who'd just arrived to battle the fire.

Apparently, nobody saw me.

In that moment, it all rushed back.

The anguish subsided for the first time in a year and numbness seeped into every part of me. Unmindful of the soot and dirt covering my pajamas, the splinters in my flesh, or even the tenderness inside my head, I struggled to my knees and from there, to my feet.

No wonder I kept coming back here. No wonder the pain. No wonder the lack of memories of one night.

A criminal always returned to the scene of the crime. Especially if she helped her friends perform a ritual to call up a demon and then a fire burned down the building and everyone died.

Everyone except me.

I wished the forgetfulness back. But that wish remained unfulfilled.

But I remembered what I'd forgotten. What we had brought to this world.

The demon was still loose.

Chapter Two—Harper

I ran all the way home. I needed to get away from that place. Rocks and pieces of broken glass bit into the bottoms of my feet, and sucking air into my lungs hurt, but I didn't care.

Oh God, a demon's loose in Moon Ridge! And it's my fault, as much as my friends. How could I forget what happened?

I noticed no lights on in the house. Good. That meant Mom still slept and had no inkling I had sleepwalked again. Relief flooded over me, but only temporarily as guilt replaced it.

I freed something that could rip my mother's soul apart. If she'd known, maybe besides those talks about sex, drugs, and being bullied, she would have added a stern lecture on demon summoning, too.

Scrambling up the oak tree that grew just outside my bedroom window, I shoved up the window that, lucky for me, I hadn't latched, and tumbled inside. After easing the window back down, I leaned my forehead against the cold glass and shivered. What could I do? I'm not even eighteen years old!

I walked out of my room and into the bathroom to grab a quick shower.

Before I did, I sat on the toilet seat and took out the few slivers of wood and a piece of glass from the bottoms of my feet and tossed them in the trash. I stepped beneath the warm water gushing from the nozzle. It felt good to wash away the dirt, soot, and the blood, but it proved harder to scrub out the memories. I stuck bandages on the sores, stuffed my dirty pajamas into a plastic grocery bag, and tossed the evidence in the back of my closet. I slipped on another set of jammies and crawled into bed. I couldn't sleep at first. The night of the fire and the demon taunted me.

Finally, exhaustion sucked me into a dreamless slumber.

****

"Harper, hey, wake up. You'll be late for school and make me late for work, too!"

"Huh?" I sat up and tried to rub the sleep from my eyes.

Mom popped her head around the door. "Didn't you hear me call you? I shouted several times."

"Yeah, I heard." I yawned and stretched.

"Well, hurry. I have to be out of here in a half-hour, latest. I have a meeting this morning."

She left the door cracked.

I flipped back the covers and climbed off the mattress. Rummaging in the closet, I dug out jeans and a black T-shirt with some hunky guy's face I thought was hot about a million years ago and dressed. I yanked on a pair of fuzzy blue socks and jammed my feet into my tennis shoes before grabbing my book bag and hustling downstairs. My feet felt sore from last night, but I could handle it.

Mom sat at the kitchen table.

Dropping my bag on the floor, I thumped down across from her. I didn't have much time to eat my breakfast of champions—a bowl of soggy cereal and lukewarm tea—before my mother herded me out the door to her car.

She dropped me off in front of the school.

"Bye, Mom," I waved after her as the car roared away, smoke following it like a long bushy tail. With a sigh, I turned and stared at the other teenagers milling around in groups while still others trod like zombies up the steps and into the building. A group of popular kids stood nearby, gossiping. Three local bad boys—Jake Hewitt, Pete Jameson, and a new kid, Tyree Washington—lounged against the cement steps as if waiting for the cue that it was all right to ditch school.

A headache pounded in my head.

Great! It's just another day at Moon Ridge High School where spoiled, snotty preppies and bullies make life Hell. Thank goodness, it's Friday. I couldn't wait until I graduated from this hellhole and went away to college outside of Moon Ridge, Virginia. Anywhere outside of Virginia would work for me. I'm still waiting to hear back from any of the colleges.

School never used to bother me. I'd always been a good student, with no problems doing my schoolwork. Nothing caused me anxiety, not even after my dad zipped out of my life. Most kids went through all sorts of difficulties when they lose one of their parents to death or a failed marriage. But I had only been a toddler when he left Mom and me.

Okay, I'd always felt different. Did I act out or do drugs or drink? No, but lately, being inside the walls of this school suffocated me. After learning the truth of a year of sleepwalking, you'd think I could handle this place better, but no.

Three guesses why? Yeah, but now, I could add a demon as another reason besides guilt about my friends, bullies, and calculus.

Wonderful. Hell on double-time: high school and a demon.

I swung my book bag over one shoulder and shuffled up the steps, staring down at my feet. Hopefully, I wouldn't attract anyone's attention.

A male voice rang out. "Hey, Harper!" Snickers from two others followed.

Jake, Pete, and now this year, Tyree. Just what I needed, catcalls from them.

Nails dug into my palm as I fisted my hands against my thighs and ignored them, only pausing when one of the popular teens, Stacey Brown, glanced my way. The girl could be a bitch; she picked on anyone different from her or didn't kowtow to her like she was some goddess. Unlike many other kids she flashed her godliness on, I never saw any need to join her entourage.

As if I didn't merit more than that glance, she returned to her friends, laughing, and I darted past her unobserved. I managed to get to my first-period class on time. Mr. Borkus was scribbling some problems across the chalkboard when I slid into my seat and plopped my backpack on my desk. I dug within its cavern and took out my calculus book, along with a pen and some paper.

I despised calculus class with a passion. I hated the way Mr. Borkus stared at us with his piggy eyes and slash mouth that always looked like he'd swallowed sour lemons. Besides that, he had busy brows that always seem to squirm like fuzzy caterpillars and a fat blob of a nose. Those caterpillars wiggled as he caught me staring at him. His nasty little smile reminded me of the Cheshire Cat from *Alice in Wonderland*.

Jazz told me last year that when someone smiled the way that cat had, it meant they were insincere. I thought that was malarkey Jazz found on the Internet, but looking at Mr. Borkus, I believed it. He constantly flashed that big grin as he told the class he wanted what was best for us, but you knew he didn't mean it.

"Wouldn't you like to wipe that smile off Dorkus Borkus's face, Harper?"

Huh? Where did that come from?

"Me."

Is someone playing a trick on me? I glanced around until my gaze met Jake Hewitt's blue eyes. Guess he decided not to skip school with Pete today. Instead, he sat big as life in his seat, across the aisle to the right of me. He wrinkled his nose and grinned.

Had he said that? Except the voice sounded feminine.

He leaned back into his chair. "What? Am I cute, or something?"

I jutted out my chin his way. "You wish, Jake Hewitt."

He leaned across the aisle and whispered. "Be honest, Harper, you like me."

I gave him what I hoped was my best 'I don't care look.' "Maybe when we were in elementary and middle school together, but since we started high school, you've been nothing but a creep."

"Miss Doyle, Mr. Hewitt, if you could join the rest of the class in opening your calculus books? Otherwise, I'd appreciate it if you'd tell the rest of us what you both find so interesting to talk about?"

God, Mr. Borkus.

I glared at Jake and flipped open my book to the page number Mr. Borkus had written on the board.

"Nothing's going on, Mr. Borkus," I said, scribbling my name across the top of the paper. "Anything Jake Hewitt has to say couldn't interest me in the least."

Mr. Borkus stared at Jake, who shrugged. "Whatever she said goes double for me."

Out of my right eye, I saw that Jake didn't open his book. He leaned back in his seat and stared up at the ceiling as if something there fascinated him. But when Mr. Borkus turned back to the board, Jake flashed me a sideways glance with an engaging grin and wiggled his eyebrows.

I studied my book as if the problems on the page had grabbed my attention.

Jake returned to looking at the ceiling.

I remember when Jake was a good kid.

We met in kindergarten and became instant buds, remaining that way all through grade school. He was smart—way smarter than me. Schoolwork came naturally to him, and he got super grades. He helped me, of course, with stuff I had problems doing. Except for English and history—I did great in those. I loved to write stories, and as for reading? Jake thought it was cool back then.

That is until he met Pete Jameson. A spoiled rich brat, Pete hung around with a nasty piece of work, Brian Woods. His father, Rick Jameson, seemed to own most of Moon Ridge. Pete ignored Jake until they both took high school P.E. in ninth grade, and he invited Jake over to his house after school. Ever since that day, Jake acted as if we had never been BFFs. And Pete didn't hang around Brian too much, either.

When Tyree and his divorced father moved to Moon Ridge this past summer, Pete took the black kid under his wing as part of his gang. Gang! Like the rich boy even knew what gangs really did. Tyree had been a nice guy when I ran into him at the local YMCA pool during the summer, but I'm fairly sure Pete changed him like he had Jake.

I wish Pete had fallen into some hole that went all the way to China.

"I can arrange that, Harper."

What the—? I looked at Jake, thinking it was him. But he still ogled the ceiling, except instead of fascination, boredom etched his face. I checked out the rest of the classroom, but everyone was busy working out the math problems. Mr. Borkus sat behind his desk and frowned. I knew the voice hadn't come from him, and I ducked my head down, deciding I imagined it.

"Harper, Harper, Harper. Do you want me to fix it so that Pete-the-jerk is out of Jake's life for good?"

Okay, that's getting creepy. The voice came from inside my head, like last night. That didn't bode well for my mental state. This voice in my head acted like some separate entity.

I've got to get Mom to call Dr. Thompson. I'll call her at lunch and get her to make me an appointment.

"Don't you dare go see that shrink, Harper Doyle! Or else."

My breath hitched. *Whoa, the voice is threatening me. I'm going bonkers.*

"You're not crazy. I'm real. Real as you."

A chill skittered up my back. "What's going on?" I whispered.

"Wait until after school, and you're home, alone in your room, then we'll be able to talk uninterrupted. I won't bother you the rest of the day. But no phone calls to your mother. Understand?"

I nodded, feeling scared and stupid at the same time.

"Now, get back to those math problems. Dorkus Borkus is watching you."

I saw that the teacher indeed had his gaze on me. Lips pursed. Lines furrowed in the forehead. Tap, tap, tapping a pencil on his desk.

My cheeks burning, I scribbled on my paper and worked out the problems. I didn't see them and felt sure that I didn't write down the correct answers. I had too much else on my mind.

The voice didn't say anything else the rest of math, or during lunch or my other classes. When the bell rang at the end of the day, I sprinted to my bus lined up by the curb in front of the school. Barely had the bus pulled to the stop down the street from my house when I got up and flew off it. I needed to find out if the voice was authentic or not.

I needed answers.

Chapter Three—Harper

Mom hadn't gotten home yet. A text on my phone from her revealed she had another meeting that afternoon. I dashed upstairs to my bedroom. The door shut behind me; I threw my bookbag on the bed. "Okay, I'm home. Who or what are you?"

"Finally, alone. Come on. You must have some idea who is talking in your head? You're not stupid. You're a brain as much as that Jake character. Even if he's forgotten how to be smart."

Could it—no, it couldn't.

"Hey, the mortal wins the prize. Yep, I'm the demon you and your friends summoned at that fiasco last year. I've been caged in a tiny section of your mind until you remembered. That sorta set me free."

I grabbed my head between my hands. "Where are you? How are you using my head to communicate with me?"

A low snicker snaked across my mind. *"You think I'm somewhere else? Oh no. I'm still inside you. We're just like bosom buddies. BFFs. I'm renting your body as my new place to live."*

"Oh, God! Possession."

"Damn a soul to Hell, don't say that name. Take a seat, Harper."

I plopped down on the edge of my bed. "Go on, tell me more."

"This is not a normal possession. Whatever you and your friends did that night, somehow, I am now a part of you. Your skin is my skin; your head is my head."

"So, it's true? I'm possessed. Did I survive the fire a year ago, thanks to you?"

"Got it in a nutshell, babe. Although, as I said, there's a problem with this possession."

Great, this didn't sound good at all. "What do you mean there's a problem?" The words stumbled out of my mouth like falling bricks.

"It appears that I can't leave your body. I can't shed you like a snake sheds its skin. Possessing you, I can speak to you or talk to others by taking you over completely. Hells bells, I can even do magic through you. We are as one, Kemosabe. Siamese twins. Ying to your yang."

"Don't give me that. I bet if I went to some psychic or a priest or someone like that, I could get you exorcised."

"Fine with me. Try it. I bet you a six-pack of cream soda you won't get me expelled from your frame."

"Ugh! I hate cream soda."

"Then you better hope you can get me evicted from your body. Otherwise, you better get used to the taste of it. I discovered in the 90s that I love the stuff more than anything else I had tasted in eons."

Not even wanting to know where a demon learned to like cream soda, much less anything else about its long-lived past, I knew I had to find somebody to help me with my problem.

Problem? Like what happened to me has to do with female issues, failing grades, or teenage angst.

The demon quieted in my head, and I went over to my desk and sat down, powering up my laptop. Maybe it would leave me alone long enough to do this. Then again, perhaps it wasn't worried. Fear left a metal taste in my mouth. The demon had its metaphysical claws in me, and it knew it.

I went online to search for any psychics locally who performed exorcisms on demons or ghosts. I didn't get a headache, and nothing else happened to me, so I figured it allowed me to do this.

Moon Ridge seemed to have an awful lot of psychics. But again, with the town's legend that a coven of witches founded it, maybe that wasn't so strange. It appeared many didn't perform exorcisms. I finally found five that did.

I peered at the link by each name and started clicking through.

The first one, Mammy Jo's Psychic Predictions and Exorcisms made me leery about contacting her—by email, much less in person. When I found out she also sold voodoo dolls that she made herself, I went onto the next psychic and the one after that. Those two sounded like money rip-offs. To be honest, a year ago, I thought all psychics were rip-offs.

I hadn't even believed that my friends could call up a demon. Heck, the spell came from a *Demon Summoning for*

Dummies book, not the *Satanic Bible*. At that time, I was more worried about spending the night in juvenile hall than dancing naked around a demon in a circle of chicken blood.

As I skimmed the fourth and the fifth psychics on the yellow pages website, I paused at the fifth one.

Can that be... is that...

Naaah, it couldn't be could it?

Jake's mom?

Pansy Hewitt.

I remembered visiting Jake's house, and how homey, how oh-so-normal, his mother seemed. The woman baked chocolate chip cookies to die for and attended PTA meetings in grade school. She bandaged bum knees and took Jake to Little League practice. There was never a whisper across Jake's lips that she was a psychic. Not any indication to me, or anyone else either now that I thought about it.

Memories crowded my head. I remember him poking fun at ghost stories or whenever someone talked about a fantastic new movie or a paranormal reality TV show on *Travel Channel* about people communicating with spirits by way of séances or Ouija boards. Not long ago—this past spring actually—he hassled a ninth grader wearing one of those T-shirts with a ghost hunting television show on the front. He told the kid it should have been called "Poop Hunters."

No, it couldn't be his mother.

But reading further down, I recognized Jake's home address. Once upon a time, I'd been as familiar with his house as much as my own.

Wow. Mrs. Hewitt had more depth to her than I'd known.

I saw her face in my mind, the sweet smile she always had for any person, and how comforting she could be. She had long blonde hair and a soft Southern accent. If there were anyone I could talk to about my problem, she would be the one.

The only glitch: Jake lived there, too.

I got offline and powered down my laptop. I stood and crossed the room to the door. Snatching my wallet and house key on the way out and stuffing them in my jeans' pockets, I clattered downstairs and slipped outdoors, locking the front door before leaving.

The demon still hadn't made an appearance.

I stared east. The Hewitts' home lay that way. Jake's face appeared in my mind's eye, and I remember how he treated me since he became best buds with Pete Jameson. The acid in my stomach gurgled.

"Are you going to let that loser scare the piss out of you? I said I would rid you of Pete-the-Creep—no fuss, no muss!"

Great. A devil is making me an offer I knew better than to take even if I didn't like Pete.

I stepped along the road, keeping to the grassy part between it and the ditch on my right. "Will you please stay out of my head for now?"

"Where are we going?"

"Nowhere that concerns you," I said. Hoping I could outsmart the demon, though I didn't have a clue how when it lived in my head. Maybe even being in my body, the devil had limits; it might need time to recharge, even just speaking in my head. *Right, it's a fricking demon!* I blurted out, "Okay, I'm going to church."

"Church? Come on, girlfriend."

"I'm going, so leave me alone or join me."

"I know you are not going to a church." Two blood-red eyes appeared in my mind. *"With a demon possessing you, though, you wouldn't make it inside the building."*

"I'm not going to a church, but I'm going somewhere where I might get you and me parting ways. Thought you wanted that done."

The demon shut up. I felt it dig deep inside my brain. I waited a few minutes, but no more peeps came from it. Maybe, hopefully, it didn't know where I was heading until too late. I couldn't be sure what it thought about exorcisms. I didn't know what I felt about them, either.

An image of a demonized Linda Blair retching up pea soup flittered through my head for a second, followed by a small cackle. Yeah, it knew what I was planning.

The sweet smell from flowers and the fresh-cut grass from lawns wafted to me with the promise of a lazy autumn afternoon. The lure failed. Fear dug a hole in me. Although I felt a chill in the air, I sweated, worried about the demon. I tried not to think of anything, but the beauty all around me. No way would I let Lucifer Junior freak me out.

A few dead leaves littered the lawns and even the road, the promise of fall to come. A breeze whooshed out of nowhere and swept up several of the leaves, slapping my face with them. They reminded me of a ballet performance, promenading side-by-side in mid-air, then dipping and twirling, only to suddenly fall to the ground. Barely breathing and my heart pummeling, I stared down at them lying inert on the ground as if nothing ever happened.

"Scared you, didn't I? Unfortunately, that's all I'm doing to you for now. I can wait for you to get to your destination. Forget the exorcism or anything else you might try to expel me back to Hell. I think my power is growing. Soon, Harper, soon—and then watch out."

I licked my lips. "That didn't spook me." Yeah-right, it freaked me out.

A mental shrug. *"I don't give a forked tongue if it did or didn't scare the bejesus out of you. It's a demon thing, you know."*

I picked up my step and tightened my jaw. The demon giggled, but I ignored it.

I stopped short of five wooden steps that led up to the sizable shadow-filled wraparound porch of a gray rancher with dark blue trim. I'd made it. Taking a deep breath, I took each step one at a time. With some luck on my side, Jake wouldn't be home. Even if he was, it didn't matter. The demon and I had to part company.

Chapter Four—Harper

Something uncurled inside my head. *"Go ahead and knock, girl. There is nothing inside that'll be able to take a demon down."*

"Cocky fiend," I muttered under my breath.

I lifted a fist to knock on the bright blue door as I'd done in the past when I saw the brand-new doorbell. Mrs. Hewitt must have had it installed since I last visited the place three years ago. I pushed the button. The chimes sang out a series of pretty notes.

A screech ripped my head apart. "Hell's bells, what is that awful angel-inspired sound?"

I didn't answer, just wiped at the few tears that bubbled from my eyes.

The door cracked open. At first, I saw an eyeball. The door swung the rest of the way open, and it was as if the three years since my last visit had never happened.

Mrs. Hewitt stood on the other side, a big, bright grin on her pretty face. She had her blond hair gathered up into a French knot on top of her head, but a few wisps escaped, tickling her forehead and ears. She wore a T-shirt with words splashed across the front: "Tarot Readers Do it By The

Cards." She threw open her arms wide, and I went into them, receiving a generous hug.

"Harper, honey! It's been a while. About time you came back here. Jake with you? Though if he were, that boy has a key and would have let you and himself in."

"Yeah, it has been some time, hasn't it, Mrs. Hewitt? And no, I'm alone."

"Well, come on in."

I strolled past her and into the living room. It hadn't changed a bit since the last time I'd been here: the same comfy couch and recliner. She still had the few antiques she had brought with her from the plantation house she'd lived in before it'd been bought and torn down. The TV was new. Instead of the tubed one she had back then, she had a flat screen that rode the wall. Beneath it, I spied a Blu Ray player on a shelf instead of the DVD player she used to have. Something else that hadn't been here before was a laptop on a desk in a corner. No doubt the psychic business was doing well for her.

She gestured at the couch. "Sit, sit. I'll rustle up some cookies and milk." She hustled toward the kitchen, but she paused and glanced back over her shoulder. "You still like chocolate chip, right?"

How could I say no to her homemade chocolate chip cookies? I grinned and nodded. She left, and I curled into the plump, soft cushion of the couch, breathing in a pleasant apple-cinnamon odor from the lit wickless candle in a container on a nearby bookcase where books fought for space.

Footsteps reached my ears, and I sat up.

Mrs. Hewitt returned, carrying a tray that held a plate of chocolate chip cookies and two glasses filled to the brim with milk.

I licked my lips with the tip of my tongue.

She set the tray down on the coffee table and settled beside me, handing me a glass.

I snatched a cookie and bit into it—the soft creaminess of the cookie and the dark chocolate chips melted in my mouth.

"Oh, there is something as good as cream soda. The woman can bake a mean chocolate chip cookie. Harper, I went along with your little charade. Did you think that you can pull this off with something like me sharing your body? What are you planning to do with a psychic medium, as if I don't already know? Anything you think in this brain of yours I know."

Great, simply great. Like I knew, it only let go because it had control of me. Worse, whatever I tasted, the demon could taste it, too. I am sure that wasn't the only thing we did together. No privacy.

Ouch! A shot of pain riveted inside my head.

"I told you so. Your pleasures are my pleasures, your hates mine, etc...."

"Hush."

Mrs. Hewitt said, "What? Is something the matter?"

"Nothing, Mrs. Hewitt." Heat rushed up the back of my neck. The fiend almost made me screw up, and now it had me blushing. The pain went away—time to spill the beans to Mrs. Hewitt. I needed to find out if she could get this thing out of my head. Even if the fiend made my entire head feel like little imps were pick axing my brain.

I put down my glass and swallowed the last of the cookie, brushing cookie crumbs off my lap. My eyes met hers.

"Mrs. Hewitt?"

"Mmmmmmm?"

"I have a problem." The pain returned, a couple of jabs. She stilled.

Okay, I got her attention.

"Nothing female in origin?" Her tone suggested that she doubted that.

"Er, no." More jabs.

She shook her head, lines furrowing in her forehead. "No, you would go to your mother for that. You have a serious problem. You know I'm a psychic?"

"Ah, yeah...that's why I'm here. I'm ah, I'm—" The agony went up several notches as tears flooded my eyes, blinding my sight.

She wiped away my tears with a tissue and peered into my eyes. Horror flashed in her own. "You're possessed by a demon."

I sat up straighter; Mrs. Hewitt must be the real deal. Maybe she could help me. I hoped and prayed that I would be rid of this entity before supper tonight.

Mumbling erupted in my head.

She gathered me into her arms and patted my back. "Let Mrs. Hewitt get rid of the nasty beastie for you. I am so glad you came to me."

I opened my mouth to tell her, but I saw its red eyes in my head. Red eyes! The demon snarled, "*Oh no, you don't!*" Everything went dark, as if it had shut off my lights. Metaphysical arms grabbed me, and I found myself thrown into some part of my brain, unable to get out.

"It's my turn, Harper. Showtime."

Chapter Five—Cresil

I struggled in the mortal female's arms, snarling. "Take your hands off me, woman!"

She drew back, her face grim and lips pursed as she rose to her feet. The New Age phone to the spirit world knew that Harper no longer had control of her body. She knew that I'd shoved the teen into a tiny section of her own brain and locked her up inside like a prisoner. The grim look on the woman's puss cheered me up. Only a little, though. I remembered that this mortal was the person Harper was going to have vamoose me back to Hell.

"Listen to me, demon," she stated, her arms crossed, "and give Harper back her body, before I bring on the big guns."

"Ha. I'd like to see that."

I leaned back against the cushions and crossed my legs, but not before I snatched a cookie and bit into it. The sinful sweetness of it melted down my throat. Mortal beings have no idea how addictive food and drink could be. Cream soda had been number one on the list of my vices. Not anymore. Chocolate chip cookies had just replaced it.

I waved the half-eaten cookie at her, and the crumbs littered my lap and the couch. "You really know how to bake a great chocolate chip cookie, woman. It's decadent enough to be Hell on Earth for me."

The medium sniffed. "I'll not thank some demonic entity that is not only making a mess, scattering crumbs everywhere, but possessing someone I know. Even if it likes the cookies that I bake, and will you quit calling me 'woman'! It's Mrs. Hewitt."

"It doesn't bother me if you do or don't. Mrs. Hew-witt." I stressed out her name before stuffing the rest of the cookie into my mouth. Too much for the small mouth of the face I now wore, I seized the glass of milk and downed the white liquid in one gulp, washing down the cookie. A tiny bit of the milk dribbled down my chin. I scrubbed at it with the back of my hand and wiped the wetness off onto the front of Harper's shirt.

The woman snatched the glass from me and the plate off the table. "What a pig. Since you can't treat that borrowed body right, you will not get any more cookies."

I snorted. "Whatever." A belch escaped, followed by a giggle.

"Rude."

"Better to burp and taste, then fart and waste."

She frowned.

I propped my feet up on the coffee table. But when I saw the human female's glower go even deeper, something made me bring them back down to the floor.

Now why did I do that? It wasn't due to any bad feelings on my part or caring how she felt.

Harper's voice resounded in the head, loud and clear. *"I made you do it, stupid demon."*

I growled, low and gritty. The mortal had gotten free of the prison in her head and retrieved control of her limbs back. In all the eons I've existed, this has never happened to me before.

Forcing her back into that spot of the brain, I mentally tied a rag around her mouth to keep her quiet, and slammed the mental door on her, locking it. I hoped this time she stayed inside.

I came back to the real world and found that the psychic lady was no longer in the room. Leaping to my feet (or is that Harper's feet?—no, our feet), I searched for her. It's never in any demon's best interest to let a medium disappear from their sight. I might get *abracadabra'd* back to Hell, or someplace worse.

There are things a human being can do to a demon that are horrible. Exorcisms are one.

Exorcisms are never pleasant for the demon. There are the summonings. Called from Hell, I could be made a slave and serve some pitiable sorcerer or Satanist. That had happened to me many times. Lucky for me, when Harper and her friends did the beckoning, they were amateurs at the business. Otherwise, I would never have gotten control of that situation. *Mmmmmmmm...I still can't figure out how a demon like me gained control out of their hands as quickly as I did, no matter the level of their abilities. None had any psychic powers I could detect.* There were dark blots in my remembering of that time. It made me uneasy.

If you're going to summon a demon, I admit that there are better ones than a lowly fiend like me—on the scale of one to ten, something like me teeter-totters on a fence between three and four.

Okay, maybe closer to one.

I stepped into what must be the kitchen, as I saw a refrigerator and stove.

"Got you, demon." The woman flashed me a big grin as she pointed down at my feet.

Oh, oh. I'd stepped into a circle of sea salt, with only one opening. The medium quickly sprinkled more of the damn salt from a bag and closed the gap. A few grains hit me and I screeched in pain.

I hate salt.

"Hell's bells, woman. That burns icy cold, and it hurts worse than being whipped with a cat-of-nine tails." I preferred the cat-of-nine whip.

"Will you stop with the woman crack, demon." She flicked a few more salt granules at me. "My. Name. Is. Mrs. Hewitt."

I screeched again. Every granule of that white crap burned! I kept my mouth shut after that.

When the pain subsided, I looked up at the ceiling and saw a large red pentagram drawn there that helped the salt circle to hold me in place.

I cut my eyes back at the psychic. *No doubt the witch intends to vanquish me back to the Pit. If I ever get free of this damn circle, I'll teach her the seven levels of agony.*

This has happened to me two times before, once in 1310 and later in 1602. You'd think I'd learned from my past mistakes. Like, keep notice of the surroundings I am in, especially if it belongs to a sorcerer, witch, or psychic medium. I smacked my borrowed head with a hand. "Dummy, dummy, dummy, dummy."

"Stop that, demon," commanded the woman. "You will quit harming the body that's not yours."

"Oh, putz." I propped both hands on my hips and looked at her. *Come closer, so I can grab you by the throat and throttle you.* "What do you plan to do with me now that you've captured me? Like I don't know what spiel you'll spout."

"Give Harper back her body."

Yeah, I wanted to shag free of this body at some point and time, but I'd be double-damned if I'd listen to the ghost radio and do it now.

"Think of what I can do for you. Wizards, sorcerers, and witches in the past have received many wondrous things by capturing demons. I bet you'd like to become rich. Be able to give that boy of yours things I know you can't give him." I lowered my voice to my most soft and seductive tone. "With money in your hands, you can enroll him in that private school you always dreamed for him. Get him away from that creep, Pete."

She frowned. "How did you know?" Her eyes widened. "Get out of my head." Her eyes narrowed; she snapped her fingers. "I am not listening to you either, hellspawn."

I lifted both shoulders. "It was worth a shot."

She snatched a book off a nearby table and flipped it open. I tried to catch the book's title, but her hand covered it. The odor of powerful magic wafted to my nostrils. A headache began to pound in our head.

The woman chanted in Latin. "Unus, duos tre oust is everto ex is somes."

My spirit self-shifted, banging against the flesh, but still not able to pass through it. *By Lucifer's blood, she's exorcising me, and it's not working*! The headache sped out of control. The words clawed through me, ripping me apart, but I couldn't leave Harper's form.

Please, no more of this torture.

It felt like constipation, but on a subatomic level. It confirmed what I already knew: that I couldn't break free of Harper's body on my own, and now it looked like I couldn't shag it by a medium's exorcising. Not by this one anyway.

"Licentia corporis, immunda animus."

Something like a thousand knives cut into our brain, and I dropped to our knees, clutching Harper's head, and screaming. Still, I hadn't popped out of the body. Through the living nightmare, I heard her saying something, and it was not in pig Latin. Had she? Yeah, the bitch's mouth moved. I read the lips. How dare she?

I bared my teeth. "Hey, I resent being called an unclean spirit. My name is Cresil."

She shut the book and laughed. "The demon of impurity and laziness? You've got to be kidding. Such a poor excuse for a bad boy."

The peals of laughter rained over me, adding insult to my misery. "How dare you make fun of me," I said with a growl. "I earned that title dishonestly. And I'm female, not male."

Damn, it felt like imps pounding on anvils in this head. Each blow made tears well up in Harper's eyes and blur my vision along with the girl's.

"All this time, I thought it was some high-order demonic entity, and you're nothing more than a wimpy—"

"Enough, you twit!" I roared. "If I was some piss-poor fiend, why am I still here? Guess you need to brush up on your dollar-store exorcising."

She grew white. "First, you call me woman, now it's twit. From now on, you better call me by my proper title, Mrs. Hewitt, you thrift-store bargain fiend."

Thrift-store bargain? That bit the big one for me. I managed to stand up on shaky legs. I wanted to kick the salt so I could escape the circle and lunge for Mrs. Hewitt's throat. Except I knew even that small portion of salt would feel like Sodom and Gomorrah on a less Biblical order. I was in enough agony as it was.

I calculated to see if it would still be worth the suffering to do that, just so I could get to her, even tried it. I found myself back on my knees. "Forget all that crap you're spouting. You'll never part me from Harper's body. She and her dumb friends screwed up somehow a year ago, and the little girlie and I may not like it, but we're stuck with each other like two sheets of construction paper glued together. I've been trying to escape her, and I'm still here. You failed, too."

A long cry echoed in my head.

Guess Harper got ungagged. She understood at last why I never tried to stop her from getting a psychic. We were as one, maybe for eternity. Eternity meaning until the fleshy prison died.

Just what I needed, going through puberty. Now that's actual Hell for me. I began weighing options of suicide. Maybe I could rush outside and let some vehicle crash into this body if I crossed a busy intersection. There were other ways of dying that I could explore. Usually, I could escape the flesh when the human died, but this possession had none of the typical attributes.

I might expire when her body did, as I had no guarantees.

The sounds of a door opening and closing reached me. A male voice that sounded familiar broke the silence. "Hey, what's going on here? Is that Harper on the floor? What are the two of you doing?"

Jake Hewitt stood just inside the kitchen, his bookbag on the floor at his feet. I must admit Harper had good taste in mortal males. The boy stood about six feet but not gangling like a lot of other teens. He had unruly raven-dark hair that brushed his broad shoulders and big green eyes that stared at me with intensity beneath long, black lashes. And though

I hated to think it, the boy had angelic features that rivaled the archangels.

I ignored Harper's frantic jabbering in the back of my brain and plastered what I hope was a sexy smile on my face, hoping I didn't show any telltale evidence of being exorcised. "Well, hello, good looking. You could tempt a devil. I bet you'd do the same for those angelic sissies up in Heaven, too."

Lines burrowing into his forehead and eyes narrowed, he stepped closer. "Okay, what's the joke, Harper?"

I cocked Harper's head to the left. "No joke, but I'm not Harper."

"Funny, haha. I see you standing in front of me, a circle of salt surrounding—" Jake glanced up at the pentagram above me, then at his mother. "I know you have the pentagram painted on the ceiling for all those silly exorcisms you do, but why do you have Harper in a circle of salt? Mom, tell me what is going on here right now! Are you doing an exorcism on her, and what for?"

The mother blurted out, "That's Harper's body, but that's not Harper. It's a demon called Cresil. It's possessing Harper."

He stared at me. "Mom, I know you believe in that entire paranormal mumble jumble, but there are no such things as—"

I finished, "—demons? Oh, but there are. Heard of the term, 'for we are Legion'? It's pretty crowded there. Keep up what you're doing, bad boy, and when you die, you'll be joining us. Though, you would be a part of the lower Escalon, unlike me, who happens to be an original fallen angel, even though I'm below Lucifer and his chosen lieutenants. I was right there with the Devil when Heaven tossed us rebels down into the Pit." I said this with pride like I'd earned a badge of honor or something. I flashed Mrs. Hewitt a look that dared her to call me a loser demon after me saying that.

Losing Heaven's grace had to mean something. That's what I kept telling myself, especially on bad days like this. There had been plenty of them over the eons. Too numerous to count, or maybe I didn't want to know the exact number. Nothing like what's happening to me now.

Jake whipped his gaze back to his mother.

She nodded. "Yes, she's right; the demon is one of the fallen, but not that high up in the order like Lucifer." She stuck out her chin as she looked at me. "She no doubt believed Lucifer's lies and found herself sent down into Hell with all the others when the Devil's rebellion failed. Not too bright."

I snarled as I snapped Harper's fingers. "Think about this. If Lucifer hadn't failed, you hairless apes would be monkey meat for us."

Jake moved until he stood across the salt from me. "Testy, aren't we?"

Damn. The mortal boy's eyes. Such depths of green, like an endless wave of grass. I wanted to jump right into them.

Whoa, what in the devil's cloven hooves was that? Mortals went crazy over me, but I had never fallen for any of them. It's like a web of seduction had snared me. I'm supposed to be doing the temptation scene here, not some bratty mortal.

I glanced down and composed myself before I caught his gaze again. "You would be, too, if you got stuck in some pit for years. The last idiot that called me up from Hell before Harper and her girl pals was a half-wit sorcerer who didn't know his way around a spell." I crossed my arms and snorted. "To tell the truth, all my 'masters' who summoned me had been short on brains. None of them held enough power, in the end, to stop me from tearing out their throats and taking their sorry souls back to Hell with me. Just like this Harper bimbo and her friends. Her friends have been toasting their toes in Hell for a year now, but Harper's time will come once I find a way to shag free of her body."

Sudden anger flared in those green depths. "So, you're saying that Harper's stupid?"

"Look, what kind of ignorant teenager would summon a demon when they knew next to nothing about doing it? The only reason Harper survived was for some reason that I don't know the how and why as of yet; we merged together to share brain and body. I can't waggle free of her skin. That has never been done before in the history of demons. Do you know what it's like to share a body with a girl going through teenage angst?"

The anger in his eyes faded, and the glint of humor took its place. "Looks like the demon protests too much. That's if you're a real demon and not Harper playing a trick on my mother and me." With the toe of his booted foot, he scraped away some of the salt.

"Jake, no!" cried out his mother in a frantic voice.

Lucifer's hate, it's freedom! I stepped through and went toe-to-toe with the boy. Maybe I wasn't as tall as him, but just wait until the brat got a load of my magic—foolish hairless ape.

"Dilos tonen." I uttered a demonic spell as I wiggled fingers at him.

Nothing happened. Jake arched an eyebrow and smirked.

That burns my hellfire.

I tried to put the whammy on him once more, but again, nothing. *I have powers, so why no juice*?

Drool leaked out of Harper's gaping mouth. I wiped it away.

Gaping mouth? Drool? What the—

Hells bells, I am fawning over some snot-nosed smart mouth like a lovesick teenage girl with her first crush? This can't be happening to me. I'm the demon here, even if I'm female. I should be leading him into depravity by his oh-so-cute nose.

Oh, so cute nose? By Lucifer's forked tongue, someone, please smite me now.

He grinned. "I don't see you smiting me or anything. Come on, Harper, fess up, and stop the play-acting."

I stepped away from him. What was going on here? My powers should be working. Even if I couldn't get out of the girl's body, my other abilities should still work.

The acid in Harper's stomach bubbled. One hand on the belly as I propped the other against the wall, our breathing spurted out in short gasps as the acid burned.

Unless...oh no! It hit me. It wasn't my powers that were wonky, but that the boy had his own. I peered at his expanding grin and realized he didn't know about his abilities at all. Jake was an untutored sorcerer. The strongest I'd ever run into, tutored or untutored.

A wave of dizziness washed over me, and I teeter-tottered. Everything swam in Harper's head, and my eyesight shorted out. Her body dropped like a load of dirty laundry, smacking the back of the head on the linoleum floor. Damn, that hurt. Like a Hell worm bored through the skull.

Hellfire. When we possess someone, we never get any inkling of how human flesh can bruise and sting so easily. Things changed for me with the custody of Harper's body.

That. Scared. Me.

I zonked out.

Chapter Six-Harper

I opened my eyes and sat up—big mistake. Pain tap danced through my head, and my vision swam. My mouth tasted funky like I'd been snacking on garbage, and if the aching muscles indicated anything, I must have survived a wrestling match.

I stumbled to my feet. An already upset stomach from the headache and dizziness couldn't handle that, and I threw up. Most of it ended up on the floor, though some painted the front of my shirt and jeans.

"Yuck." I scrubbed my lips with the back of my hands. It didn't work. My mouth still held the tang of a sewage plant.

I caught Mrs. Hewitt staring at me. I apologized as my cheeks grew hot. "Sorry about that." Like sorry would cut it, as I'd just upchucked on her floor. "I'll clean it up."

"It's all right," said Mrs. Hewitt, grabbing a couple of rolls of paper towels and beginning to clean up the mess. "Not your fault."

A bit of noise came from behind me, and I turned around. *Oh*! Jake stood so close, I could have kissed him. Like he would want to kiss me after what I'd done. Heart pounding,

I backstepped and kicked aside some salt on the floor. The stuff scattered across the linoleum.

Okay, why's there salt on the floor? Frowning, I dimly recalled being caged somewhere, unable to get free. Memories flooded my brain, making pain rip through my head. I felt like the Siamese twin who felt the binge her sister went on.

Jake grabbed my hand. "Harper?"

Through the hurting and shock of remembering, I still felt a tingle from our touch. Pretty off the wall, our touching, and yet, I liked it.

I'd have to get back to that tingle later. There were more immediate things to fret about—such as the demon and its possession of my body.

Untangling my hand from his, I stuck it and my other one in the pockets of my jeans. I scuffed the floor with the toe of my tennis shoe. "Yeah, it's me. Not the demon."

"Harper, why do you keep persisting in that story?" His eyebrows knitted together, and lines burrowed in his forehead.

"I'm not, Jake. I'm possessed by a demon."

His eyes flashed disbelief.

"Honest, I'm not making it up."

Mrs. Hewitt put an arm around me and led me over to the kitchen table. "The demon is locked away in your head for now. I'm getting you my robe and putting your clothing in the wash. No way I will let you walk home like that."

"Do you have something for headaches? I've got a killer of one."

Mrs. Hewitt patted my shoulder. "I'll go fetch a couple of pain killers and get you that robe."

I slumped into a chair, rubbing at my temples. That didn't ease the headache. It didn't help that Jake stared at me from where he lounged against the wall. Or the weird feeling his stare gave me.

Mrs. Hewitt came back and handed me a glass of water along with a couple of pills she shook out of a bottle. She dropped the folded robe on the tabletop.

I swallowed the pills and chased them down with the water yhen handed the empty glass back to Mrs. Hewitt. "May I have more water, please?" Being possessed proved to be a thirsty business.

She nodded, "I will, but go get changed first in my laundry room and place your soiled clothing in the washing machine. You still remember where the laundry room is?"

I grabbed the robe, and, keeping it away from my messy clothing, I crossed over to the closed door of the laundry room off the kitchen. After stuffing my shirt and jeans in the wash, I shrugged on Mrs. Hewitt's robe and rejoined Jake and her in the kitchen.

Jake slid into the chair across the table from me when Mrs. Hewitt handed me the refilled glass. "Ah, come on, Mom, she wasn't possessed." He swiped the glass from his mother and studied me, his brows knitted together. "Confess, Harper."

"Cut it out, Jacob Bartholomew Hewitt." Mrs. Hewitt snatched the glass back and returned it to me.

Something seemed to be digging into my head. The pain went up a couple of notches in misery. I winced, tears welling up in my eyes. "Stop it." I wiped at them, then drank the water.

Jake retorted, "Stop what? I'm not doing anything. You're the one who's faking it."

I thumped the glass down on the table and snapped at him. "I am not faking it, Jake the Snake."

He glowered.

Good. I knew Jake would hate the childhood nickname I gave him years ago when we fought over something trivial at the time. Call me a faker, would he? Still, realizing I couldn't blame him for believing that, guilt washed over me. After all, wouldn't I think the same thing? Wouldn't most people? I remembered some talk show I'd watched on television about Catholic priests admitting to sending people to a psychiatrist first to be proved beyond doubt that demons possessed them before they would perform any exorcism. Not everyone had a demon in them. Most times, it came down to being mentally ill, but being possessed change one's perspective.

I sighed. "Sorry about the nickname. That was uncalled for, but I'm not lying."

Mrs. Hewitt brought over a plate of cookies. "Have a cookie, dear. These are peppermint sugar cookies. They might help your tummy after its upset." She turned to Jake. "Jake, she's telling you the truth. A demon, Cresil, possessed her." She nodded at me. "Excuse me, while I get your clothes started in my washing machine."

With a puckered brow, Jake filched a cookie, and then before biting into it, asked, "Were you possessed in class today?"

I snatched a cookie, too, and took a bite, chewing. After I swallowed, I replied. "Yes. I learned I'd been like that for a whole year."

"A whole year—" His eyes alight with understanding. "That fire in the old Miller house? Is that where it began, where you got...?"

I leaned over the table and pressed the palm of my hand against his mouth to silence him. "Yes, that's when it happened."

Withdrawing my hand, I gobbled up what remained of the cookie and seized another from the plate. The sweet gooiness and the spice of the peppermint kept my mind off memories of that night: that, and the peculiar jolt from the touch of Jake's lips beneath my palm.

I mean, come on, we're just friends. There has never been anything between us but what a brother and sister, or even cousins might feel. Right?

Kissin' cousins...

Okay, what a stupid thought. I would never dare to press my mouth against Jake's. Not even if I had to perform mouth-to-mouth resuscitation. Well, maybe for that. I couldn't even let my worst enemy die.

Is he your enemy, Harper?

I looked up and found Jake staring at me, puzzlement in his eyes and one eyebrow cocked. Fighting to keep the heat in my cheeks from becoming a red-rosy reality, I stared back; my chin thrust out.

I almost leaped out of my chair when I felt skin against skin. It was Mrs. Hewitt. She had returned from the laundry room; I could hear the washing machine filling. Her hand covered mine while her eyes held sympathy in them.

"Oh, honey, I am so sorry that you had this entity in your body that long," she said, her voice slow as Southern molasses. "If I'd known..." She whipped her accusing gaze on her son, who lowered his. "Jake, I don't know why you haven't been bringing her over here. I swear the last time I saw this child she was—"

"Fourteen years old. Mrs. Hewitt," I finished for her. "Jake and I haven't been friends in a long while—not since ninth grade."

Her eyes widened. "Has it been that long?" She switched back to Jake. "Why aren't the two of you still friends?"

I whispered, "Because he became friends with Pete Jameson and someone like me is no longer cool enough to know in the same universe, never mind the same school and town."

Mrs. Hewitt scowled as her hand tightened its hold on mine. "Jacob Bartholomew Hewitt, are you still hanging around with that no-account little self-service prig?"

Whoa. Did that mean Pete-the-jerk no longer came over here either? Or maybe never had?

I looked with interest at both of them.

Mrs. Hewitt shook a finger at Jake.

His face darkened, and defiance glittered in his eyes as he crossed his arms.

His mother's face tightened with lines of irritation.

I seized another cookie and munched on it, keeping quiet.

Jake mumbled. "Well, you told me he couldn't come back after the first time I invited him over. So, I hang around his house most of the time."

"The little rich brat broke my crystal ball. He...he-" for a moment, Mrs. Hewitt fumbled as if trying to recall what Pete actually said, "called it a paperweight!" She blushed. "I won't repeat the actual foul word he used with paperweight." She drew a breath and continued, "He also called my ball the ugliest thing he has ever seen. After that, he used several cuss words a truck driver would be ashamed to spout. I never washed anyone's mouth out with soap, even yours, Jake, but my fingers itched to do it to him."

Yeah, Pete talks a blue streak. He did that a lot at school, but because his daddy employed most of the people here in his factory and Moon Ridge Winery—Mr. Jameson owned most of the town, too—he didn't get into trouble for it. No doubt, that's a reason why Pete never spent time in detention or got expelled from school like other kids.

I propped my chin on the hand that felt Jake's lips earlier and, with the other one, got me another cookie. All this drama would gain me some weight. Guess I'll have to work out harder in P.E. because I love cookies.

Mrs. Hewitt's eyes narrowed with suspicion. "Have you been hanging with that brat all this time?"

Jake looked back with his lips twisted with disdain. "He doesn't treat me like I'm some poor white trash kid of a crazy woman who claims she communicates with the dead."

I sucked in my breath, almost choking on a few crumbs of the cookie.

Mrs. Hewitt sat rock still, not answering.

I didn't know about Jake, but I could feel the heat of anger rising off her skin. Maybe most of the town said Mrs. Hewitt spouted nonsense, but they didn't say it to her face.

Of course, Mr. Rick Jameson did. Mr. Jameson said what he wanted because he believed he owned the town in the tight grip of his fist. Pete only mimicked what his father said, because Daddy put all the money in his pockets without making him earn it.

I remember the one time I saw Chloe Jameson, Pete's young stepmother, walking her dog at the park and she ran into Mrs. Hewitt. The woman picked up her prissy chihuahua and carried it as if it might get soiled from any close contact with Jake's mom.

Mr. Jameson said he met his second wife in New York City at some fancy get-together given by one of his cronies. He claimed that she'd worked as a model and made money. If the bimbo happened to be that great of a model, making all the bucks, why did she marry Mr. Jameson? Why not a richer man that lived in New York, or even some producer from Hollyweird?

The demon snickered. *"I see what the woman looks like in your head. Mortality is hitting her, as she appears old, turning from calf to cow with sagging—"*

Hush!

I could imagine what the next word would have been if I hadn't shushed her. The trouble was, that didn't stop her.

"Just because I shoved you in your id, do you have to do it to me? You can't believe all the junk from your memories cluttering up this place. Blech!"

Mrs. Hewitt rose from her seat simultaneously as her voice did, turning my interest and the demon's on the interaction between mother and son. "That's it, Jacob Bartholomew Hewitt! You are now grounded after school until...forever! Rick Jameson thinks he's better than the rest of this town but let me tell you this: I know where that pompous ass's father dug his way out, and it was not with a spoon made of silver or gold!"

She stomped off but paused at the doorway to look back at me. "What are you waiting for, Harper? Do you want to sit at the same table as someone who probably thinks you're not good enough to be friends with?"

I leaped to my feet and seized the plate of cookies just as Jake extended his hand to take one. His fingers wiggled at air instead. He flashed me a fierce look as I pranced out of the room after Mrs. Hewitt.

"Eat air!" The demon called back to him as I stepped into the living room.

Sitting down next to Mrs. Hewitt on the couch, I set the plate on the coffee table, and reached down to grab the last cookie when I remembered Mrs. Hewitt.

I pointed to it instead. "Did you want this cookie, Mrs. Hewitt?"

She shook her head. "No, you go ahead and eat it." She sighed. "Where did I go wrong?" She mumbled to herself, although I caught it.

My fingers went numb. No longer able to hold the cookie, it fell onto my lap. Everything froze. and it sounded like Mrs. Hewitt's speaking came from far away. First, a kaleidoscope of colors that morphed into gray, and finally black, splashed across my vision.

"Taking your body back, mortal."

"Oh no, you don't. It's mine." I fought the demon, but my spirit proved too weak. *God, I'm so tired, I felt so tired.*

"Fight the demon. You do have the ability to do so." Another voice broke in.

I blinked as a bright orb of light filled my vision. It hovered up at the ceiling. Though my teeth felt like heavy rock and my lips clumsy, I opened my mouth.

An animal growl filled my head. *"No, no. Damn busybody angels!"*

Confusion filled my head. *Angels?*

Cresil purred in my head. *"Forget that angel. He doesn't know what he's talking about."*

My soul fell back into the cell of my mind, then...nothing more.

Chapter Seven- Cresil

I snatched at the cookie teeter-tottering on my leg and shook it at the older female human. "I'll tell you where you went wrong, woman. You thought your little angel would remain that: an angel. There are plenty of demons down in Hell who did not listen to their mommies and daddies. It has been like that for eons with humankind. If they did, Lucifer would be broke, with only two little souls to rub together."

I looked at the ceiling and around the rest of the room, but I didn't see a telltale spark of Heavenly goodliness anywhere. Whoever...whatever spoke, it left after Harper and I traded places.

Had I scared it off?

I smirked at the image of an angel high tailing away from me. I admit I'm good at smirking. Call me the demon of smirkiness.

Yeah right, like any angel, will flitter off in terror of you. I dropped the smartass expression.

The bratty boy's mother stared at me. She didn't look happy.

Mrs. Hewitt remarked, "I thought we'd got rid of you for a while."

I giggled. "You can't keep a good demon down in its host." I stuffed the cookie into my mouth. Cookie crumbs flew everywhere as I cackled at what I'd just said.

Not even bothering to wipe my mouth, I snatched the plate and licked at the remaining crumbs on it, then put it back down on the coffee table.

The woman rose from the couch and, with both hands on her hips, glared at me. "You're going back under that pentagram."

I sputtered, cookie crumbs flying everywhere. "Oh no, I am not. I don't want to be in this pathetic meat suit any more than you want me to be, but there's no way you will stick me under that pentagram again." I leaped to my feet and kicked the coffee table by accident. The plate wobbled to the edge, toppling over, and falling to the rug.

Mrs. Hewitt screamed. "Jake! Help! Quickly, before she escapes."

I shot like a bullet for the front door. The woman might be a psychic, but her son wouldn't be easy to control. Had to admit though, he's cuter than my last crush a zillion years ago.

I bet he kisses great with those lips, too. Unfortunately, the way Harper shies away from him, I doubted I would ever find out. Besides, wizard-boy might blast me past the end of this galaxy. And I couldn't be sure if the feeling were more due to Harper than me. He's not my type.

Just as I seized the doorknob, two arms clasped me beneath my breasts and yanked me back hard against a firm male chest. I struggled, stomping on Jake's boots, hoping to hurt him, but it didn't work. I tried my magic, but I couldn't get it out. His own magic appeared to be blocking mine. I screeched as the anger flushed through my body, and I slammed my head back, but he pushed me to the floor, gripping Harper's arms behind her back.

"Been working out?" He whispered in the left ear. "Where are your powers, spazz demon?"

"Shut up!"

The boy lifted me back on my feet and dragged me to stand beneath the five-pointed star. I dug my feet in, but it didn't work—his strength won over Harper's body. "You're not putting me back under that." I snapped Harper's teeth at his fingers when he flipped me around.

I couldn't understand why I couldn't use my demonic powers to free myself. Was it due to the teenage mutant sorcerer himself? It appeared, even though untrained, his powers worked on me somehow. That must be it.

Another thing, maybe he ragged on about his mother being a fake and agreed with friends that she was, but in reality, he knew her to be the real deal. I could sense the truth. Not sure how this might help me, but I tucked the information away.

Stumbling, I dropped to Harper's knees as he got me beneath the drawn symbols on the ceiling. When he moved away, I bolted to my feet and put out a hand, ready to cast a spell on his mother to stop her from pouring salt to finish the circle around me. A sudden flash of pain in my metaphysical brain prevented me, and Harper's legs gave out. I ground her teeth against the agony as Mrs. Hewitt completed the circle. Just as fast as it hit me, the pain vanished. I clawed my way back upright. Our stomach twisted, and I grabbed it with both hands, trying not to upchuck.

Well, here I am again. What kind of evil spirit am I that an untried sorcerer could get me? A low-caste imp? A fricking fallen angel?

Jake snapped his fingers a few inches from my face, though he stayed on the other side of the salt. "Harper?"

I wanted to slap him. "Harper is not at home to take your calls, but if you leave a message at the beep..."

"Such a real live wire, aren't you?" His eyes held a ring of gold around his pupils, and for the first time since we wrestled, I felt his powers increasing several notches.

Shit. His power is growing.

My anger fizzled. My palms grew slick with sweat, and chills ran up my spine. Even without knowledge of how powerful he was, an untried sorcerer could still reduce any demon—except Lucifer—to ash. I might like playing with fire, but I never had plans to let it do a slow burn with me as the kindling.

"Look..."

He stabbed a finger in the air, over my side of the salt, and just inches from my face. "Look nothing. Leave Harper alone and get your pointed horns, forked tongue, and tail out of her body."

Hells bells, what these mortals believe to be the truth. I blamed it on too much bad press from poorly written horror novels and movies.

"That's a misnomer." I croaked, keeping an eye on his finger and hoping nothing zapped out of it.

"What?"

I cleared the throat and spoke up. "Misnomer. Mistake. Demons don't actually have horns, tails, and forked tongues. Not unless we use our powers to appear in that form. But it's not our real selves. We're only spirits, needing a meat suit to be able to do things like eat, kiss, rock and roll, things like that."

Mrs. Hewitt butted in. "Are you being smart with us, demon?"

I didn't respond to her, but I kept my gaze straight on Jake. I had to know.

"Do you believe you are talking to a demon now, or that Harper's faking you out, or even off her rocker?"

He blew out a breath. "I may have been stupid to think so earlier, but no, I know it can't be Harper this time. Why are you using her body?"

Yeah, why? I sure would like the answer to that million-dollar question. A bit of memory returned, a germ of one that sluggishly flitted into almost thought. But it dissipated before I could snatch it.

I shrugged. "Maybe I wanted to possess the girl for shits and giggles. What do you think?"

"That you have an attitude, demon."

I snorted. "Better believe it. By the way, my name is Cresil. Otherwise, I'll keep calling you boy. Like that, BOY?"

He grimaced. "No, I don't, CRESIL."

Touché. I sagged, not wanting to fight anymore.

I began to empathize with Harper. When I found myself sucked up from Hell, I'd been surprised to find the girls nothing more than children. Children in puberty and on the verge of adulthood, but still kids, nonetheless. Before, in past possessions, I could get out of the bodies I'd taken over. Something changed that night. Had someone whammied me to meld with this fleshy prison of teenage heartbreak and acne? Yes, I began to believe that to be the correct answer.

The question remained: who or what was behind the orchestration? The ability to do so took a lot of magical mojo. Mojo, which to my knowledge, I'm sure I didn't possess.

Mrs. Hewitt picked up that book again and started reading from it. The words formed in the air. Forceful, they wrenched at the flesh and pain scraped claws through every molecule. I fought not to cry out as they ripped me a new one.

What's going on? The inner door in Harper's mind swung open, and Harper screamed from inside. That doubled the agony for me. Was this exorcism harming her, too? I managed to slam the door shut again, cutting her off in mid-scream.

The throbbing continued to rent through me, as it shredded me with sharp metaphysical instruments. I wanted to die; no, I was dying. Except I can't die, being anything but a spirit anyway. What unnaturalness could this be that Harper was me and I was Harper? One unable to leave the other? I looked up at the clock on the kitchen wall and saw it was two hours later.

Two hours later?

Something leaked out of my eyes, trailing down my cheeks. I touched it with trembling fingers and looked at the glistening drop.

A tear?

The bodies that demons possessed never cried because we cannot cry. Only the living shed tears.

The teardrop fell, landing on a grain of salt.

"Mom, she's crying. Is Harper back?"

"No, it's still Cresil, Jake."

"Is it trying to fake us out?"

"No, Jake, it's not."

I hated what was happening. Bodies were great to possess, but I wanted to be free of Harper's. This exorcism proved I couldn't shake her. All it was doing was hurting me, hurting Harper. I begged as more tears rained out of my eyes, "Help me. Help Harper. Untwine us another way, because what you are doing is harmful to not just me, but Harper, too."

Like we were ropes twisted together and tied with a good sailor's knot. I couldn't untangle this mess. Not on my own anyway.

Through the glistening wetness, I saw begrudging sympathy in the psychic's eyes. "I'm sorry, demon. I am not sure what I can do. There's never been anything like this in my experience before. By now, I should've expelled you back to Hell."

The smart-mouthed demon in me wanted to snarl that I didn't need her sympathy. Instead, I scrubbed at the tears and whimpered. "It's fun possessing bodies, but we're supposed to be able to escape these fleshy prisons when we want, or when someone like a witch, a psychic, or a priest vanquishes us using exorcism. Instead, I'm living some teenage girl's life."

The woman tapped a finger against her chin. "Jake, I need you to go to my bedroom where I keep my books on the paranormal and find every one of them that has something on demons. Bring them all to the living room. I'm setting the demon free from its salted circle."

He glanced at me, lack of trust back in his eyes. "You sure that's a good idea, Mom?"

She nodded. "I think Cresil has as much to gain from me finding how to be set Harper free as much as we do. The demon won't do anything to me." She stared at me. "Isn't that right?"

I nodded. "Yeah, I'm not going to eat your face off, mortal."

Mrs. Hewitt rolled her eyes, but she filched a broom and swept away all of the salt, scooping it up in a dustpan and tossing it in the trash. She propped the broom against the wall and headed for the living room.

I limped after her while Jake went to collect the books. She grabbed my arm just as I was about to sit down on the couch.

She planted her face much too close for my comfort. "My name is Mrs. Hewitt. Not mortal or woman, or anything else, especially the cuss words. Same goes for Jake—he's Jake, and this is the last time I will say it."

"Okay, Mrs. Hewitt."

She dropped the arm, and both of us sat down. We didn't say anything, just stared at each other until Jake rushed in, a load of heavy books cradled in his arms.

Most of the volumes smelled like musty books you might find in a used bookstore. But an odor of magic drifted from a couple of them. I mean the really, really old kind. Whether good or evil or even the in-between kind, I couldn't tell. I just hoped not the harmful-to-demons kind.

Jake deposited all of them on the coffee table and took a seat in the recliner nearby.

Mrs. Hewitt seized a book and started flipping through its pages. She paused on occasion to stare at something on a page, wrinkling her nose before she continued turning the pages again. The first one speed-read, Mrs. Hewitt placed it next to her. She picked up two books with both hands and dispensed one to me and the other to Jake.

"You two read those, and I'll take this one," she said, snatching another tome from the pile.

Jake opened the book in his hands. "What are we looking for?"

Her forehead wrinkled as she stared down at the book she held. "Look for anything that mentions this peculiar possession happening to someone else or how to fix the problem. Surely, this has occurred before—at least, I hope it has."

I glanced down at the book on my lap. The cover was a bright blue with words in red scribbled across the leather on the extensive and heavy volume. *Kinda pretty for a book and it's giving off a scent of magic, too*. Curious, I opened it, and the smell slapped me in the face and crawled up my nostrils. I sneezed. I sneezed three more times after that. Not little sneezes but big honking ones. The magic it contained didn't like a demon looking at it; it tried to overpower me, to keep me from reading it.

I closed the book before it did more damage to me, to this body. Thank Lucifer, it wasn't good magic, or instead of sneezing, it would have burned me the minute I touched it. It still did a number on me.

Well, that's all par and parcel with being a devil. But I think Mrs. Hewitt should be more careful what she handed me if she wanted me to help.

I handed it back to her. "I'll take another book. Magic hovers over that one like a cloud, and I had an allergic reaction." I grimaced. "Make sure the next book doesn't have magic attached to it that might do something to me. Otherwise, you will burn pretty little Harper's fingers with a vengeance. You may not care for me, but I am sure you do for her."

She sniffed at one, shook her head, and took another whiff of another book before offering that one to me. Nothing came from it. Only dust motes rose as I flipped it open.

We read forever, it seemed, though in reality, only for the rest of the afternoon into the early evening. I had to stop in the middle of my reading to call Harper's mother as Mrs. Hewitt didn't want the human woman worried. She took the receiver from me and spoke to Mrs. Doyle.

She said, "I hope you don't mind if Harper stays for dinner and watches a movie with us afterward? Jake asked me, so I had Harper call to ask you. She said she forgot to grab her phone when she left home."

Mrs. Doyle said something I couldn't hear, but by Mrs. Hewitt's grin, I knew the woman had given her permission. Mrs. Hewitt passed the receiver back to me when she finished.

Harper's mother's voice spoke softly into my ear. "I am so glad you and Jake are friends again. I wondered why I never saw him over at our house anymore. I won't keep you, but maybe you'll tell me why later?"

She didn't wait for me to say anything, just blurted goodbye and told me she loved me, er, Harper, and the phone clicked off in my ear. I stared at the receiver for a while. I'd never had anyone tell me they loved me. Well, God, my Father, had, plus many of the angels. But that was before I did the traitor thing. The Fall ended all that touchy-feely stuff.

Who needed all that love and goody-two-shoes junk anyway? Who cared if I used to be an angel? Being a demon made me a tough chick.

Sharing Harper's body with her made me privy to why she and Jake hadn't been best buds for a while, but I sure wasn't going to blab out the truth to her momma. Anyway, there's no profit for me in doing so—no soul taking or anything. It sure wasn't because I didn't want to upset the woman. No, nothing like that. Still, I felt good inside, strangely enough.

"Harper's old lady bought it," I said, as Mrs. Hewitt took the receiver from me.

"Good. Although not good in that you called Harper's mother her old lady—that's rude—but good in that she believed the story. I don't like lying to her, but telling her that her daughter has the devil in her is not what I like to do. Of course, she would think I'm nuts if I said it."

I grinned. "I liked it that you told Mrs. Doyle a lie."

Her brows came together. "It's only right that we keep her from ever finding out that you inhabit her daughter's body, Cresil. Until we unbind you."

"Such a dipshit demon," said Jake, snorting with quiet laughter.

I glared at him. I opened our mouth to spout off something cuss-worthy when I caught Mrs. Hewitt's eye.

She flashed me a look and shook her head but kept silent, slipping me another book. The woman turned to Jake and said, "Watch that potty mouth, mister."

I snickered from behind the opened book on Harper's propped-up lap.

His mother hissed, "Not one more word or sound from either of you. Read!"

We all resumed reading.

Dork-breath human, I thought. Hell's bells, I'm glad his mother can't hear my thoughts.

Jake gave me a fixed stare, then lowered his gaze to his book.

As evening came on, its shadows spread long fingers through the glass of the big picture window and into the room. Mrs. Hewitt clicked the floor lamp at the couch's left side, and light chased the darkness into corners.

We lay down the last of the books and took a stretch. Nothing had been found even remotely feasible to help get me out of this meat prison. Frustrated, I wanted to run into the kitchen and grab a knife from a drawer and stab this body right through the heart. It seemed that death might be the only way I could escape.

But I knew the medium and her son wouldn't let me. Guilt filled me at considering it. Anyway, the way things were going, I might die when Harper died.

"There's nothing in any of these," I complained, pointing at the books. "They're nothing but useless trash!"

"Hush," said Mrs. Hewitt, "Not useless. It appears I don't have the right book for this dilemma."

There was no way out of this mess.

Unable to stand it any longer, I bolted and flung open the front door, streaking outside. I heard the thunder of their footsteps not far behind me. Who cared? Agony burned inside this flesh, and the inability to do anything about it was the only thing that concerned me at the moment.

I wanted to punch something, anything. Maybe I caused this predicament, but something told me I hadn't. Hell, it might be an archangel. I might as well think it: it could have been Lucifer himself.

I ran and ran, hoping I put enough distance between Jake and Mrs. Hewitt and me. I didn't stop, not until I found myself in front of the house where it all began.

Harper's lungs fighting for air, I stared at the building, the light of the bright full moon washing over its bones. The ghosts of burning wood and, worse, human flesh still haunted the nose we shared. Bile fought to rise.

I took in deep breaths of clean air. Finally, our shared upset stomach became convinced the smell came from memories and not the real thing, and subsided.

Stepping through the doorway, I pushed aside what remained of the door, barely hanging by one hinge that hadn't melted like the rest. I hated being here, but this place held the key to me being in this mortal realm. Something went wrong that night, and I meant to find out why.

"I'm the reason why, you stupid, low-caste demon."

Whoa! What the. ..? I looked around for the owner of the voice. It sounded familiar. Not human, no, not that, but... Hellish. Dark. Pure evil. The hair rose on the back of Harper's neck. A foul odor tickled the nose hairs.

I followed the smell to one shadow-haunted corner. A glimmer hung in the air, like a half-done orb, shining and yet, invisible. More darkness than light.

Orbs are the state most ghosts, demons, and angels achieve when they couldn't or didn't want to show themselves in complete spectral form. A large, gray ball drifted from the shadows.

Then the damned thing spit hellfire at me.

I stumbled like a drunk to the left to avoid it.

"Ah, you see me. Feel the heat, don't you?"

That voice—recognizable, but I still couldn't place it. I fisted my spectra hands and made Harper's fleshy ones do the same. "Show yourself. Who are you? Why did you do this to me?"

The shimmer grew more definite, the orb reshaping into a mist. From the mist, it morphed into a mass of darkness. Red eyes glowered from the top part of the shadow-being.

Spirits can become shadows. Contrary to what some paranormal reality shows tell people, most shadow-people are not evil. But whoa to the person who runs into one with red eyes. That meant they were dealing with a demon.

The one facing me loomed large. I mean, as if a grizzly bear had stood up on its hind legs, type of large. Much scarier than a bear, to be honest.

"Come on," I said through a dry mouth. Harper's heartbeat galloped beneath her breast, thump, thump, thumpity-thump, not unlike a herd of racehorses. "All the way. I want to see what you look like, know who you are." I had my suspicions about the identity of the fiend, but as humans say, "I need to see to believe." If I was proved correct, the last time I had heard and seen this fiend had been in Hell, and in Hell, we all sound different than on the mortal plane.

Dark laughter filled the room as the spectral shape solidified. The heart went into overdrive, punching at Harper's chest.

Hell's bells, it's not just any higher caste demon, but Baal, head of the Infernal Armies of the 66 legions and one of Lucifer's right-hand demon lords. He had fallen when Lucifer and his followers went against God and had been caught and punished.

I had been one of those idiot followers myself. I went from a lower angel in the hierarchy to a low-caste demon in Hell, one that Baal tormented and tortured for most of my unnatural unlife. No, not everyone ruled in Hell as that stupid book, *Dante's Inferno,* inferred. Some of us became the dirt beneath the clawed feet of the lucky ones who rose to the top of the demonic food chain

Baal stepped forward. He had an awful grin, and his glowing eyes lit up his face like a jack-o-lantern at Halloween.

I wanted to blow out his candle. The trouble was, I couldn't take him on, even if I wanted to. The evil beast could smash this body I inhabited into a bloodless pulp, sucking all the blood before he did so, and send me right back to a part of Hell demons feared to be put in: Tantalus was more than human mythology.

"I cast the spell that put your pitiful soul into that body when those brats dared to summon me from the depths of Hell. I wanted an entity trapped inside a human body so that I could keep the portal propped open. It wouldn't do for Lucifer's chief commander of his legions not to be able to lead them into the world if I hadn't done the job right. You made a good patsy, Cresil."

Shouts came from outside the building, and Baal turned to look. Hatred tightened the dissipated features of his face and he vanished.

I turned and ran into something warm and solid. I breathed in the odor of humanity, not just any human, but the boy, Jake.

"Hey, I—"

A loud crack sang in the air, and the right side of my face vibrated with pain.

Jake stood over me.

I snarled in his face. "How dare you? That hurts!"

Harper's voice blasted in the body's brain. She had gotten free of her cell, screaming *"Give me back my body!"*

I fainted right into Jake's arms.

Chapter Eight—Harper

I sat up and swung my legs off the couch. Soreness throbbed at my right cheek. *God, that smarts!* Tears welled up in my eyes. "Why's my face hurting?"

Someone patted my shoulder.

Blinking through the wetness, I saw Jake's face close to mine, concern in his eyes. Embarrassed that he'd caught me bawling, I scrub at the tears with a sleeve. Pain ripped through the cheek from the movement.

"Jake and I brought you back to the house," said Mrs. Hewitt, handing me a cold compress. "You were in that burned-out building on Morgan Street."

I laid the cloth against my cheek, being careful. The ache eased.

Jake blushed and mumbled. "Sorry. The demon was screeching, and I slapped it. I never meant to hurt you, Harper."

Something vague teased the horizon of my memories, but I couldn't catch it. I didn't remember what happened when Cresil possessed me again. Mrs. Hewitt and Jake hadn't told me why the demon was in that place, either. I only remember demanding my body back, then sometime later—now—waking up on Mrs. Hewitt's couch.

With a part of his T-shirt and a ginger touch, Jake wiped at my eyes and cheeks. "Glad to see you're back."

Even though my face stung, I leaned into his hug. He smelled good, and his touch felt comforting. For a moment, I closed my eyes and savored the moment, before I reopened them and peered up at his face. His strong chin, lips of...

What the—

I withdrew and stepped back a couple of steps.

Whoa. Jake had been my friend for years, and then he became a boy I didn't like, but now I get tingles every time he touches me? Did that demon do this to me?

Mrs. Hewitt took the compress. She looked at Jake, who stared at me as if he'd never seen me before.

"Jake? Jake! Go get me a glass of water and the bottle of pain killers in the medicine cabinet in the bathroom."

He didn't move, and I looked into his eyes. Neither of us blinked or breathed. Time stood still.

"Jacob Bartholomew Hewitt! Get me the water and pills. Now!"

Jake broke contact first and blinked at his mother, before he stumbled away.

I broke into tears.

Mrs. Hewitt hauled me against her body and, with her arms around me, drew us both down onto the couch as she comforted me and handed me a tissue from the box on the coffee table.

"There, there. It's all right. We'll figure how to get the demon out of you somehow."

I would work out the puzzle of Jake later. The demon, Cresil, was the immediate problem.

Sniveling less, I pulled away. "This time, I can't remember that the demon took over. What happens if I'm at home with Mom eating dinner and it takes over my body, or worse, while I'm at school? It might say things or do things, things that could put me in juvenile hall or worse, a mental hospital. 'The devil made me do it' won't work with most people."

She shook her head. "I don't know. All I know is that Cresil helped me and Jake read all the books on magic I own. If it had been a typical fiend, it wouldn't have done that. And by the way, it's female, at least, from what she told me. Unless it assumes the sex of the body that it possesses?"

"It's talked to me, but the demon has never said anything about being female or male. I did get its name, Cresil. But anything else, nothing. She may be able to find out anything about me from being inside my head, but she has kept her secrets pretty tight from me."

"Cresil is the demon of impurity and laziness."

"Great," I said. "Of all the demons to possess me, I get what sounds like a loser."

Jake returned at that moment. He held a glass of water in one hand and a bottle of painkillers in the other. He handed me the glass.

Mrs. Hewitt took the bottle, unscrewed the cap, and shook out a couple of pills onto the palm of my other hand.

I washed them down with the water.

Mrs. Hewitt took the empty glass and gave it to Jake. "Put this in the sink." She sat the bottle on the coffee table while Jake went into the kitchen.

Rubbing the material of my jeans, I asked, "What do I do, Mrs. Hewitt? How can I keep the demon tamped down?"

"I don't know. Yes, I am a psychic, and yes, I handle ghost possessions, but I never encountered a demonic entity in a person before. The last demon I actually had any experience with haunted a house. Between a priest and me, we rid the house and its owners of that fiend." She tucked a strand of her long blonde hair behind an ear. "But blessing a house and an exorcism of a person are two different things. Your problem is worse than that. From what Cresil told me, something crammed her in you and a regular exorcism won't be able to shake her free of you. The little devil's right because I tried it. There's never been anything of that precedence before in paranormal history, that I know of anyway. I need more knowledge than what I have in this house. If it makes you feel any better, Cresil wants to leave you, too."

"Are you certain about that?"

"Yes, I am a hundred percent sure...well, maybe ninety-nine percent sure anyway. You can never be positive of a demon—they do lie, you know."

Is the demon lying about not being able to get free of my body, or is Cresil telling the truth?

I wanted to go home to the comfort of my mother's arms. I blinked back tears that blinded my sight and scrubbed at them. "Mrs. Hewitt, I better get home before my mother freaks out."

"I had the demon give her a call, telling her that you had been invited here for dinner and to watch a movie with us afterward. Besides, do you really want your mother to see that red mark on your right cheek from Jake's slap?"

I jumped up and ran to the bathroom. After hitting the light switch and light flooding the room, I stared at my reflection in the mirror and touched the reddened cheek. I winced.

Mrs. Hewitt strolled in with the washcloth from earlier, where she wetted it with cold water from the faucet, wrung it out, and then led me back to the couch. She pressed it gently against my cheek, making sure I kept it there as she needed to make dinner.

Jake wandered into the living room, his head down, and slumped down in the chair across from me, opening up his phone to a social media website.

Okay, this wouldn't do. He was avoiding me. I didn't blame him for hitting me.

"Jake?"

He stared down at his phone, scrolling through it.

"Jake?"

Now, this is getting ridiculous.

I dropped the cloth on the coffee table and walked over to him and punched him in the upper arm.

His head snapped up, almost dropping the phone. "Ow! What's that for?"

I grinned. "Well, since you did slap me, I figured tit for tat."

He looked serious. "I'm sorry, Harper. I never meant to hurt you. I think I was freaked out. I mean, I know Mom talks to ghosts and I always denied it, but you took off...no, the demon in you bolted." His voice dropped to a whisper and he looked down at his phone. "I slapped you. Only creeps do that."

I grew serious and placed my hand over his. "Jake, thanks."

"For what? Slapping you?"

"No, for coming to my rescue." I took my hand off his and lightly tapped his cheek. "Just don't do it again and we're square."

His cheeks reddened.

I'd never seen him blush before. Ever.

He shrugged. "It's the least I could do. After all, we were friends for a long time."

"Why did we stop being friends?"

"Stop?"

"When did you decide that I wasn't your friend anymore?"

Jake kept his eyes on his phone and cleared his throat, but he still didn't give me an answer.

This was getting tiresome, with him not looking at me and avoiding giving me the truth. Anger boiled up inside me.

"I know when our friendship went away," I said. "It's when you became friends with that creep, Pete Jameson."

He raised his head, his eyes flaming, and his hands tightly fisted against his thighs. At least he looked at me and not the floor. "Pete is not a creep. He's a great friend."

"The first time you go against what he wants, he'll prove he's not the best buddy in the world."

His nostrils flared. "He's not that way. You don't know him at all."

"You're just like him, too—now. I remember a kind, thoughtful Jake. One who spent time with his old friends and didn't make fun of his mother, just because she heard and saw ghosts." I frowned. "Although you never let on about her being a psychic. Best friends don't hold secrets from each other, and yet, you treated her like a dirty secret you kept hidden from me. So maybe that part's not because of Pete, but you." I folded my arms. "That's terrible, Jake. You're ashamed of your own mother. I always thought she was one of the best mothers I ever met. You're lucky to have her. Who cares if she talks to dead people?"

He snorted. "You're such a know-it-all, always telling someone what to do. What do you know about living with a mother people in town consider a crackpot, yet come here to seek their futures from her? Not a single thing."

Am I a know-it-all? Does Jake really believe I order him around? I've never...and that hurts.

I pressed my nails deep into the palms of my hands. "I don't like to tell people what to do. But I will tell you something. You're as big a jerk as Pete is. Stuck-up, smart-mouthed—"

He jumped up, shouting, his face rosy all over, this time from anger. "No, I'm not! At least I can say I'm not a magnet attracting demons to possess. And it's not some big, bad-assed demon, either, but a pathetic one." He stomped to the other side of the room. "Hear that? You're a lame-o that only lame-o demons possess."

Tears blinded me before slipping down my face. How could he be such a brat? I wiped my cheeks, wincing at the tenderness from the one Jake struck.

"Are you saying that I attract only wretched demons to take me? If I am so lame-o, you must be, too, because we were the best of friends for a long time. You only have Pete and now, Tyree, for friends nowadays because I don't see you guys hanging with anyone else. Excuse me, except for that bully, Brian Woods. At least I had Shellie, Carrie Ann, Lisa, and Barbie."

"Yeah, and look how that turned out. They died."

How dare he? *How dare he*? I ran over and swung my fists, plummeting him like a punching bag. All the agony I felt from my friends' deaths and my life since the possession washed over me.

Jake didn't retaliate or say another word; he just stood there. The sound of my fists connecting with his flesh filled my ears, but I ignored it and kept pummeling.

The clearing of a throat filled the air. I stopped and whipped around.

Mrs. Hewitt.

I stared down at my fists and then back at Jake.

He stood like stone. A slight trickle of blood trickled from his nose, one eye was closed, and I bet bruises would appear on his face, even on his body.

I turned to Mrs. Hewitt. She opened her arms. I darted into them, crying, and she folded them around me.

She looked at Jake over my head. "I heard everything from the kitchen, Jake. How could you? It's not her fault the demon took possession of her. She's right about that Jameson kid, though. I've been telling you he's not the right sort of—"

"Friend," he finished. "Yeah, like I haven't heard it a thousand times before from you." Suddenly, he sagged. "I'm sorry, Harper. That was mean of me. You aren't a demon magnet. Damn it; you've got a mean set of fists."

I sniffed and stepped away from Mrs. Hewitt's arms. "I'm sorry for hitting you."

Jake crossed the room. "I'm sorry. I don't know why I said that. But I don't like anyone mashing on my friends." He shrugged. "Even if he can be a dick."

I stared at him, open-mouthed. First, a word I never thought he dared say in his mother's presence, and second, that he admitted that Pete was no angel.

His eyebrows knitted together like thunderclouds. "Look, I know he can be a class-A snot, but he's still my friend."

"Am I?"

He arched an eyebrow.

I blew air through my nostrils. "Your friend?"

"Yeah, you are."

He hugged me, wincing when I hugged him back. Yeah, I got him good. That feeling about him came over me again, but with his mother looking on—I tamped it down. Besides, this was not the time to examine the electrifying jolt that sparked between Jake and me. After all, he didn't acknowledge he felt it, too.

A disturbing thought hit me as I slipped from his hold and turned to Mrs. Hewitt. Did Cresil know how I felt about Jake? Or—and this troubled me on many levels—did the demon have this feeling about him, too? Could these feelings be due to the both of us meshed together like Siamese twins? My stomach churned the acid in it like butter.

Later, at dinner, as Jake and his mother chatted, I peered at him from under my lowered eyelashes. Saw how handsome he was for the first time. No longer the skinny, freckle-faced kid I always thought of as a brother, but a different Jake. I now understood why girls giggled when he passed them by in the hallways at school. Yeah, maybe the bad-boy image helped, but he was cute on his own, even without that reputation.

"Forget cute—the boy's hot." Cresil's voice echoed in my head.

Fighting the flush of heat threatening to inch up the back of my neck, I took a bite of my mashed potatoes when Jake looked at me, a question in his eyes. The food went down wrong, and I almost choked on a piece of meat scooped up with the potatoes. I swept up my glass of soda and sipped.

That helped. I gave Jake a slight grin, and he turned back to his mother. I put down the glass with a shaking hand.

I got to my feet, pushing my chair back. "Mrs. Hewitt, I need to use the bathroom."

She nodded. "Sure, sure. You know where it's at."

I fought the urge to bolt, meandering out of the kitchen. A sixth sense told me Jake's gaze was plastered to my back as I went through the doorway.

Once inside the bathroom, I closed the door behind me and locked it. Not switching on the light, I leaned my forehead against it and sighed. The wood held a slight chill to it. Feeling somewhat safe in the dark, I fumbled around and found the toilet with its seat down and sat.

My life had been changing ever since that night a year ago. Okay, my friends did the summoning. I told them it was a stupid thing to do. But I didn't expect them to succeed, as I hadn't believed demons existed.

But they did. One of them shared my body. It just let me know Jake was hot.

I got off the toilet, and my fingers faltered along the wall, trailing over the light switch. I flipped it, and light flooded the room. Standing in front of the sink, I stared at my reflection in the mirror of the medicine cabinet hung on the wall.

My cheek no longer shone red as blood. It looked pale pink now. My hair needed brushing, except I didn't have my purse—that was back at home. Using my fingers, I combed out the strands best as I could. I turned on the tap and bent over, splashing cold water on my face. Just as I reached out for the towel hanging on the towel bar nearby, I saw the image in the mirror and almost screamed.

Red eyes with no pupils stared back at me in an inhuman face with sunken cheeks. Its flesh shone pale, see-through enough for me to see the reflection of the framed picture on the wall behind me. It grinned, revealing razor-sharp fangs crowding its maw.

I gripped the edge of the sink.

"Do you think you could win the blue ribbon yourself at the county fair?" The image spoke in Cresil's voice.

Whoa! *Am I going crazy*?

"No, you're not going off the deep bend, human. It's me, Cresil, channeling your brain waves with my magic to talk to you by use of this looking glass." Cresil snickered. "Good looking, ain't I?" She cackled. "Anyway, I'm just projecting a scary image on purpose, not what I actually look like. Demon, you know." It busted out in full laughter.

I skittered backward, right smack into the wall, knocking the picture off to hit my shoulder before it landed on the floor. That hurt, but I didn't care. I didn't even check to see if I'd broken it. Not when the demon that possessed your body for a year found a way to show itself to you. It bothered me that it made this reflection in amusement, to unnerve me.

I stared at Cresil. "Why can't you just give me some space?"

"Look, if I could jiggle free of you, I would." Her terrifying image drew closer to its side of the glass. "If you and your bratty friends hadn't decided to call up a depraved soul from

Hell neither of us would be in this unholy mess." She frowned. "Again, maybe I would still be in this fix. It would just be another foolish mortal. The real problem is that you guys didn't call me, but Baal, head of the Infernal Armies of the 66 Legions and one of Lucifer's right-hand dark angels. He's not just a non-human entity. He's one of the most powerful demon lords around. Only Lucifer is stronger. Baal used magic and threw me into you. The fiend didn't do it for shits and giggles."

I could hear the underlying fear and loathing in the demon's voice and my thoughts returned to that night. My friends sweeping me along in their wake to the empty house. The *Demon Summoning for Dummies* book. The black candle and the circle made of chicken's blood. Me spewing Latin. Black mist appearing, becoming a black shadow with red eyes towering over us. Screams, all our screams. I'd blacked out, my last sight before I did, of red eyes staring into mine. I remembered dark laughter filling my head before going unconscious. I thought it was Cresil at the time, but now, I understood it wasn't her.

It had been Baal.

I broke out of my thoughts and looked at the demon in the mirror. "Why would Baal do this?"

"He needs an open portal so he and his armies can cross over into the mortal plane. Only a living mortal possessed by a demonic entity can be used to do it."

"You must have magic. Why didn't you use it against this Baal yourself?"

She cast her eyes away. "Yeah, well, ah, well..."

The truth struck me: Cresil's magic was nothing more than pathetic bragging. I saw why it used Cresil to take its place and slammed her into me with a one-way possession.

I shook my finger at her. "You don't have any magic, do you?"

The demon retorted, her eyes blazing, "I do!" But her voice grew smaller. "Okay, not enough to duke it out with Baal. He can kick my ass seven ways."

"You're nothing more than a fake. Worse, you never told us about this other demon."

"Look, I just found out myself the last time I was in the driver's seat of your body."

"You're not lying about not being able to be exorcised?"

"No, it's the truth. Baal told me what went on that night. The only way I could shake free of you would be by Baal. Not unless either Lucifer or Heaven itself stepped in and decided to help our situation. Lucifer won't, with a possessed human jamming open the portal, that will ensure his armies can cross over to Earth. As for Heaven, who knows what God and His angels think or want?" Sadness filled her eyes, taking me aback. "We're glued together because there is no way I know of separating us. I'm sorry, Harper. I wish I knew of something else to help us in our situation. I hope beyond hope that Mrs. Hewitt finds another way to help, but honestly, I don't think she will." She closed her eyes. "I'm so tired of being in you. I want freedom."

No longer did I have to worry about the demon under my skin. No, something much worse haunted Moon Ridge. Worse, every human on this planet.

"You never agreed to Baal's plan?"

"No."

"Why? I thought demons were all about chaos."

"Want to know why?"

No, not really. "Yes."

"Because I've been to Earth many times over the centuries, and I like what I have seen of it. Humans may drive me nuts, but the sights, the smells, the sounds...it's alive. Hell is nothing but death. Earth and yes, even humans, have promise. The apocalypse will end that promise. Lucifer and Baal will like that. They've always been jealous of humankind, especially Big L himself. He had never been happy that God's new children took His interest away from him."

A knocking came at the door. "Harper, are you all right?"

It was Mrs. Hewitt.

I didn't answer but turned back to the mirror. "Go on." But I only saw my reflection staring back at me.

It seemed that Cresil had fled.

Oh no: the apocalypse. What could I do about it? What could Mrs. Hewitt or Jake do? We were human, after all.

"I'm coming out." I unlocked the door.

Mrs. Hewitt peered around the door as it cracked open. "Is everything all right?"

"Yes. There's nothing wrong. Why, what do you think is the matter?" *Only the end of the world. Nothing out of the ordinary.*

The answer shone in her eyes.

She thought that maybe Cresil had retaken me. All the worry about me stressed her, and that bothered me. She'd always been gracious to me all the years I knew her, and I hated that I had brought foul troubles to her.

I wanted to go home. I wanted to see my mother and be held by her. I wanted to crawl into bed and hide beneath the covers. Most of all, I wanted time to turn back the clock to that night my friends decided to call up a demon.

This time, I would have pleaded a headache and stayed home.

No, I would have worked harder to convince them not to do something stupid and instead come over to my place to watch a movie and snack on popcorn. Then all this would never have happened. The only good thing out of this current mess was—

You and Jake are talking again. Maybe back on the road to the friendship you both once had. Trouble is, there might not be enough time to enjoy it.

Tiredness overcame me. "Mrs. Hewitt, it's just me. Harper. I want to go home."

"But—"

"I know that Cresil can take me over anytime. But I don't think she will, not tonight anyway."

She frowned. "How do you know? I'm psychic, and I can't see everything."

"I just know. Will you take my word?"

She nodded, still looking unsure. "All right, go home. But if anything—"

"Strange happens?" I finished. "I promise I will get away from my house and my mother if anything goes wrong and head right back here."

"Damn it! The spirits have quit communicating to me. They're either afraid, or something is stopping them."

I knew what kept those ghosts from spilling the beans. If Mrs. Hewitt couldn't see Baal, then maybe it was better for her if I didn't tell her what Cresil told me. For now, at least.

I walked past her to the front door. I didn't even stop by the kitchen to say good-bye to Jake, but he stood at the front door, waiting. Even though we hadn't been speaking to each other—other than insults since we entered high school—it was as if our sixth sense about each other had never been interrupted. Jake might not like his mother being a psychic, but maybe he had something of it from her, and me, too. Mrs. Hewitt said we were two souls who always understood each other.

I paused.

"You're going home, aren't you?" He reached out to touch my arm. A current of something went from him to me.

I stared down at his hand, then at him. My gaze met his, and somehow, I knew he felt the current between us, for he took back his hand.

"Yes, I'm going home, Jake." I glanced over my shoulder at Mrs. Hewitt. "I'll be back tomorrow after breakfast. We need to figure out more about this demon."

She nodded. "Good night, Harper."

My gaze met Jake's again. "Night, Jake."

"Night, Harper."

We didn't move for a minute. Then Jake opened the door. I strolled past him and into the night. At that moment, the demon got in one jab.

That boy sure is a hottie, isn't he, Harper?

I ignored her and headed for home.

Chapter Nine—Harper

I closed the front door behind me with a soft click. Not soft enough.

"Harper, is that you?"

"Yeah, Mom, it's me."

I had prayed I would be able to sneak in and get upstairs without her hearing me, but I should have known better. I should be grateful that she hadn't asked me to call home occasionally, as some parents do. She worried about me, but she wanted to give me space ever since I turned seventeen. To show she had faith in me.

I trusted her. Just not with this secret. How does one tell their mother that a demon inhabits one's body? She might go into hysterics, but more likely, take me to a psychiatrist. After all, it does sound more like insanity than pea soup and Linda Blair.

Poor Mom.

First, Dad leaves her with a young child to rear alone. She lives day to day on an income she earns from that sucky job as a real estate agent at Moon Ridge Real Estate. Finding out I was possessed by a demon would be over the top for her.

She looked up from where she stood at the stove as I strolled into the kitchen. I sat down at the table.

Mom stirred a wooden spoon in a pot. "Hi, I'm making some cheesy potato soup for tomorrow night's dinner. This way, we can take it out of the fridge and pop it in the microwave to warm up. I'll pick up crusty French bread to go with it at the supermarket on the way home from work tomorrow."

"Sounds good to me."

She returned to the pot.

A few minutes later, she turned off the burner and with her hands wearing oven mitts, picked it off the stove and poured the soup into four containers. Tops not snapped on, she left them on the counter to cool before sticking them in the fridge. She joined me at the table, but not before pouring us a couple of glasses of milk.

I felt her eyes on me as I took a swallow of mine.

"Did you have a good time at Jake Hewitt's?"

Mom, a demon has possessed me for a year. Not only that, but there is another demon even worse loose in Moon Ridge who wants to bring the end of the world. I had rip roaring fun. "It was okay."

"Is that all? I haven't seen Jake around here for a long time."

I drank more milk.

"Harper, I understand that for teens it's different than when you were little kids. That maybe you might be embarrassed to talk about your friends or have them come over while your mother is home."

I put down the empty glass and wiped off the milk mustache at my upper lip. "No, it's not that." *Okay, here goes.* "Jake and I broke up our friendship when we both went to Moon Ridge High. He became friends with this guy..."

She looked puzzled. "Guy?" Her eye lit up with understanding. "Oh, I see...as he prefers boys?"

"No, I don't mean that." I snorted.

"Peer pressure?"

"Kinda, although I never thought Jake would cave to what others thought," I said thoughtfully. "The guy is Pete Jameson."

Her mother sniffed as if she'd just gotten a whiff of something unpleasant. "Rick Jameson's son? I remember Rick Jameson himself back in high school and he acted like a jerk—still does, thinking he's above everyone else in Moon Ridge." She placed her hand over mine. "It looks like both Jake and you found each other again. He just got lost for a while. Lots of teenagers do that. But you're friends again. Right?"

"Yes, Mom, we're friends again."

"Oooh, you're lying to your mother, Harper. Shame, shame." A snicker echoed in my head.

Hush, Cresil.

I stood, stretched, and yawned. "I'm feeling tired, so I'm heading up to bed. See you in the morning, Mom."

Mom took the empty glasses over to the sink, but not before giving me a kiss on my cheek. "I want to watch the news at eleven before I go to bed. Good night. Love you."

"Love you, too."

I tramped upstairs to my room.

I didn't sleep well that night. Like the fairytale about the princess and the pea, I tossed and turned, unable to find a comfortable spot on the mattress. When I finally did drop off, nightmares raced across my mind. I became Cresil in the dreams, and from the looks of the landscape, I was in Hell. Neither hot with fire nor cold with ice; black and gray made up the color scheme, most of it shadows and mist—a depressing place. Things lurched out, terrifying and alien. Screams and insane laughter reached me. If I had lived there for all eternity, I would have gone mad.

I awoke and sat up, breathing hard and my heart in pain, clenching my comforter like a lifeline. It felt like I'd been running a race—one for my life. I clicked on the lamp on the bedside table next to my bed, and I saw the familiarity of my well-lit room.

"Now you know how I feel about that place. It can warp anyone."

My heart settling down and breathing easier, I hit the switch and lay back down in the dark. I fell asleep, this time not dreaming.

When daybreak arrived and streamed through my bedroom window to trace fingers of light across my face, I had already been awake for a couple of hours. A headache pounded behind my eyes and I stared dry-eyed up at the ceiling, not seeing it. The ceiling fan overhead whirred and whirred, the sound amplified in the quiet.

Unable to stand being in bed a minute more, I tossed aside the covers and sat up. Usually, I never got up early on weekends. When you needed to rise early for five days of the week because of school, a couple of hours of sleeping in Saturday and Sunday were luxuries.

But there would be no sleeping in this morning. I snared a glance at my alarm clock. *Six o'clock and it's Saturday?* I shuddered.

I crossed over to the window and pressed my face against the cold glass. It felt great to me. My cheek no longer hurt, and it looked as pale as the other one in the reflection of the glass. It must not have been even pinkish last night, or Mom would have said something.

The vista of the towering mountains in the distance was gorgeous. Dawn had spread her cloak over them, the sunlight lending a glow to the grass in our backyard. It also washed the glass of the window with its heat, warmth starting to win over the cold. I took my face away from the window.

I didn't mind living in a small town. I've been to Richmond and Roanoke, and didn't mind the tall city buildings, but those were visits and I wasn't living there on a permanent basis.

The only thing about rural communities that bothered me was how some members believed reading or watching science fiction and horror made you a liberal crazy or a devil worshipper if it was why you missed church one Sunday. It's not that I didn't enjoy neighbors caring about you, but sometimes, small towns got too much into your business.

I loved hiking on the many trails in the nearby mountains and taking a packed lunch with me to eat later, communing with nature. Many of the kids in Moon Ridge liked to check out the malls, but I preferred the quiet of the country, especially this time of year, when autumn lent a cloak of red, brown, orange, and yellow to the trees. With the hint of Halloween already in stores and pumpkins for sale along roads at nearby farms and the local supermarket, fall made me want to spend my days outdoors.

Not to say, I didn't enjoy spring and summer. Most of the time, summer in Virginia hovered in the nineties and was muggy, too, but I handled that well. Winter...not so much. Although Moon Ridge covered after snowfall looked picture perfect: like a postcard. I still didn't care for the cold weather.

Like most small towns nestled in the mountains in the western part of Virginia, legends abounded.

I grew up hearing about the folklore of witches and wizards, werewolves and black dog phantoms. The old-timers told ghost and soul-eater stories. I'd even heard something about a ghost of a headless horseman haunting the woods not far from my subdivision, except he wore the tattered gray of a Confederate soldier.

As a child, I had accepted the tales as truth, but when I became a teenager, I began to doubt the local ghost stories and didn't put much belief in people like Mrs. Hewitt having psychic powers. After all, this was the twenty-first century.

Now I wondered, if demons existed, how much truth prevailed in those local legends? Like the one told about Moon Ridge being founded by a witches' coven in the late sixteen hundreds.

"There are more things in Heaven and Earth, Horatio."

The demon. Why couldn't she leave me a bit of peace?

"What do you want now, Cresil?"

"Nothing, I'm just quoting Shakespeare. That man knew there were many things not of the norm. He knew the supernatural existed."

"Did you know him?"

"Did you think I spent all of my unnatural life down in Hell? As a demon, I was allowed to go forth and tempt humanity. I tried to tempt the bard himself, except I came to admire the mortal and his talent. But he also had a talent for fighting supernatural evil, as I found to my dismay."

I turned away from the window. "What do you mean?"

"He discovered that I inhabited the body of one of his actors at the time and banished me with a spell back to the underworld. It didn't make me mad. I convinced the Dark One not to send someone else in my place to tempt him. They didn't, which made me glad."

The demon of impurity and laziness surprised me with this insight. Most people wouldn't trust a demon. After all, they lied to get what they wanted, even when there was some truth in the lie.

"So, you're saying all the stories told about this town might have a bit of genuineness about them, even the town's founding?"

"I would say not to doubt the old wives' tales from any place in the world, not even here. There's always a grain of truth hidden beneath the layers of folklore. I can feel that 'something else' about Moon Ridge, even now. That may be the reason Lucifer wants to begin the apocalypse here."

A light bulb went off in my head. "Could there be something in any legend to help separate you from me? Or do you remember that spell Shakespeare used to exorcise you?"

She sighed, the sound loud in my head.

I winced.

"No. Don't you think I didn't think of that spell? I tried it when I remembered it. But I'm still here, aren't I? I could've been a word or two off in the spell casting, but I believe it's more due to Baal's magic being stronger."

I slumped down on my bed, dejected. It looked like the demon and I would be sisters forever. A sister I didn't want. A sister I would like to give up for adoption.

I rubbed my hand through my hair. The headache returned, more intense this time.

"Why don't you go away and leave me to my thoughts alone, you stupid demon, unless you can think of something more helpful?"

"You think I want to experience puberty? I am getting tired of your body, girl."

My headache pounded away. "Leave me alone."

No arguments or anything else came from Cresil, just blessed quiet.

I shed my pajamas and got dressed in jeans and a sweatshirt. I clattered downstairs and snatched a granola bar from the kitchen before walking out the door. Thank goodness my mother still slept. She never heard me leave, as she would have asked questions and made me sit down and have breakfast. I needed to get some air, maybe even go for a run.

Pausing on the front porch, I breathed in a hint of autumn. I swore I smelled burned pumpkin, even though it was still September and it can't be Halloween, as it was six weeks away. Most if not all pumpkins remained uncarved that I knew. *That's not to say someone hadn't already carved and lit one.*

Damn it! I was becoming suspicious of every little sound or smell; it smacked of paranoia. Next, I would be thinking our neighbors next door were Government agents spying on me or alien clones.

I pranced down the steps and crossed our front lawn to step off onto the street. I wanted to run away from myself and my life. I did just that, breaking into a jog. Maybe I hoped that I could run back in time before the demon entered my life. Dazed, barely hearing the pat-pat of my shoes, with the wind whipping through my hair, the scenery blurred past me.

When I stopped jogging, I found myself standing on the porch of the Hewitt house, nestled between the screen door and the front door with my hand raised in a fist as if prepared to knock.

I know I told Mrs. Hewitt I would return here, but that was after breakfast. Besides, I'm sure Jake and she are still asleep.

I heard something and turned around.

A large black shadow hovered by the oak tree in the front yard.

It's my imagination—right?

I blinked and looked again. No, it still lingered there. A foul odor—like sewage—wafted to my nostrils. Bile rose in my throat. I fought to keep it down as hair rose on the back of my neck, chills creeping up my spine.

"Cresil?" Now, how stupid is that? Calling out to some shadow person like it was Cresil when I felt her shifting in the back of my mind.

"Knock on the door. Get inside."

Cresil's fear joined mine. Sweating, I dug my nails into the flesh of my palms and made fists.

"Damn it. Pound on the door, will you?" Cresil's voice raised several octaves in hysteria.

I banged on the door with both hands. "Mrs. Hewitt, Jake, it's me! Open up! Let me in!" I wasn't sure anymore if the words came from me or Cresil.

I snuck a peep back over a shoulder.

The shadow stalked closer.

Sweat ran down in torrents, plastering my top to my skin. I battered on the door, screaming. It swung open, taking me back in surprise.

Jake stood there, dressed in sleep pants only, blinking sleep from his eyes.

Breathing hard, I darted inside and shoved him aside, slamming the door shut behind me. As if by invisible hands, the lock clicked and locked. I stared at the door, shivering. Had Cresil done that? It reminded me she had said she could do a few tricks.

"Baal's out there, Harper. We're both in bad juju."

Jake rubbed his eyes and frowned. "What's going on, Harper? What the hell are you doing here this early?"

I didn't answer, just tensed, as Cresil did, too. Just as Jake opened his mouth again, hammering erupted at the door.

"What the—?" He furrowed his eyebrows together and stepped toward the door.

"Hell's bells, Harper, he's going to open the door! Don't let him! Stop him!" Cresil grew even more frantic as a sharp pain shot through my head.

Clutching my head, I begged, "Don't, Jake. Please don't touch the door."

He looked at me. "Someone's clobbering the door so hard I'm surprised they don't punch a hole in it. It might be your mother, probably upset because she found you gone. It's early, you know." He touched the knob.

I shook my head and winced at the throbbing pain. "No, no, that's not Mom. She would have called on the phone first."

Cresil screeched. "Can you not sense it, monkey boy? It's not human!"

I didn't understand why Jake would sense anything, unless she meant the possibility of him being psychic like his mother? Her screeching grew shriller, and I dropped to my knees in agony as her voice resounded in my head.

Jake's face whitened. He took his hand away from the doorknob as if it had burned and backed away. Both hands in tight fists, every line of his body rigid.

"Hells bells, the hairless ape can hear me."

He narrowed his eyes at me. "What do you mean, it's nothing human? And what's with calling me a hairless ape?"

I licked my lips. "I saw you go pale, Jake. Don't deny it. I never said a word to you."

"Okay, so I felt weird." He whipped his head around to stare at the door. "Demon?"

He whipped around and snatched me by the sweatshirt. "There's a demon out there? How do I know what it is? Is that why you were screeching?"

I nodded. I didn't understand how Jake knew a demon waited on the side of the door or that he heard Cresil. It only mattered he didn't open the door. The headache eased, but not enough. Cresil was still frightened out of her ethereal self.

Mrs. Hewitt padded into the living room, dressed in a robe that hung open and showed her pale-blue flannel nightgown. "What's going on?" Her face grew pale as she stopped and looked at the door. "Oh God, there's a demon on my porch!" She took a step back, her hand out as if to ward it off.

I bent over, clutching myself; Cresil's anxiety enveloped me. I gritted my teeth. "Yes. It's a big, bad monster of one. It's the actual one my friends summoned last year. He's got Cresil at sixes and sevens so that she's giving me one nightmare of a headache right now."

Jake drew closer to the door again.

Mrs. Hewitt stumbled over to us and grabbed Jake by the arm, yanking him away. "Jake, listen to her. Don't let it in. With all my charms surrounding the front and back door plus all the windows, it can't get in. At least, I hope not. If you open the door, that is tantamount to inviting it to enter our house."

"Don't worry, Mom, I'm not going to do that. You're not the only one who can sense it." He sounded confused. "Why would I sense it, Mom? You always said I'm not psychic like you."

"Harper, it's me, your mother." The voice came from the other side of the door. It sounded so much like my mother, soft and persuasive. The doorknob rattled.

"You know it's not her. It's Baal. Let him in and he'll eat Mrs. Hewitt and you for dinner and have me possess Jake. Jake has powerful magic and will make a stronger portal. Baal knows it."

My head still aching, I shivered and stared at Jake, not understanding. I asked, "What do you mean, Cresil? How could Jake have any powerful magic?"

"Mrs. Hewitt may only be a psychic, but her son is way beyond that. He's an untried sorcerer. Who the blasted hell was his father?"

I shook my head, still not understanding. I tried to reach out to Jake as I lurched to my feet and tottered like a baby on its first, unsure steps.

"Harper. HARPER!" Okay, that hurt—like a gong of a giant bell in my head. *"Harper, tell Jake to plant the palms of his hands on the door and make Baal leave."*

Make Baal leave? I didn't quite grasp what it was that Cresil wanted Jake to do, but I said, "Jake, Cresil said to lay your hands on the door. Just get the bad thing to leave."

"I heard your freaking demon, Harper. She wants me to lay hands on the door. Wants me to command the other demon to go home or something?" A bewildered look crossed his face. "Is she nuts or what? I can't do that. That would be Mom's mumbo jumbo department."

I started to shake my head when pain jabbed at it again. "For some reason, she thinks you have power that can drive it away."

Mrs. Hewitt gave me a funny look, but she nodded. "Jake, do as Cresil has told you."

Jake positioned his hands against the door.

Mom's voice still called from outside. It rattled me that it parroted her so well.

Jake looked like he wanted to step away but stood his ground. The door began to shake. It paused. Then the wood bent in and out, like a pair of lungs taking deep breaths. Jake closed his eyes and cocked his head to the left.

"Begone, foul spirit."

"Really? Begone, foul spirit? Is that the best you can do, some half-cracked line from a movie? Spout that at me, and you find me laughing my head off."

The noise ceased.

Blowing out a breath, Jake unlocked the door and peeked out. He looked over his shoulder back at Mrs. Hewitt and me. "No one's out there."

Cresil eased inside me. *"Wow, that actually worked! Baal's gone—for now."*

I said, "Cresil is right. Begone, foul spirit? That's all you could think of to say? No abracadabra or something more spectacular?"

Jake shut the door. His skin shone red with embarrassment. "Well, that's what Mom always says."

Mrs. Hewitt frowned. "No, I don't. That is way beyond corny."

He grinned self-consciously, rubbing the back of his neck. "Well, all right, I heard it when Pete and I watched some horror movie at his house one night."

"I knew I didn't say clichéd stuff like that. However, it appeared way too easy to get rid of that entity. If what emanated from it is true, it's one powerful creature. I'm sorry, Jake, I don't doubt your abilities as my Tarot cards always left me hints over the years, but that fiend left on its own, and it's not due to you. I don't know why it did, either. I don't need to be psychic to know it'll be back."

She turned to me. "Who's here: Harper or Cresil?"

"Both. Neither. Oh, I don't know anymore." I threw up my hands and stomped over to a chair, dropping down into it.

Mrs. Hewitt followed, with Jake close behind. "What do you mean by that crack, Harper? Cresil?"

"Right now, I guess it's me, but Cresil has been talking in my head. She was freaking out, bad enough to give me a nasty headache, but it's gone now."

"That's because badass Baal's gone. Mrs. Hewitt's right—the bad boy didn't leave because of Jake. He'll be back."

"The demon might come back?" I asked.

Mrs. Hewitt said, "So, Cresil agrees with me?"

"Yeah." I still didn't understand how Jake could hear Cresil, but psychic-medium Mrs. Hewitt couldn't.

"It's because I cannot keep a sorcerer from hearing me, but I can keep a medium from doing so. Psychics are not that strong, at least, none I have ever encountered. Jake's mother isn't that strong."

Jake frowned at me. He drew close and whispered, "That's my mom you're talking about, dumb demon."

Mrs. Hewitt took my hand and helped me up out of the chair, leading me over to the couch where we both sat. "Here, let me try something. I have a million questions for that little imp. Now, you have to trust me. Understand?"

"Um, yes, Mrs. Hewitt?" I didn't understand.

She put her face close to mine, the tips of our noses touching. "I'm sorry, Harper, but I'd like Cresil to take over so the she-devil and I can talk. Talk, without a middleman, so to speak."

I wanted to prevent Cresil from retaking control of my body, and I opened my mouth to refuse when Mrs. Hewitt began to hum. The ditty sent little shocks riveting through my body. I fought but knew I was losing as colorful lights shifted and danced before my eyes.

"Oh no," I said with a moan, "when do I ever get to remain in my body long enough?"

My lids dragged down as if rimmed with lead and dropped over my eyes, and I remembered nothing.

Chapter Ten—Cresil

My mouth felt dry as a desert, and when I tried to open my eyes, I couldn't. No, that's not right. It's Harper's mouth that tasted desiccated and her eyelids that refused to open. I'm a disembodied demon. The body no longer belonged to just Harper but both of us. I never volunteered to be the brain and voice of Harper for this latest possession. I felt like a jack in the box, boomeranging back and forth.

At last, I popped the eyelids up. Blurry at first, my sight cleared until it filled with the fleshy tone of a face with two blue orbs close enough for us to bump noses. I yelped, startled, and kicked out, almost upending the coffee table. Things on it did fly off.

Jake began picking them off the floor.

Mrs. Hewitt chastised. "Hush now, Cresil."

I folded my arms and sniffed, jutting Harper's chin out. "I'm just fooling. Did you think you startled me? It takes a lot more than that to scare a demon."

"Whatever you want to believe if it gives you comfort. But I know something does frighten you, another of your kind."

"Why did you call me?" As if I couldn't guess.

"Tell me what happened that night, to Harper and the others."

I sucked in a breath. Never having been alive as a mortal, it felt good to breathe, even if it was second hand.

I told her about Harper and her friends summoning a demon last year. How the girls had succeeded, but that I'd discovered they didn't call me or just any old one. No, the specific one of their beckoning was Baal, one of Lucifer's right-hand dark-angel lords. Baal commandeered me by magic, and they ended up with me instead of him. He freed me from the pathetic circle they made to keep me in and slammed me into Harper's body. Worse, the bastard had used his powers to kill the others by conjuring a fire that spiraled out of control—and then made Harper forget what happened. He put me to sleep. And how I'm sure he had fixed it, so there was no trace of Harper in the building that night, just her friends. It wouldn't do for his plans to have her arrested.

I uncrossed Harper's arms and stared down at Harper's hands. Pink-painted nails trimmed nice. "I'm just as much an idiot as Harper's friends. Baal used me and only he has the power to keep me stuck in Harper's body." I looked into her eyes. "Baal did this for a specific reason. He told me why, too, with sinful pride."

She looked at me like she didn't believe me. "You never remembered being magicked by him? That's a likely tale only the demonic could conjure up."

I fisted the soft hands, digging the blunt nails into the skin. "It's the fricking truth, lady. May I let you stick a cross on me if I am telling a fib."

She glanced at Jake. "I believe her."

Jake opened his mouth, but she cut him off. "Jake, my sixth sense is backing me up."

Jake asked, "What's Baal's gain in all this?"

"Baal wants an entity trapped inside a human body to keep open the doorway between Hell and the mortal realm."

Mrs. Hewitt gasped. "Dear God, he's planning to lead a demonic army into our world, isn't he?"

I winced at Mrs. Hewitt using God's name, but I nodded. "If he does, he'll win, and Lucifer gets control of this realm. From there, the next step will be to breach Heaven's gates."

Jake snorted. "He'll find himself battling missiles, guns, and more from the armies and navies around the world."

I turned to him. "Get your head out of your video game and into reality. Baal will be leading legions—which means more than your mind could comprehend—and all will have the power of Hell behind them. The only equal to that would be from Heaven. Armageddon in those video games and movies are one thing, but the real McCoy would be literal Hell on Earth."

I rose and walked over to a window, lifted the end of the blind, and peered out. I didn't see anything out of the ordinary—for now. The sun shined upon an almost quiet neighborhood, the only sounds coming from a lawnmower and a bird's trill. It did not look like the end of days was approaching.

Too damn bad it wouldn't be peaceful for long. With my imagination, I could see the wasteland that Baal's armies would create. No plant life would grow, except weeds, a sky covered in dark gray clouds that the sun's rays couldn't filter through, buildings in rubble, rotting carcasses everywhere, and inhuman things stalking the land. Maybe someone should tell that guy to forget the mowing; there wouldn't be grass after the demons marched through his lawn. No mower or person, either. Both would be dust wafting over the barren world.

I remembered my spot of Hell. It had been arid, with nothing solid anywhere, just endless cells of darkness. I'd hated it. Mortal souls who ended up in Hell went mad after a while, unable to stand for long the insanity of the place. Those who got kicked to my portion of the Pit lost it within seconds, spinning over the line to heels-over-head insane.

That's not to say we inhuman things fared much better. It's just...we knew the score when we Fell. If humans knew where they would end up and what would happen to them, maybe they would not let their dark side take over. Yeah, tell me a fairytale. What I knew of humanity didn't give me much hope, but Harper really didn't deserve what happened to her.

I dropped the blind and turned around.

Mrs. Hewitt and her son stood side by side, their features guarded.

This didn't bode well for me. Demons know never to trust a human. We know all they are suitable for is to ride hard until they dropped, or someone banished us from them. The mortals should never trust us, either. After all, look at the demonic track record. I wanted to be trusted. I wanted to be free of Harper, and I sure didn't want to go back to Hell. Not too much to ask, right?

The nastier side of me whispered, insidious. *Are we getting soft, Cresil? Is the mortal you inhabit finally getting to you?*

Who knew? Maybe later, I would turn on these mortals. Perhaps I would rip free from Harper's body once Baal and the demons flooded into Earth and help them destroy the planet.

"You won't, Cresil."

Harper?

"Who else could be talking in my head? You'll help, won't you?"

I grimaced and answered out loud. "I can't believe I am saying this, but yeah, I'll help, Harper. Though what a minor-league demon can do remains to be seen."

"Time to let Harper have her body back, Cresil," said Mrs. Hewitt.

I rubbed our arms. *The flesh is so weak, but I have to admit it feels so...good. I'm tired of being nothing more than a voice in the girl's head, an insubstantial spirit.*

I may cry foul about wanting to exit this flesh, but I wanted to be flesh, not spirit.

My thoughts must have shown in the eyes, or maybe the body's posture revealed it, for Jake stomped over, his eyes blazing with power.

Though unconscious of his capabilities, the boy's untapped power appeared to be growing stronger. Jake could blast me out of Harper if he realized what he could do, but I doubted he could at this time. Not much longer, though, but when he figured it out...wham. I might find myself in Tartarus in pieces spread all over it with a snap of fingers, and that was the untrained version. What if he ever became trained?

I almost shivered at the truth.

I held up a hand. "Don't worry. I'm giving Harper her body back." I added, "I wish I could leave, but until Baal is defeated and his power taken away or destroyed, or we can figure out how to unwind his spell, it appears Harper and I will be like a peanut butter and jelly sandwich."

Mrs. Hewitt touched Harper's forehead. Pure white light burned me back into secondary status.

Chapter Eleven—Harper

I awoke to Jake's arms around me, supporting my weight. He slipped his arms beneath my shoulders and my knees and lifted me. Holding me against his chest, he carried me over to the couch and laid me down, slipping a pillow beneath my head. His eyes were filled with concern

I forced my lips into a smile. "I'm okay, Jake."

He pursed his lips and lines scrawled across his forehead.

"I truly am."

He peered into my eyes for a few seconds before nodding. "I can see the demon didn't do anything dreadful, but it's taken some of your energy."

"The demon has a name. It's Cresil."

He didn't say anything.

"Since she possesses my body, I'm beginning to tell when she feels hurt, and she wants to be known by her name, Cresil."

He raised an eyebrow.

"Yeah, I know, me defending the demon that's possessing me. I know now that she didn't do it to me on purpose, and if she had, I would have been far more affected than I was."

"Okay," he said, "Cresil, didn't do anything too vile to you. Happy?"

I lay my head back down on the pillow. "You know, Jake, you're not that bad."

"What do you mean?" He narrowed his eyes.

"You're halfway to being the old Jake that I knew growing up. Maybe Pete doesn't have as firm hold on you as your mother and I believe." I struggled to sit up again, managed to, and reaching out a hand to his face, bringing it closer to mine. "Thank you." I kissed him on the cheek.

His cheeks reddened.

He's embarrassed!

Jake said, "Why did you go and do that, Harper?"

"What Cresil knows, I know. I realized you would have used your powers on the demon to oust her from my body even though it wouldn't work. You're a decent guy. Just like a superhero."

His eyes widened and his brows reared up like exclamation points. "Powers? What powers?"

"You're a sorcerer."

Cresil's voice filled my head. *"He's more untried at the moment. Apprentice more than the master."*

Jake straightened, the look in his eyes indicating he thought I'd lost my mind. "A what? I heard you say something like you did earlier today, but your mouth didn't open that time."

"That's Cresil," I said. "You can hear Cresil speaking in my head. Like a telepath hears thoughts."

"Some freaky demon thinks I'm psychic like Mom, and you—"

"No, not psychic, though I suspect maybe that's part of what it is. You're a sorcerer, like those guys who wield magic in those fantasy movies. Such as—"

He stabbed a finger at me. "I heard that! Don't you dare say like that wizard in those books by Tolkien, demon! Or that little green guy with the big, pointed ears."

"Kinda. Though maybe more modern like—"

He broke in. "Not that JK Rowlings crap either."

"I see you still know your fantasies," I said in a teasing manner when Cresil shut up. "I remember when you used to read those books."

He scrunched his nose. "I don't read that junk anymore. Don't watch it, either."

I swung my legs off the couch, forcing Jake to back up. "We even went and saw those kinds of movies in the theater. Remember?"

He didn't look at me. "When I was a dumb kid."

Standing on wobbly legs, I took his chin, forcing him to look at me. His green eyes never looked greener. An electric shock snapped between us. I had always liked Jake as my best friend, but now? *I'm falling for him*! When had that feeling of friendship, even dislike for him over the past three years, changed? Had he bewitched me or something?

Cresil whispered, *"No doubt he's feeling that mortal ickiness ,too, even with all his denial. Although, he might have accidentally hocussed pocussed you with a sort of love spell, which explains why I acted goofball stupid over him."*

Deflated by the thought that maybe he might have unknowingly abracadabra'd me, I tried to steer away from Jake, but still unsteady, I almost fell. He grabbed me and helped me sit back down on the couch.

He appeared not to hear Cresil that time, maybe because she whispered. Again, most likely he had. It didn't matter because I knew what I felt had nothing to do with Cresil, only me. My heart ached in misery because he probably didn't care for me.

Cresil whispered again. *"Don't worry, Harper, he likes you, too. No matter his denial. Magic that tries to seduce you doesn't work unless the spellcaster feels something. Love or lust..."*

As if a resident of Hell knew about love.

"Maybe I do! Well, about lust anyway."

When Jake looked toward his mother, I dropped my voice to a whisper, "Shhhh. He'll hear."

"Nah, I put up something like a force field or something, so he can't. At least, I hope not."

Jake turned his gaze back to me, an eyebrow arched.

"I didn't say anything," I said.

Suspicion clouded his eyes. "Not you. What did the Hell bimbo say?" He wrinkled his nose. "I mean, I'm not trying to hear her in your head. Not on purpose." He shut up and jammed his hands in his jeans pockets.

"I'm not a Hell bimbo! You tell that sorcerer wannabe; he should find a wand and stick it up his—"

I closed my ears to her ranting. I looked at Jake and shrugged. "Don't worry. She didn't say anything worth repeating."

"I heard what she said, Harper."

"The fricking force shield failed!" whined Cresil.

"Oh." Dear God, how much did he hear? I fought the blush threatening to erupt.

Cresil kept screeching, but I ignored her even though it hurt my head.

Jake headed into the kitchen, but not before he said, "Stay on the couch and don't move. And tell the foul-mouthed devil she can quit screaming the abuse. Or I might try and see if I'm powerful enough to zip her mouth."

She shut up. The headache settled into a dull ache.

I whispered, "He's right. You are foul."

"I bet my shield didn't work from the beginning, the big faker. Zip my mouth, will he? I ought to take you over again, then give the boy a piece of my mind and some magic with it, too."

"Oh, no, you won't. It's my body, and besides, I've got to get up and go home. Mom will be worried if I'm not in the house by nine latest. You don't want me grounded if we need to find out how to separate you from me and stop Baal. Besides, I got some math homework due Monday."

Cresil sighed. *"Yeah, yeah. Do you have to go to school?"*

"Yes, I do. I have the rest of my senior year before I graduate, and you're not going to ruin it for me. Maybe you'll learn something."

"Oh please! Like existing eons hasn't taught me a thing or two. I know more about history than your school's stupid books could ever tell you or that you would even want to know about."

She kept chattering, but I felt tired, closed my eyes for a few seconds, and drifted off. Cresil quit talking and left me alone.

I felt someone shaking me and awoke, and sat up, looking around, confused.

"Harper, it's Mrs. Hewitt. Lunch is ready." Mrs. Hewitt stood over me and smiled. "Unless you'd rather remain sleeping instead of having homemade chicken noodle soup and a toasted cheese sandwich."

I scrambled to my feet. "Oh, I'm starving."

She chuckled and led me to the kitchen table where I plunked down across from Jake. He was already eating, so I waited until Mrs. Hewitt sat down before I picked up my spoon. The soup smelled good, tasted good, too.

Jake and I played a couple of board games after lunch, with Cresil being the third player. Surprisingly, she didn't try to cheat because any moves I made or cards I had, she knew the same as I knew hers, keeping hers next to mine.

Mrs. Hewitt made phone calls to other psychics she knew. Even not overhearing the conversation, I knew it concerned Cresil, Baal, and the possible end of the world.

Close to five, Jake headed into the kitchen to take the trash out to the trashcan outside. Mrs. Hewitt was in the kitchen, making their dinner. Not waiting for his return, I headed for the front door.

"Hey!" Jake's voice stopped me.

I looked back over my shoulder.

Jake stood just inside the living room, frowning, his mother right behind him. The light from the kitchen silhouetted the both of them like a halo.

I said, "You know, Jake, a frown is just a smile upside down."

He stomped over to me. "Well, you shouldn't be leaving."

"That's fine and all, but I need to get home before Mom raises the roof. And I've still got to finish my math homework due Monday."

"I know that. I'm in Mr. Borkus's class, too."

"I need to get home, demon problem or not, end of the world or not. If you want to stop Baal, getting me grounded is not a good thing."

He rubbed the back of his neck. "Let me grab my jacket, and I'll drive you home in my truck. That demon may still be out there."

Mrs. Hewitt agreed. "With Baal on the loose in our world, I think that's a good idea. I am sure Jake can handle him."

I agreed. "Okay. I know that Cresil can't, but I wanted to walk."

Jake replied, "Then, I'll walk you home."

Cresil snapped, *"Thanks for that slap to my incorporeal face."*

Mrs. Hewitt hugged me good-bye, and I wandered out the door with Jake. It wasn't evening yet, just late afternoon, but already I saw shadows lingering at the base of trees and fences and the air held a hint of chill.

His hands in his jacket pockets, Jake walked beside me. He didn't say anything.

I snuck a peek here and there. The promise of his manhood showed in the dimple in his chin, the strong jaw, and aquiline nose.

Cresil settled down inside me. No terrible demon attacked us.

We strolled past a park where a few kids played.

Mrs. Fritter, who lived a few houses down from Jake's, walked her tiny, fluffy poodle, Maisie, on a pink leash. The animal wore a pink bowl on top of her head, and she paused to stare up at us. We stopped and I leaned down to pat her head, but didn't as she snarled and snapped, missing the tips of my fingers.

"Stupid mutt," growled Cresil.

"Maisie!" said Mrs. Fritter, yanking on the dog's leash. She apologized. "I don't know why she did that."

"She ought to muzzle the psycho fluff ball."

I backed away as the dog went another round of yipping and snarling. *Maisie senses you in me, Cresil.*

The countless times I ran into Mrs. Fritter and Maisie, the animal was always friendly to me. I remembered how ghost hunters in paranormal reality shows claimed animals could see and hear ghosts, and technically, since demons were spirits, too, it should be the same.

"It's all right, Mrs. Fritter." I dragged Jake away, the dog still choking itself as it pulled at the leash the older woman held tight.

Wearing a bemused expression, he whispered, "I never cared for that ugly animal myself."

Cresil snickered.

We turned the corner at my street. Not long after, we found ourselves standing before my front door.

I grabbed the doorknob. "Thanks, Jake."

"See you in school?" Jake's boot heels clicked on the porch as he drew a little closer.

I shook my head and pushed open the door. "Outside of the classes we share, I don't think that'll happen."

His eyebrows knitted together. "You need me."

"In what way? It will be the same as it always has been pre-demon troubles. Pete won't tolerate me."

He sputtered. "Pete can get screwed. I won't let you go unprotected. That de... Cresil, either. I can't do anything about the classes we don't share, but there's those we do, plus we have lunch period at the same time. I'll be by your side as much as I can. Is that clear?"

He really believed what he was saying. Today anyway. But when we were at school with Pete, it might be a different story.

I shrugged. "Sure. See you in Dorkus's calculus class."

"I'll be waiting at the bus loop."

I opened the door and entered. Once I had closed the door behind me, I leaned back against the wood, hardly breathing as I listened.

Jake still stood on the porch. I wanted to go outside and rush into his arms, but a wealth of conflicting emotions filled me. So I didn't.

I still didn't feel sure of him, and I didn't understand these strange new feelings. How could I be sure that the demon hadn't anything to do with them? Maybe Baal did it by remote control for whatever he had in mind.

"I've nothing to do with them, you silly girl. Believe me, fricking emotions connected with love is not Baal's M.O. Face it, you got the hots for wizard boy."

I took a breath and closed my eyes. "Yes, Cresil, I guess I do. But even if he likes me as a boy likes a girl, I doubt he cares for me. Three years of him not being my friend, and suddenly, he cares. We'll see what Monday brings."

"Harper? Is that you?"

My mother stepped into the living room, wiping her hands on a dishrag. Though we had an automatic dishwasher, she still liked to wash many of our dishes and cups by hand. She said she could think about the next day's schedule at work or other problems while doing them.

I smiled and crossed the room, sniffing. "Yum, smells good. Are we having chicken and dumplings tonight?"

A smile crossed her lips. I love Mom's smiles. They always reached all the way to her eyes.

"I figured you'd like your favorite meal for tonight's dinner. Did you have a nice time at Jake's?"

"Mrs. Hewitt fed us lunch. Chicken noodle soup and toasted cheese sandwiches. Jake and I played a couple of board games afterward, and we lost track of time. Jake walked me home." I shook my head. "I should have woken you this morning and told you where I was going. I'm sorry."

"So, you're not telling your mother about Baal?"

I whispered. "Hush, Cresil."

"What did you say, Harper?"

"Nothing, Mom. Just sorry again."

"Well, next time, tell me where you're going. I got worried when I woke up to make us breakfast, and you were nowhere around. I called your phone, but I heard it ringing and traced it to your bedroom. That worried me, so I called a few of your friends, but no one had seen you. It scared me. I didn't think about Jake at all, not until his mother called."

I felt guilty I had forgotten my phone. Worse, I should have told her I was going outside for that jog. *A jog that ended you up at Jake's house.* Nothing else, I should have taken my phone with me and called her myself. The Baal situation and Cresil messed me up.

I hugged her. I caught the surprise in her eyes, and she hugged me back. She smelled of chicken and dumplings, dish detergent, and her favorite perfume, a light flowery scent; she smelled of comfort. She smelled of all that had been good and constant in my life.

No way would I tell her about Cresil and the other demon. I didn't even know how to tell her about the apocalypse.

"She's good, Harper. You can't keep all this from her forever."

Watch me!

Arm in arm, Mom and I wandered into the kitchen. I set out utensils on the dining table. She ladled chicken and dumplings from the crock-pot into two bowls and placed those on the table. We sat down at the table after Mom made us hot chocolate.

We talked more than we had in a long time. How I was doing in school, Mom's job and the crazy characters she worked with, but when I broached about Dad, she quit talking. You'd think since I was graduating high school in a few more months and turning eighteen in June, she would finally open up about him. But he was still a forbidden subject. What I knew was that she'd never divorced him, nor had she received divorce papers from him.

I kept close-mouthed, too. I didn't tell her about Cresil, or an evil demon named Baal and the destruction of our world hanging like a cloud over us. Cresil was right, I needed to tell her, but like my father, this subject felt forbidden. Besides, she had enough to worry over.

Even with the secrets between us, I'd never felt closer to my mother than now. I'd never felt so remorseful, either. Life never seemed such a downer before.

I curled beneath the covers in bed that night. Unable to sleep, I got up and sat at my desk, the lamp on, and finished the math problems due Monday. The potential end of the world didn't stop me from completing any homework assignments due.

"I can't sleep either, Harper."

"I assumed demons don't sleep. You're like a ghost—right?"

"Yes, I'm a spirit, and you're right, we don't sleep in our normal state of being. Demons are like a human soul or angels, incorporeal. But sharing a living being's body enables the possessor to feel what the possessed feels. With me being in your body longer than normal, your feelings are seeping into me." A sigh crawled across my consciousness. *"Your guilt and worry have become mine. Hell's bells, I...I...oh hell, I think I feel your love for your mother and friends, too. You're ruining me."*

I closed the book, and shoved it and the paper into my bookbag on the floor. "I'm not going to say I'm sorry. Maybe being stuck inside me is the best thing that has happened to you, Cresil."

"Please, like you feel it's the best thing that's happened to you. I know all your thoughts, girlfriend."

"Girlfriend? Isn't that too modern for something I bet is ancient?"

Her snort vibrated in my head.

I wrapped my arms around my body. "Cresil, how are we going to stop Baal?"

"I don't know. What I do know about Baal is a drop in a bucket, meaning not much."

She sounded like a scared child, which unnerved me. Cresil knew me, and I think I knew her. Not as much as she allowed, being in my head and in control of letting me know what she wanted me to know. Except, I think I learned more about her than she realized.

This Baal was her boogeyman, her Achilles heel. Maybe it was more up to me to get information about him somehow. And since in my view, knowledge is in books, the school library and the one in town might be my best bets. If not there, maybe searching online might unearth something. I could use one of the four PCs for patrons at the Moon Ridge Library if I couldn't find a helpful book on the occult there. Or I could search online on my laptop here.

I didn't try to hide my plans. It would be hard to hide much from Cresil anyway. She didn't try to stop me or mumbo jumbo it out of my head. No doubt she wanted me to learn the information.

Either that or she knows you won't find anything useful at all.

I yawned as tiredness overwhelmed me. Believing I could sleep at last; I switched off the lamp and headed to bed. I snuggled under the blanket and fell asleep when my head touched the pillow.

****

I spent a quiet Sunday watching TV, helping Mom bake bread, and reading. I went to bed early.

Cresil remained silent during all that time.

Monday morning arrived, and after a quick breakfast, I made a bagged lunch for a quick feed as I planned to visit the school library at lunchtime. If I didn't find anything there, then after school, I would check out the Moon Ridge Library. Surely, one of them might have a book on demons.

Seeing I only had five minutes to catch the school bus before it got to my street, I raced out the door. I made it in time as the bus just pulled up. The ride was uneventful, not even chatter from my demon.

When I stepped off the school bus, I saw Jake stop talking to Pete and Tyree. He left them and walked over to me. Pete didn't look happy about being deserted. As for Tyree, he didn't look like he cared one way or another. Maybe he thought this would be a good time to become Pete's new best friend.

I left Jake to catch up and hurried to my locker to drop off books and my bagged lunch from my bookbag, except the math book. Then, I snatched two others from the locker for the following classes after calculus.

"Hey, in a hurry to get to Dorkus Borkus's class?" Jake grinned and fell into step beside me. Shocker, he actually has his calculus book.

"Won't Pete be upset you're talking to me?"

He led me over to a corner free of the crowd of kids surging to their classes and planted his face right in mine. "Look, Harper, I told you I would watch out for you, didn't I? Pete will have to get over himself." Jake narrowed his eyes. "Where's the demon?" He laid the palm of his right hand against my cheek and his warmth seeped into my skin. I wanted to purr like a contented cat, but I didn't. "Maybe, she'll stay quiet long enough for us—"

Cresil chimed in. *"The demon's still here, wizard boy."*

Jake dropped his hand as if scorched. "Always listening in, aren't you?"

"Hey, I can't get out of quarantine, and you can't do anything about it. So, lump it."

"That's not my fault or Harper's." Jake hissed in a low whisper. He drew closer again, placed a hand on the wall beside me, and leaned in. He shook his head. "I'm sorry, Cresil. I don't understand anything about this untapped magic. Do you know how much I can do?"

"Do you think Heaven and Hell let me on all their secrets? No, I only can feel the magic mojo in you, bad boy."

"Quit the bad-boy stuff, demon," he said with a growl.

"Touchy, are we? Maybe it's because I hit a sore spot? Remember how you treated Harper once upon a time? You didn't have a demon possessing your body as an excuse."

"I'm sorry, Harper," said Jake.

My gaze met Jake's. Neither of us appeared to want to break eye contact. Then he shifted. Make that he drew closer. I couldn't look away or move. Instead, I knew how a deer caught in a car's headlights felt. When his lips touched mine, I pulled back, unsure.

"Jake?"

He straightened; his cheeks deepened to a rose color.

"Ah, come on, Harper; don't tell me you didn't like the touch of his lips on yours? I sure did secondhand."

I felt the heat of my embarrassment creeping up the back of my neck. I hope Jake hadn't heard; I knew he had. The problem was, Cresil was right. I liked Jake kissing me. Maybe we had been friends, but it was about time to take it to the next level. I drew close to him again.

His gaze met mine. "Harper?"

I nodded...and pressed my lips to his.

"Hey, Jake, what are you doing with her?"

We broke apart.

"Great, it's your friendly neighborhood jerk, Pete Jameson. Want me to send him on a fast bus to Hell?" asked Cresil.

Chapter Twelve—Harper

Pete tapped his right boot as if in time to some heavy metal rock tune. Except, the music came from kids talking and yelling, locker doors slamming, and feet stomping like a large herd of horses rambling down the hallway. Baggy designer jeans hung below his hips, and an oversized sweatshirt with some famous football team's emblem on the front hid his skinny chest. He must have dumped Tyree somewhere, as I didn't the other teen.

Not that Pete ever cared about football or any sports. But he liked to show how much money his father had in the clothing he wore. He didn't care about being skinny, either, as he bragged that being thin was better than the fatties, as he called most of the kids at school. You'd think that being rich didn't mean being a creep, not that Pete cared. "I can say what I want. My daddy owns this one-horse town," he'd said with a sneer when the principal once pointed that out to him when caught being mean to another kid.

I looked at Jake out of the corner of my eye.

He stuffed his hands in his pants pockets and scuffed his boots against the floor, eyeing the wall. So much for him being my hero and me a damsel in distress. It appeared that

Jake would hand me over to Pete the dragon to be flame-broiled with no qualms about it.

Slinging my book bag over my shoulder, I stuck my nose in the air as if I'd detected a fetid stench and stomped past Pete.

His arm flashed out and he hooked my arm.

"Take your hand off me," I stated, flashing him a dirty look.

His grip tightened. "Don't think so."

"Let Harper go, Pete."

Maybe my hero still existed in Jake somewhere.

Pete dropped my arm. "Okay. She's not worth much in amusement anyway. It's not like you care about your old friend here anyway. There are prettier girls in school."

To my surprise, Jake stepped over to me and wrapped an arm around my shoulders. He shrugged his other shoulder.

"Guess I felt it was time to rebond with those I'd been ignoring for quite a while. Besides, I think Harper's pretty, and that's all that matters—at least to me." He grinned at me. "Let's go. We don't want to be late for our first-period class. Math is just about as much fun as an amusement park." His grin grew wider. "Not!"

I stepped away with him but not before snatching a glance over my shoulder. Pete's mouth hung open, and his eyes were wide, round ovals of dirty brown. He looked exactly like one of those dead fish you see at the fish market.

I felt myself switching places with Cresil at that moment.

"Better close your mouth before a fly sneaks in," I heard Cresil mouthing off at Pete. Her snicker rolled out of my mouth.

At that moment Pete's mouth slammed shut, then he coughed and choked, only to reopen his mouth, spitting. A tiny black buzzing thing flew out.

"Gotcha," said Cresil once more inside my head. She'd given me back control of my body.

"Cresil? What did you do?" I sputtered.

"Did you think I was going to let that jerk get away with anything? That a bug happened to shoot into his mouth to give truth to my words?"

Pete kept spitting and coughing.

Jake drew me away from the scene.

Cresil did have powers that she could use, but that didn't sit well with me. I may not care for Pete, but that she magicked some fly into his mouth revealed what she could do.

"Now you understand why I am worried about Baal. Think of my powers times a hundredfold stronger. My abilities aren't close to the invocations that beast can do."

Jake and I arrived at class just as the bell rang. Mr. Borkus had been writing on the board but did a Linda Blair turn of his head that creeped me out. No, it gave me the out and out willies. Shouldn't that have hurt his neck? His head swiveled back to the board.

"Seats, please." Mr. Borkus's voice sounded deep, not his usual scratchy nails on the chalkboard tenor pitch.

I slid into my seat while Jake thumped down in his with a loud scrape. He put his book down on the desk and crossed his arms, a bored look on his face.

Mr. Borkus put down the chalk and cleared his throat, turning around. "All right, class, I have some problems on the board for you to write down and solve." He pointed at the clock on the wall. "You've got thirty minutes, so go."

Had I imagined the deeper tone? This sounded more like the Mr. Borkus I knew.

Groans filled the air as classmates scrambled for paper and pens from their bookbags and notebooks; I did, too.

Jake leaned over the aisle and whispered to me. "Paper, please. I have a pen."

Borkus's eyes zoomed in on us. His hairy brows merged into a unibrow.

Just what I need today. Another run-in with Mr. Borkus. I snatched a few blank sheets of paper and thrust them at Jake.

He seized them before they fell to the floor and, taking a pen out of his jeans pocket, pushed his book aside to scribble on one of them.

I jotted down the problems on my own paper and went to work solving them. They looked easy, not at all like the usual calculus problems. I wondered why Mr. Borkus had chosen them. As I scratched down the answers, it hit me: they were problems I'd had back in ninth grade algebra class. I stopped and stared down at them on the paper.

"Like them, Miss Doyle?" The whisper curled into my ear.

I jerked my head up.

Mr. Borkus crouched down beside my desk. I couldn't understand why he was there. He looked odd. His Cheshire cat grin seemed worse than usual, and his eyes were meaner, too.

There were other things about him that seemed out of character. His hair (what he had of it) stood up as if electrified and uncombed. Black specks splattered on his yellow teeth as if he hadn't brushed for a couple of days. Worse, it looked like a piece of skin from something had gotten caught between the two front upper molars. I remembered the man as always being clean and neat.

A nasty odor floated over, and I realized it came from him. Not just unwashed or bad breath, but something long dead. I wrinkled my nose and covered my nostrils, fighting not to gag.

Desks screeched across the floor. It appeared the other students nearby finally noticed. Some just moved their desks; others jumped to their feet and moved away. All had their noses scrunched and waving their hands in front of them as they retched. A few muttered "Gosh, the stink!" and "What died?" filled the room.

Didn't he even take a bath this morning? I thought. *You'd think he slept in a garbage dump last night.*

"Well?" He drew closer, and the stench worsened if that could even be possible. *It smells like a whole morgue filled with rotting corpses.*

I fought not to throw up breakfast from this morning as the reek slithered up my nostrils. It was hard, though.

Cresil yelled, *"Get out!"*

"What?" I didn't understand Cresil. Yes, he stunk to high—

The demon's voice grew more frantic. *"Scrape that desk back and get the blankly-blank out of there. That's not your teacher anymore; it's Baal!"*

I scooted my chair back into the desk behind me, getting a "Hey!" for it and snatched my bookbag and bounced into Jake's waiting arms.

I muttered. "It's—"

"Baal? Yeah, I heard Cresil loud and clear. Besides, I think my inner sorcerer alarm went off."

I kept my eye on our former teacher as he stood, a scary jack-o-lantern expression carved in his face. "When was this—when we first walked into the room? Or just now?"

He led me away. "I couldn't tell who it was going off on when we walked into class, so I figured I would—"

"—wait and see what happened. Really, Hewitt? You think you and the demon inside me would give a girl a head's up!"

Mr. Borkus's whole frame began to shake. He seemed to have grown taller. His face no longer had eyes, nose, or mouth, just an endless carousel of flesh whirling around and around.

The man shot up to the ceiling and his skin cracked open like a nut. Students screamed, and running feet echoed in the room, but neither Jake nor I took our eyes off the horror.

My former math teacher was reenacting the thing from outer space deal. If it had been an alien, guns might have worked. But no, we needed magic, because it's Baal. Supernatural, not science fiction.

"Jake, cast something."

"No can do. I tried when Borkus became a growing staff of flesh, but nothing."

That left... "Cresil, use that mumble jumble of yours. Take over my body."

"Excuse me? Remember, when I said I'm on a lower scale than the one Baal inhabits? Think of a Tyrannosaurus Rex against Godzilla. It would be like pitting a pea shooter against a cannon. Nada, nothing, zip."

I grumbled. "Of all the demons to possess me, I get the loser."

Jake dragged me down the aisle after fleeing teenagers. "Come on!"

Just as we reached the door, Cresil chimed in. *"Jake, you'll have to do it."*

Jake and I skidded to a stop at the doorway. We appeared to be the only students left in the classroom.

Jake said, "Look, I tried my magic, and it didn't do a thing."

"Your mojo isn't enough to take on one of Lucifer's bad boys, but if I told you a demonic spell and you repeated it out loud at the same time, what would be nothing more than a pea shoot from me or you alone, might be a lightning bolt that'll zap the big baddie. Combining our talents might give us time to get ourselves out of this school to safety."

A roar shook the room.

We turned to see scattered pieces of the former Mr. Borkus littering the floor and desks. A rising column of shadow towered in the middle of it all. A whirling tornado of papers whipped around it.

Jake called out, "Okay, Cresil, start blabbing away."

Cresil's voice rang in my head. *"Ex copiae copie of incendia a relevo telum plactum down everto ex meus finxis."*

At the same time, Jake yelled, "Ex copiae copie of incendia a relevo telum plactum down everto ex meus finxis."

Lightning bolts zapped from his fingers, and something sizzled from me, both striking the target. A loud sizzle and a rank smell burned the air.

We bolted from the classroom. Just in time, too.

Kaboom!

The room exploded, pieces of the roof spinning up to the sky. The walls outside where we stood split, and chunks of drywall fell into the hallway. We merged into a mass of screaming, stampeding students and teachers, everybody surging toward the exits. Everyone jack-rabbited for their vehicles and those who didn't own one kept running down the street. When Jake and I got to the student parking lot, we turned to watch the building do the Watutsi.

The school's outside wall beside the front double doors crumbled into dust, and something massive stomped out. No longer smoke or shadow, Baal had taken flesh.

The din from screams of those still trapped inside and Baal's angry roars fought for noise space. We let the tide of last-minute escapees wash us to the area where Jake's truck was parked.

We broke free of the crowd. Jake inserted his key in the lock of the driver's door and unlocked it.

I kept my eye on the demon as it bashed down more of the school.

"Hey!"

Pete Jameson and Tyree Washington jogged toward us, petrified looks on their faces.

"Jake, it's Pete," Pete called out. "Tyree's with me, too."

Jake opened the driver's door. "Yeah?" He left it ajar and walked around the front of his truck to where I stood and unlocked the passenger door.

I touched Jake's arm. "Maybe we should give them a ride."

Pete asked, "Hey, what the hell is that thing?"

I blurted out, "A demon."

He gave me a brief annoyed look while Tyree spoke up. "Come on, Jake; help your main man, Pete, and me out. That thing, whatever it is, looks nasty."

Pete shrugged. "I have to say, it's doing us a favor by destroying the school." He flinched when Baal roared again. "Still, I don't plan to hang around."

Jake nodded. "Okay, get in."

I grabbed the handle of the passenger door so that I could slide in, but Pete shoved me aside, almost knocking me to the cement, so that he could climb in. Jake grabbed him by the back of the neck and yanked him back out. Tyree alternated watching us then the demon.

Pete rubbed his neck. "What the—*cough, cough.*"

Jake shook a finger in Pete's face. "Look, Harper gets in first."

"But, but..."

"No buts. No rude creep attitude, either. There's a demon loose, and it wants to destroy the world. Most of all, it wants Harper, and I am not letting that happen."

"I thought we were best buds, Jake." Pete glared at me. "Don't know what bug got up your butt but leave this twit here and let's get outta here."

Jake assisted me into the truck. The door still open, he turned back to Pete. "I'm not leaving Harper and no name-calling from either of you. Get in or not. Cause it's heading our way."

Tyree's eyes widened and I swore his dark skin paled. "He's right, Pete."

Jake left to go around to the driver's side and climbed in. Baal threw a chunk of the wall. Lucky for us, it flew over the truck and hit a tree instead.

Tyree shook Pete's shoulder. "Hey, there's Brian Woods. Let's catch a ride with him." White as a ghost, Pete slammed the door shut, narrowly missing my fingers as I snatched the seat belt and yanked it around me to snap into place as Jake stuck the key in the ignition, turned it, and the truck's engine roared to life.

I watch Pete sprint after Tyree. Both boys argued by Brian's SUV, but when another piece of the building made a crater not far from them, all three leaped inside. Seconds later, they raced with us out of the parking lot.

Behind us, the whole school building danced and shuddered. Heavy chunks of cinderblock and more flew into the parking lot, demolishing what remained of parked vehicles and crushing a couple of people.

Cresil screamed as one side of the shattered metal of the school's double doors shot past us. *"Get us out of here."*

KABOOM!

I looked in the rearview mirror and saw the whole school become a giant pile of dust. "School's out—forever. What's going to happen to us?"

Jake didn't answer, just drove.

I stared out the passenger window at the scenery blurring into lines of colors. My life lay in shambles. My math teacher was dead, putz or not. Worse, the whole world is headed to Hell for real. Was it only a year ago that I thought not being allowed to stay up until eleven on school nights had to be the worst thing that could ever happen to me?

Guess my priorities had gotten set straight now.

Why hadn't I convinced my friends to watch a girly movie that fatal night? No, Barbie got it into her head that we should summon a demon since we couldn't think up anything that didn't bore her. She'd laughed at the thought of getting some entity to plaster acne on some of the bitchy cheerleaders' faces. Maybe we could score 'A's in an upcoming math test. Make some cute boys glance our way. Barbie had even admitted to having her eye on the queen's crown for the Snow Ball in December. Problem was, none of us believed we would get an actual something from Hell, Barbie most of all.

The only thing Barbie received was a six-by-six plot in Moon Ridge Cemetery. Her only dance? Set to Lucifer's tune.

Chapter Thirteen—Harper

Jake stared straight ahead, not looking at me or even in the rearview mirror to see if the demon pursued us. I looked at his hands on the steering wheel and saw they'd whitened like a corpse's.

I cleared my throat.

No reaction.

I cleared my throat again.

He spared me a glance before returning his eyes to the road. "What?"

"Take me home, Jake."

"I think we better head to my house. Let Mom know about what happened. If it's not on the news already."

"I want to go home."

He looked aside at me and opened his mouth to say something, but I twisted one of the straps of my bookbag and said, "Please?"

His gaze back at the windshield, he sighed and nodded. "All right. But understand this, I think it's not smart, but I will take you home."

"I do understand, and thanks. I know this is as scary and off the wall for you as it's for me."

I leaned my head back against the headrest and closed my eyes, hoping for a bit of peace.

Jake called out. "Harper, we're here."

When I opened my eyes, Jake had pulled into the driveway. Mom's car wasn't there, and dread squeezed my heart until I remembered she went to work today.

Jake said, "Remember, I agreed to take you to your place. Did you doze off or something?"

"No, I only closed my eyes for a bit." I frowned. "That's weird."

Jake frowned. "What is?"

"Mom usually leaves a lamp on inside to discourage burglars. She does that every day she goes to work. Not unless she took the day off, but then, her car would be in the driveway."

"Let get inside and check it out. The bulb might have gone out."

I unsnapped the seat belt, opened the door, and stumbled out of the cab. Mom hadn't even left a light on in the living room, as usual. She did this to deter thieves from breaking in, making them think someone was home. I walked around the truck, heading toward the porch as Jake stepped out, slamming the driver's door shut.

Nodding, I slipped the house key out of my bookbag. "Yes, you're probably right. It could mean the electricity died." I looked across the street and saw a lit bulb outside the Thompsons' garage. I swept my gaze around the rest of the neighborhood and saw indications of power at other houses. I didn't say anything to Jake as I gripped my house key in a death grip.

"Here, hand over the key," Jake said. "I'll open the door and enter first to make sure nothing's wrong. Like I said, most likely a bulb out."

Cresil piped up. *"Yeah, simple as Baal."*

"Shhh, demon," said Jake. "Keep your opinions to yourself."

Cresil didn't say anything else.

We crossed the lawn and tiptoed up the steps to the porch, quiet as we could. One of the porch boards creaked when I stepped on it. Not breathing, we waited, but we went up to the front door when nothing came at us.

Jake inserted the key in the lock and turned it. The lock clicked, and he turned the knob and pushed the door open a few inches. To my ears, it sounded loud enough to wake the dead, even though nothing more than a whisper of a low scape.

He shoved the door open all the way with his shoulder and stepped inside. "Remain out here," he ordered me.

Really? It's my home. Even though I knew he would be upset with me, I poked my head inside and watched him cross over to the lamp on the table by the window and hit its switch. *Click. Click.* No light came on to banish the darkness in the living room.

"Either the bulb is dead, or the power's out." He turned around and walked right into me. I let out a squeak and he grabbed me as I almost tripped.

Jake frowned. "Didn't I ask you to stay outside?"

"No, you didn't. You ordered me like some big tough man." I snorted and jutted my chin out. "Anyway, it's my house."

He threw up his hands and rolled his eyes. "Whatever. Hit that light switch by the door. Let's see if the power is working."

I tried the light switch on the wall. Nothing happened. I snatched the landline phone. Mom kept it on the same table as the defunct lamp. The light was out, but I heard the sound, letting me know the telephone still worked. I made a call to Moon Ridge Real Estate. Mom picked up after the second ring.

"Moon Ridge Real Estate. How may I assist? Wait, the caller ID says it's my house. Harper?"

I blew out a sigh of relief. "Yeah, it's me. Jake brought me home."

Her voice changed. "What's wrong? Why aren't you at school? Are you ill? Why didn't they call me to come to get you and why did they allow Jake off to take you home?"

"No one at work told you anything?"

"Harper, will you quit playing around. Why would anyone here tell me anything?"

I took a deep breath and got right to it. "Mom, something terrible happened at school a short time ago. There's no more Moon Ridge High School. The building blew up. I think most of the students, faculty, and office workers made it out. At least, I hope they did."

"What?" A crash from the other end told me she had shot up from her desk, knocking something off.

"I know you guys have a TV in the break room. Please turn it on. There might be news."

A bang told me she'd dropped the receiver. The background sounds from a television filtered through the phone to my ear. Frantic, raised, shocked voices rose, adding to the TV's noise.

A scrabbling noise of someone fumbling with the phone, and I heard Mom's voice. "Harper?"

"I'm still here."

"The news is reporting that the entire school building is no longer standing. There are thoughts that it might have been an earthquake. It could even have been a bomb, maybe a homemade one. Emergency crews of firefighters and police are combing for any people still alive or for bodies of the dead. The reporter said the Governor is sending authorities to determine the cause."

"I just hope most if not all got out of there, like Jake and I did." Mr. Borkus's image popped into my mind. I knew they wouldn't find Borkus, not in pieces, not his corpse, never.

"Harper?" Mom's voice no longer sounded horrified, but in full parental mode.

"Yeah, Mom?"

"I'm getting off work right now and coming home."

Baal's image arose in my mind. I needed to stop her from doing that. If Baal knew where I went to school, he might know where I lived. Her life might still be in danger at her workplace, but I knew for sure her most significant risk lay here. After all, he could be in the house right at this moment. If the rest of the neighborhood had power, that meant the demon had shorted out our house.

"Good. Your mother is mortal. I put out magic feelers and I don't sense Baal here or nearby. Have wizard-boy take you over to his house. We need to get our heads together on some plan to stop Baal."

I spoke on the phone, my heart pounding, "Mom. Please stay there. If it's an earthquake, it could hit with an aftershock while you're driving. Please, please, please, stay there. I don't want something to happen to you."

"All right, I'll stay here. Remain indoors and don't run out if an aftershock does hit. I think experts say to huddle in an open doorway or something. Understand?"

"I'm with Jake, and I'll have my cell phone on me. The lights are out here, and I can't be sure the phone will ring if you call."

Okay, I told Mom a lie, but it was a white one. I would be with Jake, just at his house. Cresil was right; his mother would be the best person to talk to about this. She believed in ghosts and demons. Mine would only freak out, and that's if she even believed me. She's a grounding sort of person, and I'm sure she didn't believe in anything supernatural. Still, she might come running home, and that might mean right into Baal's arms. I loved her too much for that to happen.

We both said goodbye, and I hung up. I turned to Jake, who had been staring out the front window.

Let's get to the wizard-boy's house.

"Jake, we should head over to your place."

He dropped the edge of the shade and looked at me. "I told you that we should have gone there first thing."

"I know. Let me take out what I have in this bookbag and collect other things we might need and stuff them inside."

I left my school books, a pencil, and my notebook on my bed, but I kept a pen and stuffed an empty notebook inside the bag. Sweeping my gaze around the room, I saw my laptop. I unplugged it and crammed it and its mouse inside a laptop bag, snatching a thumb drive also. It might be helpful, even if we used it to search online only. Before I walked out of my room, I grabbed my cell and its charger, stuffing them in my pants pocket. I ran downstairs.

"I grabbed my laptop, too," I said, handing it to Jake.

"But we have Mom's computer at the house, and I have a laptop."

"Yeah, but just in case. All three of us can get online to search."

He took it and tucked it under his arm.

We left the house after I locked up and got back into Jake's truck. As we raced away, I peeked around. No demon. The house's windows stared at us like dark, blind eyes.

"Don't worry. Baal is lying low for now. I think he used his magic to make the students and teachers forget he caused the school to come crashing down. Otherwise, your mother would have said the news reported weird stories from them. The demon lord's not ready to show that demons exist in the universe. Not yet anyway."

We arrived at Jake's house without any problems. Cresil was right, which surprised me. I thought Baal would have tried to attack us on the drive over.

"Baal is arrogant. Thinking that either you're stupid and scared, or if you do tell the authorities, they will think you're crazy or pulling a prank. Haven't you noticed your mother not mentioning one word about monsters or demons from any survivors of the school's catastrophe on the news? I suspect Baal used magic for those who saw him to make them forget."

Jake killed the engine after he pulled in behind his mother's car in the driveway. He grabbed my laptop, and with my bookbag slung over my right shoulder, we ran up the porch steps to the front door.

The door swung open in our faces. I jumped back, my heart hammering my chest. Mrs. Hewitt's face peeped in the opening, tears in her eyes and her blond hair in dishabille. Her face broke into a watery smile. She snatched Jake and my laptop to her breast.

"Thank the Lord. You're both alright."

I slipped past them. "You saw the news then?"

Mrs. Hewitt freed Jake and closed the door, turning to look at me confused. "News?"

"On TV."

She shook her head. "The cards let me know you were in trouble."

Entering the kitchen, I spied her Tarot cards spread across one side of the square, glass-topped table.

Jake followed her in. "Tarot cards. Mom?"

She took my laptop from him and placed it across the table from the cards. "Jake, it's my living. I had just finished a client's reading over the phone a half-hour ago when something told me to do another one. I think it was my father." She looked at Jake. "He wanted me to do yours."

She fell into the chair and tapped one of the cards. "They didn't tell me if you were alive or not, though. Just that some tragedy happened, and all connected to a demon, and not Cresil. I tried calling the school office but got only dead silence. That scared me."

"It's okay, Mom." Jake hugged her. "As you can see, Harper and I survived, and I think most of the other students and teachers escaped, too."

She wrapped her arms around his frame and shuddered. "Oh, Jake, I love you." Letting go of him after a minute, she snatched me to her breast and hugged me. "I'm glad you're fine, too, Harper."

"Ugh! Enough of this sickening love and hugging. It's time to put into plan a way to stop Baal."

Jake snorted, just as Mrs. Hewitt grabbed him again for another hug. "I heard that, Cresil."

"Tell me what happened?"

"Baal possessed our calculus teacher—"

One of the cards rose in the air and flipped over, revealing an old Native American man. A knock came at the front door.

I jumped, startled.

Jake froze. "The demon?" He narrowed his eyes.

Mrs. Hewitt shook her head. "No, I don't sense anything demonic on the other side of that door," her eyebrows knotted together, "and I will tell you both, there's no old man on any of my cards."

Jake agreed. "I don't care if that's not a demon outside. Whoever—whatever it is, can't be human." He walked into the living room and snatched a metal figure off an end table.

Mrs. Hewitt joined him, with me not far behind. I'd snatched a knife out of her knife block when we heard another round of knocks. Not because I believed it would stop a demon or anything supernatural, but it made me feel better to have a weapon.

Mrs. Hewitt walked up to the door and before she laid a hand on the doorknob, it swung open. A short shadowy figure stood outside on her welcome mat. It stepped inside and the door closed behind it with a decisive click, and the locks set as strange, glowing sigils appeared on the door, and the windows in the living room.

The light of a nearby lamp on a table came on.

An old man dressed in white, with features carved in a brown face with a ton of wrinkles, stood there. He wore his long obsidian hair in two braids slung down his back, and a Native American necklace of turquoise surrounded his neck. It looked like the man on the Tarot card.

Solemn, he bowed with his two hands together, his braids flipping to his front. "I am here to teach an untrained sorcerer who resides in this home."

"There are no untrained sorcerers here." I crossed my arms with bravado. Inside I quivered as I remembered Cresil calling Jake one.

The man flashed us a wide grin full of bright, white teeth. "I can smell his power here, the same power that led me to him."

Mrs. Hewitt brightened. "You're talking about my son, Jake, aren't you?"

I glanced at Mrs. Hewitt. I don't think she should have said that. After all, this person could be a demon.

"He is not a demon, Harper."

Jake put up a hand. "No, thank you. I have no powers. I'm not even psychic like my mother." He narrowed his eyes. "Just who are you?"

Cresil piped up, *"Yes, you do, dummy. You have powers."*

Jake glared at me, or I should say, Cresil. "No, I don't, you stupid demon."

"Who has a truckload of power inside his pathetic soft flesh? Quit being a whiner and listen to this angel face."

The little man peered at Jake. "Hush, demon of impurity and laziness. Jacob, you do have power, much power. We cannot have magic, such as you possess, fall into Baal's hands. With you under his control, it would double his chances of winning. Do you want that to happen?"

Jake stepped back a few paces from the man. "No, I don't. But I am not some Jedi type. I don't even read fantasies. And I don't remember you introducing yourself. Who are you?"

"You're correct, Jacob. I did not. I am an archangel of Heaven, though on a lesser degree to Michael and the other major seven. I am called Sotuknang, at least by the People. The Hopi thought many angels and demons were gods or mighty spirits. Something that should have been disputed, but Heaven did not. I can see why demons would, but us angels?"

The man stepped around Jake and stopped before Mrs. Hewitt, where he patted her shoulder. "I promise you, Mrs. Hewitt, I will make him into something you will be proud of."

"I know you will." Mrs. Hewitt turned and shuffled back into the kitchen. "I am going to brew tea. Harper, come and help me. I have freshly baked lemon cookies on a plate in the fridge that you can put out."

I snuck a quick look back at Jake and the man as I followed her. The man held a twinkle in his dark eyes, while Jake didn't look happy about us leaving him with the man, er, angel.

The stranger flicked his fingers. "Yes, yes, go, go, help Jacob's mother."

Is he really an archangel?

"He is. Get me away from his glory alleluianess. It's like a sun to a vampire."

The archangel turned to Jake. "Jacob, come sit with me. We must talk."

Jake replied, walking over to the couch. "It's Jake, not Jacob. I'm not a sorcerer, tried or untried."

"We shall see, Jacob. We shall see."

Not waiting around to see how Jake took Sotuknang ignored using Jake over Jacob, I hurried to the kitchen. Cresil made me sick in her desperate need to get away from the archangel. Opening the fridge, I seized the plate of cookies and set them on the table that Mrs. Hewitt had cleared of the Tarot cards. I darted over to the doorway to peer into the living room and listen.

Cresil whined. *"He's a freaking angel, no, he's an archangel. That makes it two times worse."*

Jake sat in the chair while Sotuknang sat with his legs crossed Indian-style and floated in the air before him.

Cresil sighed. *"Of course, Heaven would send Sotuknang to do the training."*

"Sounds like you know him and don't like him."

"He's an archangel, so tell me why I should like him? He's the archangel who taught the other warrior archangels the skills they needed to crush demons."

"So, Heaven sent him to whip Jake into sorcerer shape."

"I'd never imagined they would send him to teach Jake. Heaven appears to have its own plans for Jake and Baal's war."

I ignored the grumbling in my head and accepted a cup of hot, fragrant tea from Mrs. Hewitt. Even without any sweetener added, one sip let me know how delicious it was. When Mrs. Hewitt left the kitchen, carrying a tray crowded with three cups stacked, a teapot of herbal tea, napkins, packets of sugar, a sugar-free alternative, and four spoons, I grabbed the plate of cookies off the table and carried them and my cup of tea, following her. She set the tray down on the coffee table and perched on one of the couch's arms. I placed the plate of cookies down and remained standing, drinking my tea.

Jake had his arms twisted together and his lips in a slash. "Why me? What makes me so important?"

Sotuknang sighed. "Heaven has written that you are a part of the three prophesized that will block Baal from leading Lucifer's armies to destroy Earth. If he isn't stopped, then Heaven's gates will be next to be breached."

Jake narrowed his eyes. "Who are the other two defenders?"

The little man grinned and nodded at me. "Harper," his smile dropped, "and the demon, Cresil."

"Well, la di da, the fricking archangel is not happy to have a demon helping save the Earth. Wait a moment, what did he say? I'll help defeat Baal?" I heard the shock in Cresil's voice. *"I'm included in the prophecy?"*

The archangel did a complete turnaround and floated over to me. "Yes, demon, you heard right. I double-checked to be sure, but it says you are needed for it to work."

"I'm the lazy ass demon, more about sassy mouth than hero stuff, remember? If I'm part of any foretelling, someone messed up somewhere."

I was dumbfounded. It wasn't just about Cresil, but that I was included in the three to save the world. What could I do? Jake is a possible sorcerer and Cresil is a demon with magic, but me? I'm nothing more than an ordinary teenage girl.

Sotuknang spoke to me, touching me above the brow with a finger. "I am sorry to do this to you, Harper. For this to work, Cresil must be yanked from your body. It will be excruciating if you are conscious, so I am putting you to sleep." He drew his lips close to my ear. "Shhhh. Sleep."

Cresil yelled, *"Hey, fluffy wings, what the double hexes, do you—"*

Chapter Fourteen—Cresil

Double dang devil's foot, I'm back in charge of Harper's body again. Freaking archangel. I wouldn't call this getting me out of her.

I hissed at Sotuknang, who floated away so I couldn't swing at him. Before Harper dropped like a stone to the floor, the archangel must have magicked her body to the sofa.

Jake stuck his puss up close, and I shoved him away.

"Hey, get out of my face!" I zapped my magic at him.

Wizard-boy didn't budge.

The magic should have worked. Confusion ran rampant through me, or was that through Harper? I'd been a part of her so long now that I didn't know my own identity anymore.

I swung Harper's legs to the floor and Jake stuck out a hand. He'd called me a pitchfork hussy, and yet, he's offering a hand to me? I took his assistance anyway.

Harper's legs wobbled like jelly, and I ended up right back down on the couch. I opened Harper's mouth to cuss when I saw Sotuknang's eyes glowing. I didn't need the atomic level pain the archangel could inflict on me, so I kept quiet.

Sotuknang sat down in the recliner and crossed his legs like the creepy little medicine man he resembled. I expected him to go indigenous witch doctor and shake a gourd full of dried beans and chant.

Jake stood near his mother, who watched with wide eyes.

Sotuknang rose of the chair—still crossed-legged—and hovered over me. He had a grin on his face, stretched from ear to ear.

I itched to knock that happy expression off his face.

He lowered himself until we locked nose to nose.

Why does everyone feel they need to get in my space? "Move. Let me get up." I used him to try again to stand, though teeter-tottering was more like it.

The archangel remained serene. Didn't anything ruffle him? A demon put her paws on him, for Hell's sake. In the old days, I'd have earned a smiting or something on that level.

Dunderhead, I'm in the mortal girl's body! Smite me, and he destroys her pretty little face, too.

As if he heard my thoughts, he spoke. "So, demon, you want a smiting?"

I buffaloed him as I leaned against the wall, hoping it made me appear cool instead of shaky. "You put the girl's body to sleep. Her brain, too, but I'm a demon. Remember? We demonic types gotta be fracking smartass to Heaven's own. It's all about our reputation." A wave of—*is that dizziness?*—overcame me.

Sotuknang snapped his fingers and both the dizziness and weakness vanished. I straightened and took my hand from the wall. Time to drop the bravado act.

"What's this about me, Harper, and padawan boy here, stopping Baal? Except for a few magic tricks up my sleeve, I am not a smidgen in Baal's league. Or yours, either."

Sotuknang lowered himself on the couch. "Heaven sent me to instruct Jacob Hewitt, to bring out his inner sorcerer. When he is ready, he will be a force to reckon with."

"Still, Harper's human and I'm a small-potatoes demon. Why are we needed? Jake could lead the world's militaries."

"Harper has her part to play, and that is all I am at liberty to say for now. You do, too. Just wait and see."

Angelic inscrutableness—I hated when they pulled that, even when I was once an angel myself. This is why I rebelled—for the most part, although Lucifer and his head demons did the same thing.

I shrugged, acting as if it didn't matter. "If you say so." But I peered at him and the others in the room.

Jake's posture indicated boredom.

I didn't feel so sure about the powerful sorcerer thing concerning him. As for me, I'm nothing but a low-class fiend whose only claim to fame was rebelling against Heaven and impurity and laziness. I'm rather good at those last two things.

When Lucifer sent demons to tempt Sodom and Gomorrah's citizens, I managed to get out of that by finding an oasis in the desert and snatching some zzzs. I think whoever Heaven had in charge of prophecies should fire the idiot. What could I do against a Hell lord of Baal's strength? He magicked me into Harper's body in the first place without raising any sweat. As for the human, Harper, the first chance she got near a part of the Legion, she would find her throat slit.

"How long do we have?" asked Mrs. Hewitt.

Sotuknang said, "We need to be ready by Halloween."

Jake sputtered and dropped the boredom act. "What? You're going to have me trained and ready in a few weeks? I heard it takes six weeks of boot camp for the military to train soldiers, then they still go to school in just as many weeks, if not more. How long is the police academy? Doesn't it take years before one earns a black belt?"

Sotuknang laughed. "Ah, but those are mortal teachers. I am not mortal. Trust in God's plan." He grew serious. "If you are thinking actual training face-to-face, like in those karate movies, think outside of the box. I may do some training with you while you are awake, but most of it will be while you sleep, in your dreams."

Jake didn't look convinced.

I sneered. "With a snap of your fingers or your angel wings, the boy will become a grand sorcerer. That sounds so much like a hero's journey. What about me? Are you going to tell me that with Harper and me sharing one body, two think better than one? I know my magic sure isn't the best among Hell's minions."

"Ah, but little demon, I have the ability to separate the two of you. Remember?"

"What did you say?" He had said that before putting Harper to sleep.

I almost smiled, but I didn't. I knew better than to let the Heavenly goodie understand what I thought. It would hurt, but Sotuknang might just be able to undo what a demon lord had done.

Get free of this mortal frame, pretend I would help, and jump ship to the other side when the time came for the actual battle. I knew better than to go against Baal or Lucifer. Any demon worth her or his vaporous form knew how it would end for them if they fought for Heaven, and Heaven lost.

Eternity in the worse place of Hell would be their prison.

Thank Lucifer's evil heart, that Harper was brain dead somewhere in her noggin and didn't know my thoughts. Otherwise, the girl might find a way to blab to the do-gooders.

I put my hands behind my back, fingers crossed on both. "That sounds dandy. I'm in."

Jake narrowed his eyes. I know he couldn't hear my thoughts when I was in control of Harper's body. I hoped he didn't. To be safe, I inched closer to Sotuknang.

I asked, "Can you magick me out of this body now?"

Sotuknang nodded and began to chant, "Amo Siamese concero, illa duos es unus. Iam per lux lucis ex meus pennae scindo is unus."

The room began spinning like a top, whirling faster and faster like some amusement park ride.

Jake yelled above the noise. "Hey, Sotuknang, what are you doing?"

Sotuknang replied, "Bringing forth destiny. I am drawing the demon out of Harper's body."

I didn't know about destiny, but it felt like a heavy four-wheeler roared through Harper's head. Lucky girl, she got to remain unconscious. Her body began to shake, rattle, and roll. "Lucifer's Fall, it's killing us. Let me rephrase that. You're killing us."

Agony dug deep through me. It made Mrs. Hewitt's exorcism like using a pea shooter to this bomb explosion. I slipped and sloshed like a wet mop. *What's happening?*

"Harper?" She didn't answer. Her stomach roiled, and I leaned over to throw up. The tea she'd drank earlier and whatever else she'd eaten and drunk since breakfast spilled out and over the cookies and the tea on the coffee table. I thought Harper and I parted ways, but it looked like I still shared the rent on her form. Another round of sickness unsettled me, and I vomited again. Nothing came out. It hurt something awful. The misery crawled from the stomach along nerves and skin, slamming the brain.

I twisted around and grappled for the archangel, but he remained out of reach. His image reminded me of a distorted funhouse mirror. I blinked.

Damn. The distortion grew worse.

I fell to hands and knees. *Oh, no, not another cookie tossing time.* Nothing but a tiny bit of saliva came out. A nasty sting cut through the belly, and I rolled over onto Harper's left side.

I screeched, "This is torture! Do something, you haloed pain in the—"

He leaned over, and his fingers grazed like cool feathers across the burning forehead. "Shhhh."

I hate archangels, and I want to tear Sotuknang's wings from him and—

****

I opened my eyes. I laid on something hard as my vision blurred, then cleared as I looked up at the ceiling. A couple of smashed dead spiders and several spots speckled the plaster.

Mrs. Hewitt really needed to clean up there.

No doubt, Sotuknang failed.

I winced. Damn, this body feels bruised.

That meant Harper's body must have hit the floor bad when he mumbled jumbled us. I tested different areas. "Ouch. Ouch."

Even the ears and lips hurt.

I sat up, too quickly, and my vision somersaulted. I lurched to stand, and the gymnastics grew worse. So that I wouldn't let loose the stomach's contents—which were nil— I closed the eyes and took a couple of deep breaths. Finally, the dizzy spells subsided.

"Sotuknang," I snarled.

"Yes, Cresil."

"Come closer, so I could use Harper's hands to throttle you. I know I can't kill you with our weak digits, but I plan to give it the Girl Scout try."

Sotuknang's voice came from behind me. "Tsk, tsk. You can't make Harper do anything as you're not in her body."

"When your face mottles..." I whipped around to face him. The wooziness returned, and once again, I rode a merry-go-round, the room spinning. Finally, the lightheadedness subsided. "Wait a minute, what did you say?"

He thumbed at a mirror on the wall. "Check it out."

I stepped toward the mirror.

Whoa! The dizziness slapped me silly again. I waited until it calmed down. When my head quit doing the samba, I continued to the mirror, taking it slow and easy. Hands flat on the wall to keep me on my feet, I peered at my reflection.

Harper's face didn't stare back at me. Neither did my regular demon face or the shadow one, both usually having red eyes. Instead, the face of a young woman with mocha colored skin and long dark brown hair stared back in wide-eyed amazement. Her eyes were dark pools with flecks of gold that widened even more prominently as I pressed my face against the cool glass of the mirror.

I blinked. The reflection blinked her eyes. I stumbled backward and flapped my arms like wings to keep from falling. That's when I saw that the girl in the mirror wore only her birthday suit as she, too, flapped her arms.

I looked down.

Oops, naked. *Just like the girl in the mirror. Hey, I got boobs.* I squeeze them. *Not shabby at all.* I turned to look at the others to get their impressions.

Jake's jaw had dropped, and his eyes zeroed in on my body. He blushed as he caught me watching him and darted down the hallway.

I turned my head to see how this affected the archangel. Nothing. Really? I got boobs, and he's not affected by them?

Hush! A voice that sounded like Sotuknang's filled my head. *There's no time for your dirty-minded demonic musings.*

Mrs. Hewitt rushed over to me and wrapped a sheet around my body. She fixed it sarong-style, covering the naked parts that needed covering.

Seeing her waiting, I understood. "Thanks." *Humans have too much to remember. Being a demon for eons didn't teach one the niceties.* I touched the sheet poking forward, where my new breasts were. They didn't pop like balloons and deflate. *Cool. But if I am in my own human body, where is Harper?* "Where's Harper?"

Sotuknang said, "Ah...she's..."

I looked around, only a bit frantic. "Has yanking us apart harmed her?"

An expression appeared on his face. *Could he be sheepish?*

"No, it appears cutting you free from her didn't have the effect that normal exorcisms have."

I narrowed my eyes. "What do you mean?"

Jake stuck his head out of a doorway from down the hall. "Harper's on Mom's bed in here."

I managed to walk down the hallway and pushed past Jake into the bedroom, where I saw Harper stretched out on the bed. I turned to Jake.

"Harper's not dead, is she?"

He didn't answer.

I called out to Sotuknang who appeared in the bedroom. "Sotuknang, so, what the Hades did you do to Harper, and how do you expect me in this frail human flesh to fight demons? Mortals break easy. Remember, mortality? Fix it."

"I cannot make you a demon again, Cresil," said Sotuknang. "I did not do this to you. When I pulled you from Harper, the form you have now is what appeared. But I had nothing to do with you taking flesh."

"Well, who in the frack did it? Santa Claus? The Easter bunny? No, wait, it's close to Halloween. Maybe it was the queen of the fairies? Or maybe my fairy godmother."

The archangel rolled his eyes. "Who else do you think has the power to make you a human being?"

"Are you saying," I pointed at the ceiling, "God did this?" I skimmed my hand along my new body.

Great. I get to go through puberty for real. Either this was His joke, or God still has it in for me for joining Lucifer's rebellion. You'd think He'd have gotten over it after the first eon. I couldn't see any other reason for Him to make me like this.

I stared down at my clenched hands. They were nothing but slim, tiny things with dainty fingers. Dainty! What could I do to Baal with these? With this frail, oh-so-human body?

I swore I saw pity in Sotuknang's eyes. I didn't need sympathy from angelcakes.

"What does God think I can do with this sad sack of a body? Do I still have my demon mojo?"

"It is not for me or you to know God's plans, but I believe He has a purpose for you like this. Besides, I sense you still have your powers, so you're not all powerless."

"Right, and the powers I had before did me a fat lot of good against Baal?"

Mrs. Hewitt entered the room, and I began to weep like the wimpy human I now was.

"I'm nothing but a pathetic bag of bones. Baal would kick my butt to the end of time and back. He would splat me into a bloody blot on the ground, even with my loser demonic powers."

Jake said, "Cut being a whiney brat. Harper would have tried. All you've done for her since you popped into her life hasn't done her any good."

I scrubbed at the tears staining my cheeks. Damn, the boy pissed me off. Mr. Big and Bad thought he could call me about being a whiner? A brat? That I made Harper's life awful since I zapped into that summoning circle?

"How dare you? You're no better. I can say my excuse is being a demon. What's yours? Being a dumb mortal?"

Jake frowned and crossed over to Harper. He looked down at her. "You're right. I let some jerk seduce me to the creep side." He looked at Sotuknang. "I'm ready to embrace my destiny. I want to kick demons back to Hell, and then some."

Sotuknang nodded. "Good. I will whisk you away to a place where we can work undisturbed."

Jake looked mulish. "One thing before we go, I want Harper awakened."

Lines on Sotuknang's forehead bee-lined down to the dark brows over dark eyes growing darker. More lines formed around his downturned mouth. "I cannot do it."

Jake crossed his arms. "Then, there'll be no teaching me. Not until she's no longer a sleeping beauty."

I butted in. "Pansy archangel."

Sotuknang didn't glare at me, but the air around him grew hot. "I was sent to teach Jacob, nothing more. Everything else is God's will."

Ignoring the thunderclouds of growing anger around him, I poked a finger at his chest. "What happened to Harper and me is being a part of God's will? Are we a lesson God felt needed teaching or something? I think that you can do more than you claim."

Jake said, "Wake Harper up, or find some other untried wizard."

"Sorcerer," I corrected.

"Great, sorcerer or whatever the heck I am supposed to be." He turned back to Sotuknang. "Whatever you want me to be, please bring Harper back to us."

The anger fell away, and Sotuknang sighed. "I wish I could, but I really can't. I'm sorry, Jacob. I'm an archangel, but not on the level of Michael or Gabriel." He perked up. "But maybe you can."

Jacob frowned. "How can I do anything if an archangel can't?"

Sotuknang replied, "Go inside yourself. Find the spark that resides within you. I am betting you can do it. I have faith in you."

Jake moved away, looking unsure. "But I thought you said I was untutored." He wandered over to Harper. "You say I have the magic to maybe help halt a demonic apocalypse, but I'm just a seventeen-year-old boy. The smartest thing I have ever done was being friends with Harper and look how I screwed that up, thinking Pete the better buddy." He looked over his shoulder at Sotuknang. "You're the archangel. You have to do it. There's no way someone like me can do it."

Sotuknang gave him a warm smile. "This will be your first test. To see how much you can do at this moment."

I did something a demon would never do and laid a hand on Jake's shoulder, tried to say something encouraging, but I couldn't. I cleared my throat and tried again. This time the words came out. "I believe you can do it. I know you can do it." Okay, that felt bizarre. Demons were supposed to make humans do evil acts, not encourage them in something that could be helpful. This body invoked all manners of strange feelings. Feelings I couldn't cope with, and yet, feelings that caused this outlandish warm fuzziness.

Mrs. Hewitt said, "Jake, do it. Quick, before she heads into the light."

I saw the tight lines around her mouth and the worry in her eyes. I switched my gaze to Sotuknang's serene archangel face. Not quite tranquil. His one eye twitched at one corner.

That's when it struck me. *The light...oh no*!

I turned to Jake. "Jake, snap to it. Call her back to us. She's in that in-between place between life and death. The longer she remains there, the more the call of the light will lure her into entering it. When I got drawn out, so did she and she's astral-projected herself over to the other side."

Jake touched Harper's face and he sat down beside her on the mattress. Caressing her skin, he leaned over, and for a moment, I thought he might kiss her. Instead, he whispered into her ear, asking her to come back.

The power saturated the air, and fragments of it broke away, filling the room. I not only felt it, but I could also taste and smell it, and if I squinted, see the power itself. A slight buzz came to my ear like an overabundance of pop rocks crackling and popping.

I fell to the floor, whimpering, blood flowing out of my nostrils and ears. The same happened to Mrs. Hewitt. It didn't affect Sotuknang.

As for Jake, he didn't keel over, but a thin line of blood trickled out of his ears and nose. He kept whispering.

Nothing happened at first. Maybe the sorcerer's apprentice didn't have it in him to save her.

I hoped he did.

He kept it up, doing what he could to wake up the sleeping beauty. Maybe he should have done a fairytale on her and kissed her.

One of Harper's feet twitched. The other one joined the first foot. The twitching went wild. It looked like they wanted the whole body to get up and dance.

Snap! Crackle! Pop!

Chapter Fifteen—Harper

I'm alone in an endless, black void. I can't see anything, even in front of me. The place didn't feel cold or hot. No air, either. Just pure nothingness.

I don't understand. Am I alive? Without oxygen, living things died. Maybe I'm dead. Had I become one of those spirits who suddenly died and didn't realize it?

What was that? Faint, like bells tinkling in the distance.

All right, I shared this nowhere place with someone or something.

Though knowing better, I called out, surprised I could talk in a place with no air. "Hello? Is somebody there?"

Silence. Maybe I was wrong about hearing a sound.

That's when I heard the tinkling again. This time it sounded closer. Kicking out my feet, I moved away. Not fast enough, though, as it trailed me. Finally, the noise grew less and less as I outdistanced it.

Boom. Boom. Boom. This terrifying new sound hurt my ears, so I headed back toward the tinkling noise.

I paused and floated mid-space, realizing the booming sound came from my own heartbeat, a signal that I still lived. The tinkling broke in, louder and more demanding. Frantic,

I used my legs and arms, dog paddling through the emptiness. No air in my lungs; still, they hurt as if I had sucked in loads of it.

I couldn't get away from the tinkling. It rang right beside me.

"Who's doing this?"

Nobody answered.

I fisted my hands. "Look, I won't let you do anything to me without a fight."

A whisper. "Harper."

My heart dropped to my stomach. "Go away. Leave me alone."

"Harper, please wake up. Come back to us."

It sounds like Jake!

"Jake?" How did he get in here? It must be a trick.

I swam away. The whispers dogged my flight, and I stroked harder, swishing though the nothingness. Just when I was about to give up and let the blasted thing catch me, a light appeared in the distance. Cool and white, it didn't blaze in the darkness, but beckoned like a soft beacon. A need overcame me to go to it.

I headed for it.

The thing behind me drew closer, using Jake's voice, and it became more commanding in tone. "Harper, wake up."

Oh yeah, like I'm asleep. I wouldn't fall for that.

I stopped just short of the light. It didn't hurt my eyes, and I felt the urge to pass through it.

The voice behind me boomed louder, and the void shook, causing an effect of ripples of zilch everywhere. "Harper. Don't go into the light."

Afraid of what might happen next, I escaped through the light and right into the four arms of a large and terrible shadowy being. It had a smile only a monster could love.

"Hello, sweet thing, thanks for going into the light and not listening to that stupid mortal sorcerer kid. We finally meet in my world. I won't say it's good to meet you, as I am never up to any good, only evil." The voice sounded male. One of his hands caressed my hair. "The name's Baal." The demon pressed his face right against mine. "And I love to play games with lost souls." His breath smelled foul, of death.

I squirmed, trying to get my face away from that malicious thing. His grip became tighter. His face tautened, and his eyes went dead. "But first, I need to know how you got that lousy excuse for a demon out of you. With Cresil no longer in your body, the way into your world no longer works. I can't lead Lucifer's army into it without that open portal."

Two hands circled my neck, and Baal began to throttle me.

I choked and coughed.

Fighting back, I scratched at his face, but my fingers passed through him. Frightened, I understood he could be physical with me, but I couldn't with him. He had more than two arms, and, using his other ones, he yanked my arms tight to my sides while he still kept choking me.

I wanted to pray for a way out, but if I were in Hell, then Heaven wouldn't hear me. Worse, if I had listened to Jake's voice on the other side of the light, maybe now I would be back where I belonged.

My heart's pounding grew fainter and fainter. The devil was winning. I felt sure that if he killed my soul (what else could I be?), then my body would slip away, too, back with Jake and the others.

His grip on my neck still rigid, Baal paused. Through the dancing lights in my vision, I managed to see his narrowed eyes. "There's something about you, monkey girl." He sniffed me. "Even your smell is wrong, not all hairless ape."

What did he mean by that crack about my odor?

Jake's voice popped into my head. "*Harper, come back to us.*" Except how do I escape Baal and back to the void? Forget the void, back to the 'other side?'

Jake's voice boomed, this time outside of me. "Harper."

Baal snarled. He'd heard Jake calling me. His grip on me loosened, and I managed to jerk free. Giving him a swift kick in his nether parts, I soared away from the demon lord, and the army of fiends I saw waiting behind him. Behind them, stood a yawning chasm like a great mouth of a snake waiting to swallow me. The entrance to Hell? Not staying around to find out, I reentered the light. Halfway back through it something yanked me out.

Baal roared, the sound becoming fainter as I felt myself rising. "You may be escaping me for now, but I will find another way to reopen the portal!" He called out. "I will lead Lucifer's armies as foretold, and when I find you, I will find out what is different about you from the other humans."

I awoke and sat up, screaming, before I hunched over, my breathing huffing out like a choo-choo train shifting into coughs. Someone patted my back until I stopped, and I realized it was Jake. He helped me swing my legs over the edge of the mattress. Something dripped off my chin. *Yuck.* I wiped at the drool.

He mimicked a little girl from an eighties ghost flick. "She's back."

Three others crowded around the bed. I recognized Mrs. Hewitt and Sotuknang right beside her. But who in blazes was the third person? Did we now have someone else in our apocalyptic secret? Why is she wrapped in a bedsheet? A lovely teenage girl I estimated to be about my age with long dark brown hair and dark eyes leaned over and hugged me.

I untangled myself from her and demanded, "Who are you? Where's Cresil?"

"I'm Cresil." She wrinkled her nose. "Yeah, hard to believe." She hooked her thumb at Sotuknang. "The archangel claims God did it. That before Sotuknang could yank me out himself, Big G sucked me out of your body and made me a fleshie." She snickered. "Personally, I still think Sotuknang did it."

Sotuknang rolled his eyes. "I told you I did not make that body for you, hellspawn. I do not have the power to do that, only the All-Father."

"Don't get your halo in a dander, angelcakes, but I have my doubts. Even if I know archangels aren't supposed to lie."

"Water," I said, barely able to get the word above a whisper.

Cresil said, "Hey, Harper wants water."

Mrs. Hewitt bustled out of the room. "I'll get her a whole pitcher of water with ice. The poor thing deserves it."

I tried to stand, but weakness overpowered me.

Jake pushed Cresil aside. "Here, stay in bed." With his assistance, I sat back against the headboard.

"Hey," said Cresil. "You could have asked, and I would have moved. Just because I'm a demon doesn't mean you have to be rude."

"I'm sorry," he muttered, though he didn't sound like it.

I smiled as he plumped up a pillow and placed it behind me. "Thanks, Jake."

Mrs. Hewitt bustled in, carrying a pitcher of ice water and a glass. After pouring some water into the glass, she handed it over. "Here. Now, drink it all up, but take it slow and easy." She set the pitcher on the bedstand.

I relished the cold, wet liquid snaking down my throat. After a second glassful, I felt able to talk.

"Will somebody please tell me what happened? Why is Cresil a human girl?"

Sotuknang shrugged. "I did not do it as she says, but I think God has His hand in it because I think that in this mortal body, Baal will not realize it is Cresil. I think God wants her hidden from him and Lucifer."

Jake replied, "I bet it's so she doesn't scare off people with that ugly puss she wore as a demon. She can't freak out the general population."

Cresil smacked his arm.

"Hey."

Sotuknang pressed his hands together. "Whatever and why God did it, I am assured it is for the best. For now, Cresil is a human girl. Outside of this room, we will play on that and give her a mortal identity. Admit it; this is much better. You will not be talking to something many others cannot see."

I swung my legs off the mattress and stood. Unfortunately, they still wobbled like I wore unfamiliar high heels. "Ah, yeah, we can't have the residents thinking we're crazy because we're talking to ourselves. That's fine with me."

"As if one of us doesn't already have that reputation, talking to ghosts," said Jake, and glanced at his mother.

She didn't retort, just sniffed.

I took a step. *Whoa*! My sight whirled. Except there weren't little pretty ponies spinning on some carousel, but a kaleidoscope of colors twirling. I licked dry lips and took another step. *Baby steps, baby steps. One giant step for mankind, tiny baby steps for...* I saw my reflection in a big mirror hung on the wall and sighed.

Cresil grinned as she stood beside me and admired her reflection, combing fingers through strands of her thick hair. "Not everyone has a claim to beauty. Damn girl, your skin is white as the ghost you almost became." She skimmed a hand along an arm. "Not such a lovely chocolate color like I have. If God did this, he has good taste."

Mrs. Hewitt loomed behind me and smiled. "Don't listen to the demon. With your face bathed and hair combed, you'll be the belle of the ball."

Chapter Sixteen—Cresil

I stared at my reflection in the mirror. When I was a demon, I admitted to being ugly. As an angel eons ago, my form was a lovely bright light.

I thought I looked pretty darn cute as a mortal.

How many angels up in Heaven right now are having conniption fits by my transformation. I imagined most, if not all, of the haloed buggers.

I noticed Mrs. Hewitt in the mirror. *What's that leaking from her eyes*? Something tugged at my heart. I wanted to walk over to her and wrap my arms around her and hug her.

Am I becoming a hairless ape like the humans here? I looked at myself in the mirror and realized that is indeed what I'd become.

Demons—the true non-human ones—don't have feelings, at least not good ones. We flush the wrong emotions out of mortals. Our calling is to pick at a mortal like a sort of scab until anger, jealousy, lust, and the other nasties that make up the seven deadly sins erupt. True evil doesn't have feelings or morality. Good feelings and morals belonged to the department of Heaven.

I found myself taking step after step after step until I stood in front of Mrs. Hewitt, and I swept my arms around her in a big bear hug. It made me feel all warm and fuzzy, like some teddy bear owned by a kid and dragged through the muck and yuck because the kid loved it. I never felt so dirty and a goody-two-shoes at the same time. The seven deadly sins never made me want to dance around a room.

"I'm sorry, Mrs. Hewitt."

Shocked, I dropped my arms.

Did that piece of morality just slip out of my mouth? Sorry? I'm a sorry-assed demon for sure. Demons are never remorseful. It's in our job description to tempt the foolish mortals and lead them astray. Whisper something enticing in their ear to make the desperate and weak do something to hurt their body or mind or cause harm to another. It's an empowering sense of accomplishment—a mark on Hell's rating system. But today, I felt like the lowest lifeform on this planet for causing Jake's mother to cry.

What's happening to me?

The woman wrapped her arms around me and squeezed.

It felt good. It let me know how mortal I'd become. I should hate this soft skin, I should hate the heart that pounded and the lungs that took in oxygen. One stab of a knife and the heart stopped. Hands choking the throat, and the lungs expired from lack of oxygen. I didn't know how mortals protected their souls in their bodies. When I inhabited mortals' bodies as a demon, I never felt their pain when I did harm to the flesh. Now, in my own 'real' flesh and blood, pain cut at me.

I stepped away from Mrs. Hewitt. "Hey, hey, that might bruise my new skin."

She wiped at her eyes. "Sorry, Cresil."

I flicked my hair over my shoulder, trying to get it together. "That's okay."

Harper's eyebrows knitted together as she looked at me, her eyes full of confusion. "Cresil, I still don't get why making you a human girl would be an asset. Even if it does keep you hidden from Baal."

I shrugged. "Who knows? I sure don't know. Ask the archangel fruitcake. Maybe he has some explanation."

Sotuknang ignored me and came closer to Harper. "Baal appeared to you, Harper, did he not?"

She nodded. "Yes, Baal did. That wasn't a nightmare, was it?"

He tapped a finger against his head. "No, you went to the other side. What happened?"

"He wanted to know how Cresil got freed of me. I didn't tell him anything because I didn't know that's what happened."

Sotuknang stared at me as I joined them. "Cresil is part of defeating Baal and his plans. I know God wanted me to separate her from you to help when the time is right. I thought once exorcised, she would be a demon once again. Archangels have powers way beyond regular angels, but no one, not even Michael, can change a demon into a living mortal girl. Only God can create."

I butted in. "Well, the Big Guy upstairs is mum on this. Are you sure, He's behind this, and it's not some demonic plot?"

Sotuknang shrugged. "No, it's not. Lucifer is not that powerful, no matter what he says and believes."

Yeah, I didn't think my new form was the result of evil. Hell's bells, devils are vain creatures. If any of them, especially Lucifer, could do this godlike thing, they would boast to all and sundry about me being a product of their dark magic.

I sat down. A headache pounded behind my eyes. *Ah, the wonders of being human. Aches, pains, and headaches. Being alive sucked. What next? A frilly dress?*

I snorted and crossed one leg over the other. No way would I ever wear a frilly dress or let someone put me in one.

Come, one and all, and see Cresil at the freak show. She began as an angel, then fell and became a demon, but now, she's nothing more than a costume of a mere mortal teenage girl, acne and all. Come watch as she goes back to high school and flunks math. Will she get to go to the prom before the end of the world? Stay tuned.

Harper said, "Baal told me that he sent Cresil in his place to possess me, for a portal to keep the doorway between here and Hell propped open. That way he, and Lucifer's armies, could march through into the mortal world. He became angry and tried to kill my spirit."

I said, "I don't think he will give up, either. He'll find another foolish mortal to possess, using another lowly demon."

Sotuknang lowered until he stood on his feet, and he paced back and forth. "One thing, Cresil, you still have your demonic powers. This could be used for the right side of this oncoming battle. We have wedged the portal shut on Baal's face for now and if he tries to get it to reopen, we can stop him with yours, mine, and Jake's powers combined." He paused by me and patted my shoulder. "Besides, as Harper's cousin coming to stay for the rest of the school year, you can keep an eye on her and her mother."

I said, "Excuse me, did you say, cousin?"

"The cover story will be that your parents got this chance to go to South America as part of their church's missionary program. Your parents arranged to have you stay with your aunt and cousin, as they will be gone for the school year."

"My parents are church-going freaks? Hellfire, how will we convince Mrs. Doyle that I am Harper's cousin?"

Harper said, "News flash, Mom knows her relatives, and my father supposedly has none. That's what she told me anyway."

Sotuknang's eyes flashed. "I am an archangel, remember?" He snapped his finger and smiled. "It is done." He turned to Jake. "Now for beginning your training. This will be live; you will get more in your dreams tonight as you sleep. Call the dream training, a crash course."

He vanished with monkey boy.

I couldn't believe it. Heaven would not only tell a lie by giving me a cover, but an archangel was going to whammy some innocent to ensure that cover went through.

My headache grew in intensity. "Can someone please get me a couple of painkillers? I have a headache and it's getting worse."

Being alive had its downfalls.

Chapter Seventeen—Cresil

Sotuknang never said exactly what he did to Mrs. Doyle, but the woman welcomed me to her home like a long-lost relative. I suffered the kiss she planted on my cheek as she ordered Harper to carry my suitcase upstairs to the empty bedroom next to Harper's.

"It's so wonderful to have you here, Cressie," said Mrs. Doyle, backing up to give me space but still keeping her hands on my shoulders. "I hope Jerry and Amal don't get into any trouble in South America. I know Amal always believed in helping others, and my brother, Jerry, does whatever she asks, he loves her that much. Maybe my marriage ended badly, but I am so glad Jerry found Amal. Having you made the both of them so happy."

"Uh, yeah," I replied. "I hope, uh, Mom and Dad will be okay, too." You can't take lives from made-up people.

Her eyes glistened with tears. Oh, hell's bells, she believed and worried about the fake Jerry and Amal. Just as I couldn't understand how I reacted to Mrs. Hewitt's pain, I hugged my pretend aunt. "It's all right. They'll be fine. I know they will, Aunt—" I fumbled around for her first name—

Harper had told me earlier, "—Clara. Aunt Clara, thank you for letting me stay here with you and Harper."

She smiled and wiped the tears from her eyes. "How could I not let my niece stay with us?"

She slid an arm around my shoulder and walked me into the house. "Come see your room. I know you'll love it. After you unpack, we'll have dinner. I made your favorite. It's being kept warm in the oven."

Favorite? Okay, what favorite? The only thing I had that I ever liked was cream soda. Okay, that included chocolate chip cookies now. I brightened. "Do you have cream soda? And chocolate chip cookies?"

"Cream soda? I don't remember Amal telling me you drank that."

"Mom doesn't keep soda around the house, but I love it. Can I have a glass of that with my dinner?" I cajoled. "Please?"

"Well, uh, I'll have to drive to the store and get some, but sure, I think we can do that."

I remembered the bet I made with Harper about cream soda when I possessed her and told her I loved it. I grinned.

"As for the chocolate chip cookies, we do have a couple of packages of them in the fridge."

"Not homemade?"

"Sorry, but with me working a lot at the real estate office, it doesn't give me time to do much baking. Maybe this weekend you, me, and Harper can try our hand at baking some cookies? Does that sound good?"

"Sounds great to me."

Aunt Clara and I entered my bedroom; Harper placed my suitcase on the bed.

Oh no. I refuse to sleep with that, that, that thing hanging over my bed.

I drew closer to the foot of the bed, my gaze trained on the offensive painting on the wall.

Harper said in a low whisper, "Like it? It's Sotuknang's and my idea."

I replied back in an equally low tone. "Wait until you see what your mother is running to the store to add to our dinner tonight. I bet you'll just love it."

A freaking painting of an angel? If any other angel had given this to me, I would think they're being serious, but Sotuknang? I expected this to be a sly bit of angelic humor. He needed to stick to training Jake and leave me alone.

An angel to watch over me as I sleep.

"Aunt Clara, got any painkillers? I got this killer headache coming on."

I wished I had cream soda to wash them down.

Chapter Eighteen—Cresil

Laughter echoed in my head as Harper forced herself to drink from the glass of cream soda. The first time she took a sip, she almost spit it out. That would have gone over great with her mother. Aunt Clara partook a small taste, too, but I could tell from the distaste on her face that it would never be something she would buy for herself. She drank the contents down until it was all gone. She drank water after that, remarking about watching her figure.

I'm a demon, despite this frail human body, and I can smell a lie a mile away, Aunt Clara.

Harper just sipped hers on occasion, which was not that often.

I smiled and lifted my glass, chugging down the contents. I flicked the tip of my tongue to capture the few precious drops on my lips.

What Harper and her mother couldn't stand, I loved. This was only my fourth glass. I plan to drink more as Aunt Clara had bought several bottles of it. It'd been a while since I had this drink of the gods. As a demonic spirit in a human body, I had enjoyed it vicariously. In my newly crafted human flesh, having my own taste buds doubled the pleasure.

Aunt Clara spoke. "Well, isn't this nice? It's been a while since we last saw Cressie, hasn't it, Harper?"

She nodded as she scooped more of the casserole onto her plate that Aunt Clara believed was my favorite.

Favorite? *Corned beef and cabbage? Yuck*! The couple of bites I managed to swallow with some of the cream soda curdled in my brand new stomach. Why had Sotuknang inserted that Aunt Clara knew me as Cressie? It sounded like a namby-pamby lamb's name. Either that or the name of some stupid poodle.

I despised poodles unless they were deep-fried and covered in mushroom sauce. What Aunt Clara would say if I told her that was my favorite meal? I doubted she would have let me stay here with her and Harper then.

I took another bite and swallowed, forcing the stuff past the lump in my throat. Sitting back in my seat, I flashed a grin at my newfound aunt. "This is great, Aunt Clara. It makes me want to hug you for being so thoughtful." I wanted to barf it all up right back on my plate.

Aunt Clara smiled. "I can make this anytime you want it. How about having it once a week?"

Demon claws, pretending I crave this rot every week? "Ah, Aunt Clara, that's nice of you, but how about my other favorites? I'd love to try yours and Harper's favorite dishes, too." I picked up my glass that still held traces of cream soda. "But I will take cream soda for dinner anytime. And you guys don't have to drink it, either. I can tell it's not your cup of tea."

Harper shot me a smile. "Sounds good to me, Mom."

Aunt Clara sighed.

I said, "But you can serve corned beef and cabbage every once in a while. Like at St. Patrick's. I'm here for the rest of the school year."

Hopefully, this apocalypse would be long over before that holiday swung around. Maybe I could use my demon powers to make sure the grocery store in town didn't get any corned beef in. Cabbage, either.

After dinner, I offered to dry dishes while Aunt Clara washed them. With a wave of the dishcloth, she told me to go ahead and spend time with Harper.

"You both have school tomorrow, and though you're already enrolled, Cressie, you can ask Harper about what school might be like at the high school in Dogwood. I'm sorry it's not Moon Ridge High School, but the high school here was destroyed in what they still think might have been an earthquake." She stopped washing. "They still can't find any proof, as they did in Louisa County. They can't rebuild the school until the town, the State, and the Government quit arguing if FEMA is needed or not."

Harper sank to the floor in my room, where she sat with her arms wrapped around her knees. I plopped down on top of the bed.

Harper spoke first. "So, you're to go to school with me tomorrow." She looked up at me. "Have you ever been to school? I mean, other than the times when you possessed me?"

I lay down on my right side and plucked a thread from the comforter. "There have been a few times. Though, not like your kind of school. Back in the 12th century, this young man who lived in another nobleman's household had just become fifteen and was about to become a lord's squire when I took him over. I got to swing a massive sword, things like that." I left the comforter alone and looked at Harper. "I cut off his lord's head with the knight's own sword, and they burned the boy at the stake for witchcraft after I dodged out of him."

"That's a terrible thing, Cresil!"

I mumbled. "Well, I was a demon at the time and expected to get his soul muddied enough to get it sent to Hell." I stuck my chin out. "Anyway, if it helps, he had been awful before I got him as my assignment. He always got into fights, gambled, and he lied about a young serf, accusing the young woman of stealing from the lady of the castle's coffers when it had been he himself who did it."

"Oh."

I decided not to tell Harper what happened to the knight's family and the rest of the household, after me as the squire chopped off his head. The brat may have been a terrible kid, but I made him twice as bad. I made him into a monster. Because that is what demonic entities did.

I sat up and forced myself to go on. "Another time, in the early 1800s, I possessed this young woman sent to finishing school. In 1814, she was caught sleeping with the headmistress's husband. Next, I shared the frame of a young

French girl who had this governess. I puppeteered the girl into doing all sorts of nasty things. She died when the Germans destroyed the house her family lived in during World War I, and her soul forfeited to Hell."

I'd forgotten doing those terrible things in the girl's body. Not just her, finishing school girl, or the squire, but all the other countless times I had possessed an innocent, to get more souls for Lucifer. I reveled in it at the time, but after it ended and I found myself back in Hell, I had felt a tiny bit of remorse. Not enough to make me stop, but I kept it secret from the others.

Mortals think demons enjoy being villains and hurting people and taking souls. Yeah, most do. It's what makes them demonic. They don't feel guilt, and they indulge in the gore and agony.

I had discovered I'm not one of those.

Oh, I never let on. Otherwise, Lucifer might have sent me to Tartarus, which still happened. Believe me, anything that scares a devil is not something to take lightly. Tartarus is the only thing, other than Lucifer himself, that the demonic truly fear, and yet, I had ended up there until Baal used me for the portal.

"How do you live with yourself, Cresil?"

I broke away from my memories. Harper's upset face filled my vision.

I grimaced. "I'm a demon, Harper. Demons don't care— they're evil, remember?"

"But you been in my head, Cresil, and I get this impression that you're not all that bad. You could have had me do all sorts of terrible things to get me in trouble."

I sighed and sat up. "All right, guess that's why I am in the lower echelon in Hell. Guess angel guilt remained with me after the Fall. How did I handle hurting people or causing trouble for those I possessed? Most demons reveled in that shit. I wasn't one of those, as I learned after the first time. But I faked it. I had to; I didn't want to end up in Tartarus."

Harper sat beside me. "I thought Tartarus belonged in the Greek myths." She arched an eyebrow. "I do remember reading about it in English class in seventh grade."

"It's no myth, the place is real. Terrible and frightening, no demon aspires to end up in it if they can help it. Baal is in charge of it, and he gets to pick your own particular form of torture that you relive over and over. There's not just the pain, there's the unrelenting terror."

Aunt Clara poked her head around the cracked-opened door. "Hey, you two, showers, teeth brushed, and then to bed. You have to get up at five in the morning."

Harper groaned and stood. "Mom! That's early."

"Sorry about that, but remember there's no high school in Moon Ridge anymore. At least they managed to get all you kids into Dogwood High. You ought to feel sorry for the teachers and staff at Moon Ridge. They reassigned some to the elementary and middle school, some got hired on at Dogwood, but most are without jobs." She shook her head. "Not a good thing to be these days, being unemployed."

She left.

Harper stretched, before crossing over to the door. "I better go. See you tomorrow morning, Cresil." Her body at the threshold, she looked back over her shoulder.

"It's going to be weird in two ways."

I slipped off my tennis shoes. "What do you mean by that?"

"Because I no longer share my body. It's only me. Plus, the demon who had will be a classmate of mine in school, pretending to be my cousin." She smiled. "I'm glad on all fronts that's it's you and not some other demon. You're not as bad as you like to pretend you are."

"Hate to point this out, but we still have this big problem."

"What's that?"

"It's called the apocalypse."

Harper lost the smile and walked out, the door slamming shut behind her.

Chapter Nineteen—Cresil

A voice kept butting into my dreams. "Go away," I grumbled, burrowing deeper under the covers.

"Hey, wake up. It's your turn to shower. We only got an hour to get ready and eat breakfast before the school bus gets here."

Huh? What? School—what? I crawled out of the mound of blankets, yawning and blinking sleep out of my eyes, confused. It hit me: I'm now a real flesh-and-blood mortal teenage girl.

Harper stood beside the bed, wearing khaki pants and a blue long-sleeved T-shirt. She tossed a towel at me. "Hurry. Mom got up extra early to make us bacon and scrambled eggs. She only does that for the weekend. If you're not down there in ten minutes, I'll eat your portion, and you'll be chowing down cereal." She bounced out of the room.

I tossed back the covers and climbed out of bed. After slinging the towel over my left shoulder, I found a pair of black jeans and a hot pink T-shirt with a cutesy devil on the front folded on the dresser. *Is this Harper's idea of a joke?* I hate pink. A glance at the alarm clock on my bedstead revealed no time for a change of shirts, so I snatched the tennis shoes and socks and juggled everything in my mad dash to the bathroom. I dumped everything on the linoleum and took a quick shower. Once done, I rubbed my body with the towel, enjoying the feel of its softness against my skin.

Never ever having had flesh before—other than use of the possessed—it felt good. I broke out of my self-absorption and dressed. Combing my wet hair, I stared at my reflection in the mirror, fogged from the shower. I wiped at the glass.

I looked at my reflection and saw the wide grin on the mirror girl's face. My eyes gleam ink dark, and the ends of the wet hair curled as it began to dry.

My stomach rumbled. I looked down, not sure what that meant. It made the same sound again. I ached, too.

Then I understood. The stomach's growls and the ache meant hunger. I tossed the damp towel, plus the dirty T-shirt and sleep pants, into the hamper nearby and bolted out of the bathroom and downstairs. As I strolled into the kitchen, I saw Harper tucking into her bacon and eggs while Aunt Clara leaned against the kitchen counter, drinking coffee.

The odor from the food and the coffee wafted to my nostrils. I breathed it in, and my stomach growled again. I sat down at the table and went to work on my breakfast. Yummy, melted cheese covered the scrambled eggs. The bacon crackled between my upper and lower teeth as I chewed a slice. The orange juice in the glass tasted like the gods' nectar—almost as good as cream soda. The taste and the smells bewitched me.

I must have been showing my ecstasy, as Harper leaned toward me and whispered, "Don't get used to this. School mornings, it's either milk and cereal or oatmeal with toast. We still get the OJ."

Aunt Clara washed out her cup and put it upside down in the dishpan beside the sink. "Harper's right. I have enough to get myself ready for work. You guys usually will get yourselves your own breakfast." She shook a finger. "And yes, you will eat something. No slacking off breakfast on school days. You make your own bagged lunch, too, except Fridays. I'll give you money to buy lunch in the cafeteria on that day."

I scarfed down the rest of my food, then followed Harper's example on washing my plate, utensils, and glass and putting them in the drying rack. We both bolted into a half bathroom downstairs to brush our teeth, crowding each other at the sink.

Aunt Clara called out. "The bus is coming!"

Harper pointed at a bookbag. "That's yours, it has a notebook and is jammed full of paper, pens. and pencils, and whatever else you might need today." She slung hers over her shoulders and I followed suit. "Don't get used to me doing this for you, you'll have to learn to do your own after this time."

We ran out the door. I skipped around a sizable orange pumpkin on the top porch step that Aunt Clara also bought at the store last night, pranced down the steps, and beat Harper and the school bus to the bus stop. Some teens waiting at the bus stop looked half asleep, others were awake but texting on their phones, and two guys jostled the other kids to get in front of the line as the bus's door swung open with a hiss and a creak. As if there was a system in place already, everyone formed a line, shoving at each other.

I checked off the list as each person climbed the steps onto the bus. *Ah, bullies go first, the snooty, popular girls next, then the jocks, and last but not least, us losers.* I was a loser in Heaven, a loser in Hell, and in mortal flesh— apparently, still a loser.

Harper and I found seats across the aisle from the two guys. She grimaced, shrugged, and grabbed the spot by the window. The dark-skinned one on the end grinned at me.

I thumped down in my seat, flashing him a shark's smile. It should have turned him off.

It didn't.

Too bad.

He leaned across the aisle and whispered. "Hey, what's your name? You must be new, as I never saw you before."

"No, really? That must be a news flash or something."

My sarcasm sloughed off him like water off a duck's feathers. "My name's Tyree Washington. My father and I just moved here this past summer, so I guess I'm new in Moon Ridge, too. He got a new job in Roanoke, so we moved from Chesterfield County in June."

I cocked my head. "Oh, you're that friend of Pete Jameson. Harper told me." She hadn't. I remembered him from when I possessed her. Not that jerky turkey here needed to know that.

He frowned.

"Harper? I saw you come on the bus with her. Did you become friends with her?" He didn't let me say anything but went right on blabbing. "You should know she's a loser—doesn't hang with the cool kids."

I managed to get a word in. "Cool kids? Like you?"

He flashed a watery grin. "Yeah, like me. I like a girl who knows who is cool. That's why I need to—"

"—warn me? That's okay. Harper's my cousin. Dad's her mother's brother." I leaned out across the aisle, closer to him. "My parents are missionaries. They went on some mission to South America. You know, church-thumping fanatics. I like to sing hymns myself. It gets me all excited. You know, for—"

He looked uncomfortable but brightened at my prompt. "Oh, to do this?" He made a lewd gesture with a finger and his other hand.

Oh yes, mortal boys and their dirty minds. I nodded, and as if I suddenly understood the gesture he made, magicked warmth at my cheeks with my demon magic. Pretending to be shy, I fluttered my eyes and stared down at my lap. "Yes, although I've never done anything like that for real. It just wouldn't be seemly for a daughter of the church, you know."

I looked up into his eyes. *He's not too bad, as human boys go. His eyes are like a raven's wing. WTH!*

I'm going bonkers. I mean, thinking that this jerk didn't seem half bad.

I looked away and kept my gaze at the back of the seat before me. A boy and a girl sat in it.

The sound of flesh slapping flesh came from there. "Take your hands off me, or I'll tell the bus driver."

"Go ahead and see if I care. You think you're too good for me. I know where you live, Annie. You're lucky I want to touch you. Now, shut your mouth."

I shut his mouth for him, mumbling a small spell under my breath. "Shut bovis os conclusit!"

I'd glued Annie's tormentor's mouth shut. I thought about gluing his hands together when he began thrashing and making sounds best as he could, not being able to open his mouth. I decided that would be enough, and I leaned back in my seat, snickering.

Tyree spoke up. "Hey, what's your..." but I never let him finish as I touched his forehead and said, "Shhhh. Sleep." His chin dropped into his chest, and he began to snore. I looked at him with affection. *Such a jerk.*

Just as I closed my eyes for a bit, I heard something.

"Cresil."

I cracked open my left eye. Harper was glaring at me. With a sigh, I popped the other eye open.

"What?"

"Did you do something to Brian Woods?"

"Brian who?"

"The creep sitting in the seat in front of ours."

"Oh, that guy. Yeah. He was being rotten to that Annie girl, so I helped her out."

"You shouldn't use your demon magic."

I shrugged. "So? He's not bothering Annie, right?"

"Yeah, but—"

"No buts. Buts are irritating. I also put Pete Jameson's buddy, Tyree across the way to sleep, too. He tried to hit on me."

She hissed, "You can't go around—"

"—doing demon things. Yeah, I know, but I count this as being good. It's peaceful. Right? Brian's not doing the creeping hands and rushing fingers. And cute boy across the aisle isn't driving me crazy. So, we're good. Right?"

"Okay. But once the bus gets to the school, snap them out of it, but don't let anyone else catch you doing it."

"Sure, sure, fine with me. Now let me get a few winks of shut-eye before we get to the school."

I closed my eyes.

Chapter Twenty—Harper

I couldn't believe what Cresil had done. I leaned over the seat in front of me to check on Brian. He struggled to open his mouth but couldn't, and when he looked at Annie, she ignored him by staring out the window. He whipped his head around, and I saw tears glistening in his eyes. Wow. I'd never seen the bully crying—ever. His victims, yes, but not him. I wondered why he wasn't driving his car to school. Maybe he got in trouble and his parents wouldn't let him? Personally, I didn't care, except that meant he took my bus to school and back home.

It's not nice what Cresil had done to Brian, but a tiny part of me loved it. The bully got his comeuppance. Guess that made me as bad as Cresil.

I scrunched down in my seat, worried. Maybe that's why she took me over and not the others when the four of us summoned the demon. That deep inside of me lurked a bad person. Someone who might be able, without a qualm, to harm others without concern.

Knock it off, Harper Doyle. It's not because you were bad—just dumb luck of the draw. Baal wanted a human body for possession. He didn't care if it'd been Barbie or you.

Eased by my logic, I hugged my bookbag to my chest and relaxed as the bus took the exit off I-81 and rolled toward Dogwood on a busy street.

It didn't take the bus long to arrive at Dogwood High. We passed a large parking lot full of parked student-owned vehicles. The bus turned right onto a paved driveway that made a loop. Crowds of students stepped off other parked buses while teachers with whistles blew them and gathered some of the teenagers to them like lost chicks.

"Guess some of those must be Moon Ridge kids." Cresil peered over my shoulder out the window. "Wonder where they're going to take us?"

"I think either the auditorium or the gymnasium. It depends on which building has the most space. I hope that one of those places doesn't end up a classroom of ours for the rest of the year. They'll need to organize us for classes and lunchtimes." I climbed to my feet as our bus rolled to a stop. Others stood, too, as did the unhappy Brian. He didn't say anything or bother Annie, who squeezed by him to get to the aisle. She ignored him and merged with other students heading to the front of the bus. Tyree still snored away; his face mashed into the seat in front of him.

I said, "Wake him, Cresil."

Cresil reached over and tapped him on his head. "Awaken."

He woke up with a snort, muttering. Drool rolled down his chin and dripped down the front of his T-shirt. A few guys and girls giggled.

Something told me they would spread the news about his drooling by lunchtime. Especially as Tami Reed, the biggest gossip of Moon Ridge High, was one of those giggling.

Tyree rose and snatched his bookbag from the floor. It looked new and no doubt was. Even though he hung out with Pete, I felt sorry for him.

Cresil saw my glance at Brian as we merged with the line, and she snapped her fingers. I almost stopped her after remembering things he did to others, but I didn't.

Brian sputtered, "I...I can talk!"

Nacelle, another of the girls behind Cresil and me, giggled. "Yeah, and still nothing smart pops out of that mouth of yours."

Everyone laughed, except Cresil, me, and Tyree, of course. Brian's face grew red with anger as he turned and narrowed his eyes at her. She whitened, not saying another word.

He stepped away from his seat and pushed against others, forcing his way to the front of the bus. No one liked him—except Pete Jameson. He had always been a rotten bully and enjoyed hurting animals and other kids. Pete Jameson may be a jerk, but nobody I knew matched Brian for sheer viciousness.

When a teacher came over, she herded us over to a group waiting nearby. Jake stood on the fringes of it, and his face brightened when he saw me. He took my hand and pulled me closer.

"Hi," he said.

I felt heat on my cheeks and prayed no one noticed. "Hi, Jake." I met his gaze. "You must have drove here."

"No, Mom dropped me off. She has business here in town. Told me to catch the school bus home."

"Hey there, Jake." Cresil jostled me for space.

He drawled, "Hi, Cressie."

Her face darkened. "Don't call me that. It's Cresil."

He shook his head. "Sotuknang said your name is Cressie Doyle. So, get over it, Cressie." He broke into a grin. He handed Cresil a large brown envelope taped shut. "Here, after he spent teaching me in my dreams all night, getting me into sorcerer shape, he told me I would find this packet on my dresser when I awoke. This has your birth certificate, records from your old high school, plus the shots you've had. Sotuknang said that even with his angel magic, it would be smart to have paper backup."

Cresil grimaced at the envelope as if it were a germ under a microscope. "What do I do with it?"

Jake explained. "Give it to the office staff as technically, you are a new student and have never been to Moon Ridge High. Welcome to the world of red tape, Cresil."

"Sounds exactly like Hell to me," muttered Cresil.

The bell rang.

"Attention, Moon Ridge students!" called out a male voice.

It came from a tall man dressed in a blue suit and white shirt, with a bright multicolored tie that stuck out like a sore thumb. He stuck his hand up in the air.

The other students—those not from Moon Ridge—surged through two double doors of the main building. All of the buses had left.

"I am Mr. Johnson, principal for Dogwood High. Follow me to the gymnasium, where you will be checked in and assigned to your classes. This way."

He took off at a long-legged pace, and we all trotted after him to a large rectangle building painted in the school colors of red and green. That's right; someone must have had it in for this high school to assign Christmas colors to it.

Chapter Twenty-One—Harper

The building was the gym, and it stunk of old socks, athlete's foot, and sweat beneath whatever cheap cleaning product they used. Just like the gym at Moon Ridge High, the cleaning product didn't work.

I sat on the first bench on the north side. Jake plopped down next to me. Tyree perked up when Cresil grinned and started to head his way. His bright look grew dim as she walked past him and plopped down next to Pete Jameson.

Pete looked uncomfortable when she began chatting to him. He scrunched down like a turtle into its shell and looked everywhere but at her. I didn't see Brian anywhere.

"Looks like Cresil is going to bug Pete," said Jake, snaking an arm around my shoulders.

"Speaking of Pete, Tyree, plus Pete's buddy, Brian, rode our school bus."

"Did that creep bother you or anything?" An underlying current of anger ran in his voice.

"No, he sat next to Annie Deeds and was bothering her, when Cresil took care of him. She put a whammy on him, and he couldn't talk the rest of the bus ride. She also put Tyree to sleep; I think he must have bugged her."

"Good for her." He smiled and took my hand.

I should have removed it from his grasp, but I didn't. He brought it up to his lips. That's when he did the unexpected and kissed it.

I snatched it away and placed it on top of my bookbag. The spot on my hand tingled when I looked at him. He reached out and tucked a loose strand of my hair behind my ear.

He leaned over and whispered, "I wished I could have kissed your lips and not your hand. But we're in school at this moment."

Oh God, me too. I have cared about Jake ever since we were little kids. He was the brother I never had, and I figured he thought of me as his sister. We were both only-children. Then we split apart and became enemies. It hurt me when he ignored me and later picked on me. Now it appeared our friendship had morphed into something more.

Jake whispered again. "I know we have problems normal teens don't have, with demons, angels, and the apocalypse, and we can't do more than hold hands at school, but surely we can find time to be together that has nothing to do with all that?"

I inched closer until my left shoulder touched his right one. I so wanted to move my hand over it, but he was right. We were at school and among a room full of other kids, teachers, and the principal. I straightened, and Jake shifted a few inches apart from me before others noticed. But his hand nearest to me hovered near mine, fingertips brushing. I looked at him and mouthed, "Later."

He nodded.

Mr. Johnson walked up to a podium in the center of what looked like a basketball court. He talked into the microphone, his voice booming almost inaudibly until a dark-haired woman in a tracksuit jogged up. She fooled with the microphone, stepped aside, and when he spoke again, his voice still boomed, but we could understand him.

He nodded at the woman. "Thank you, Mrs. Johnson. Give a hand to Mrs. Johnson who fixed our minor problems—she's not only one of our gym teachers for the girls here, but also my wife."

Almost everyone clapped. The sound deafened as it echoed in the gym. When it subsided, the principal resumed talking.

"Before we go on, those of you with cell phones or tablets, please turn them off. Welcome, students from Moon Ridge High. When your tragedy happened, the council of our county volunteered our new school as a place you can learn until they rebuild your high school." He stopped to clear his throat and resumed. "Now, Dogwood at its old location had temporary classrooms in trailers when we overflowed with students before they built this new one. Considering the overflow with all of you here for the rest of the school year, they brought those trailers back. Except for a few classrooms in the buildings that can take in extra students, most of you will be learning in them along with the auditorium.

Staggering your class schedules and lunch, we should be able to fit you all in."

I glanced around at the other bleachers and saw disinterested faces while others listened with rapt attention. Quite a few stared down at their cell phones and texted or held theirs to their ears and chatted to someone, ignoring what Mr. Johnson ordered not to do.

As I swept my gaze along, I found my eyes looking into Brain Wood's, not far from where Jake and I sat. He didn't smile and totally ignored Mr. Johnson's speech, but he noticed Jake with me and appeared to catch Cresil with Pete. He looked at me again and sneered.

It unsettled me.

I unzipped my bag and dug inside, taking out a notebook and pen. Not looking at anyone, I paid more attention to Mr. Johnson and the next couple of adults who talked, writing in the notebook.

Jake noticed. He leaned over and whispered, his breath stirring loose the hair that he'd earlier placed behind my ear. "What's wrong?"

I gripped my pen in a death grip. "Nothing."

"Don't tell me that. Your knuckles are white. Is it a demon?"

I shook my head and stopped writing, turning to look at him. "No, nothing demonic." I glanced at Brian.

Jake followed my gaze. His features tightened, and his eyes darkened.

"Brian? I see him staring at you. I told you to tell me if he does anything."

"Oh, but he isn't. Stares can't hurt anyone. Besides, he's not some demon you can defeat. Though mean and ugly, he's still only a human being." I went back to scribbling about something Mr. Johnson said. "Forget about him. I'm sure he won't try anything on school grounds. His only friend is Pete, probably Tyree, and I bet none of the Dogwood students will have anything to do with him once he shows his mean side to them. You know no one at Moon Ridge cares for him, especially as I'm sure he has bullied everyone that went to school with us."

He chuckled. "Pete hung around me more than Brian when we became friends in ninth grade. I think it was a stick in Brian's craw, the way Pete dumped him and became my friend." His eyes lit up with glee. "After the way he bullied me most of my life, it's justice to me to take away his only friend."

"Are you sorry you don't hang with Pete anymore?"

"Naw. Brian can have him back." He flashed a grin. "I got someone better to hang with." His eyes twinkled. "Even with Demon Girl hanging around her."

Eventually, we had to get up and meander over to line up to get our schedules and lunch times. To my delight, I found that Jake shared most of my classes with me—and Brian none. Cresil shared three out of five periods with me. The only classes we didn't share happened to be P.E. and English. I hoped she behaved since I wouldn't be there to make sure she did. I said the same to her once we were alone.

Cresil grinned, popping gum some girl gave her earlier. "Don't worry your pretty mortal head. I'll be fine. I'll handle it like a pro." She blew a bubble and popped it, sucking it back in.

I took a tissue from a nearby table and held it in my outstretched hand. "You're not supposed to chew gum in school, Cresil. Take this tissue and cough it into it, wrap it up, and toss it in the trash can over there."

"But—"

"None of that. You've already made a mistake that could get you into trouble with the faculty here."

Grumbling, she spit the wad into the tissue. She crumpled it up and tossed it into a nearby trashcan.

"Tonight, at home," I said, "we'll go over the dos and don'ts of high school."

With a shrug of a shoulder, she replied, "Whatever." Her face brightened. "Hey, it's Pete." A wide grin splashed across her face. "Want to see me bug him?"

"No, not really."

She didn't say anything else, but before I could restrain her, she strolled over to him and Brian, who stood next to him. I didn't follow her. Not with Brian there. Maybe with her demon powers, she could take care of Moon Ridge's bully, but I also prayed they weren't flashy enough to garner the attention of anyone on the faculty. Or any of the students either, especially Pete or Brian. We didn't need to explain her magic.

Chapter Twenty-Two—Cresil

I sauntered over to Pete, who was too busy talking to Bully Woods to noticed me. I draped an arm over his shoulder and blew into his ear. He shivered.

"Hiya, cutie."

He jumped and whipped around. "You!"

"Of course, it's me. Who did you think it was?" I waved at Woods. "Hey there, Woods."

He didn't answer, just glowered.

"You don't have a sunny disposition, do you?"

He didn't answer.

Such a jerk.

Pete could be, but I had to admit the boy intrigued me. Not too unpleasing to the eye, either. Besides, Daddy has all that money. He'll provide me relief in a time of boredom when we aren't battling evil. The brooding buddy, though, needed to go.

Besides, I noticed the creep staring at Harper meant nothing in her best interest. Maybe kicking a demon lord like Baal in the nards took guts for a lower caste fiend like me, but a piggy like Woods didn't scare me. I may wear the outer casing of a pretty teenage girl, but beneath this exterior lurked a fiend with all her magic intact.

First things first, get Pete interested in me. Nothing but a bit of abracadabra might do it. I mumbled, placing my hand over his pounding heart, "Planto fossor cado mihi." A red glow emulated beneath my hand.

The glaze of being smitten replaced the freaked-out gleam in Pete's eyes. The fool even drooled for me. I took a tissue and wiped it off his chin. *How grossly sweet.*

Pete snatched me to him and began to kiss me. Worried that this might be too in-your-face for the teenagers crowding around, besides upsetting the adults, and that Harper might be freaking out and getting Jake to come over, I tried to pry myself from my eager swain's octopus arms. Not too much success. I think I overdid it with the love spell.

Brian butted in. "Hey, Pete. Why are you smooching her? She's with that dumb bitch, Harper. Get away from her."

Finally, someone strong-armed Pete away from my not so eager arms. "All right. We'll have none of that, er, Mr., can someone tell me his name? And hers?" It was Mr. Johnson. He pointed at me while hanging on tight to the squirming Pete.

A girl flipped her long, streaked blond hair back. "I can, Mr. Johnson.," she said in a candy-sweet voice. "I don't know her name, but she was with Harper Doyle this morning, so I bet she knows." The girl wrinkled her nose when she looked at Pete. "That's Pete Jameson. I think he was French kissing her."

I craved to put a whammy on her, but the love spell broke the quota of my screw-ups for today.

Mr. Johnson wiggled his finger like a worm for me to follow him and Pete. "Let's go, you two lovebirds. Already your first day and you broke a rule here. Shame, shame."

Are we going to the principal's office? Maybe Pete's not a winner in many departments, but he's a senior for Lucifer's sake. As for me, damn, but I have more years on me than this man a zillion times over. I wiggled my fingers in readiness for a spell when I caught Harper and Jake shaking their heads.

I didn't say anything, just tramped after Mr. Johnson and Pete. Snickers and murmurs trailed us until we left the gym.

Woods shadowed us, the sore puss never-ending on his face. I might have to use a sleep spell on him on the bus ride home.

Chapter Twenty-Three—Harper

I didn't see Cresil for the rest of the day, Pete either. As for Brian, he appeared to have vanished. Just for today, lunch was in the gym, brought to us by cafeteria workers. No charge either. That would save Mom money as she'd given both me and Cresil some cash for lunch today.

Trying not to think about Cresil, I chatted with Jake at lunch. The trouble was he knew where my mind wandered.

"Harper, she'll be okay. The principal just took her and Pete to the office. I'm sure he placed them in separate rooms."

"I'm not worried about her." I set down my empty pudding cup on the tray. "More about the principal, and even though I think Pete deserves a lot of things, she used magic on him. One minute he looked like he wanted to run away, the next, he's giving her mouth-to-mouth resuscitation." I leaned over my tray and lowered my voice. "You're supposed to be a sorcerer. Can't you remove the enchantment?"

He rolled his eyes. "No, I can't. Sotuknang hasn't taught me that, even if he plans to. I think he's planning to gear me up for Armageddon, not dumb love spells an idiot demon cast."

"I know Pete's a creep, but I thought he's your friend."

He sighed. "It doesn't matter. I don't know how to do it."

The lunch roiled in my stomach. I took my tray and trash over to a cafeteria worker. The woman took it, tipped it, and the garbage fell into a trashcan. She plopped my tray on top of a stack of other dirty ones. Jake handed his tray to her, and we returned to the bleachers.

Jake and I sat down, but I didn't say a word. Worried, I chewed on my pen, wondering how long before Cresil blew it. Pete might be enamored of her now, but sooner or later, her spell over him would fade. Worse, Mr. Johnson could discover the truth, and when he did, I'm sure Cresil wouldn't be flunked out of school or put in detention, but something way worse.

I bolted for the girls' restroom, Jake not far behind. He stopped at the door as Mrs. Johnson walked up, shaking a pen. I stopped and listened at the door.

"You can't go in there, mister. That's the girls' restroom."

"I know that, Mrs. Johnson. But Harper needs my help."

"In what way does she need your help?"

"I think she feels ill."

"I'll go check on her."

I ran into a stall and locked the door. Pulling my jeans down, I sat on the toilet.

The restroom door creaked open, and I heard the sound of tennis shoes squeaking across the linoleum. They halted in front of the stall I hid in.

Go away, go away, go away.

"Ah, Harper? It's Mrs. Johnson. Are you all right?"

"Yes, I just needed to tinkle."

"Okay. I'll let the young man waiting outside know that you're fine. He thought you were ill."

"Thanks, Mrs. Johnson. You can tell him to go back to the gym and wait for me."

I heard her footsteps as she left me, the door opening, and slamming shut. Rising on shaky legs, I pulled my pants up, and quickly whipped around to lean over the toilet. Just in time, as I threw up my lunch. It only took the one time. Feeling better, I used toilet paper, wiped my mouth, wadded it, tossed it into the toilet and flushed.

I left the stall and crossed over to the big mirror above the sinks stretched across the wall. My reflection revealed a pale face and dark under-eye circles. I turned a tap and cold water gushed down. It felt good to dip my hands in the chill of the wet and splash it on my face. The faucet shut off, I dried my hands and composed myself before leaving the restroom.

Jake hadn't returned to the gym. He leaned against the wall just outside of the restroom. He straightened as I walked out and slipped an arm around me.

"Are you all right?"

"Guess you didn't believe what I told Mrs. Johnson?"

"Heck no. You looked white as a ghost when you ran for the restroom."

I leaned into him and sighed. "Jake, I'm worried about Cresil."

"I'm not even sure what she sees in Pete."

"Well, jerk or not, he's not bad looking."

"Better looking than me?"

I grinned. "Oh, no, you have Pete beat hands down. It's not just your looks, Jake. You're a good person, too."

He flashed a smile. "I'm glad."

"Glad you're a good person or that you beat him in the looks department?"

"Glad you prefer me, period."

We headed back to the gym before Mrs. Johnson decided to find out what took us so long to return. Jake dropped his arm from my shoulder before we pushed the double doors open.

Mrs. Johnson waited just inside, tapping her pen against her hand. We both ignored her, though I could feel her eyes on our backs. You'd think we would begin a make-out session right there.

The bell rang, and we sat down as another teacher walked to the podium to talk to us, introducing herself as the head of the math department. I took out my notebook and pencil, jotting down more notes, occasionally looking at the closed gym doors and wondering when Cresil would be back.

An hour later, the English and history department heads replaced the math department teacher in talks, and still no sign of Cresil.

Chapter Twenty-Four—Cresil

I squirmed. The seat of this chair felt stiff and rigid on my buttocks. How long had we been here? It felt like hours to me. At least they brought us lunch. Except, the meat tasted fake, the mashed potatoes were soggy and bland, and I hoped never to eat Brussels sprouts ever again.

Pete sat in his chair across the room. He had his chin propped in his hand, boredom etching his face, and he'd ignored me the past hour. Had my spell on him worn off? Maybe being in this human shape weakened my powers. I hoped not.

I called out in a whisper. "Pete."

He sat up and turned around to stare at a picture on the wall. It had a man in gray carrying a saber as he rode a galloping gray horse. The tag beneath it read "General Robert E. Lee on Traveler." Somehow, I didn't think Pete cared about a dead Civil War general.

Maybe he was mad about being here, and blamed me.

"Pete. Quit ignoring me."

He swung his gaze to the floor beneath his feet. I began feeling irritated.

A door from an inner office swung open, and Mr. Johnson stepped through, papers in hand. He stopped to talk to the woman typing away on the computer and handed her the papers, before he crossed the room to the front door of the school office. His hand on the doorknob, the man turned and swept his gaze from me to Pete.

"School ends in another hour and Mrs. Leland here will take you back to the gym so you can catch your buses. You'll get your classes and whatever else you need to know for your school year from her."

He walked out, the door closing behind him with a quiet click.

"Pete, he's gone. Will you look at me now?"

Pete finally turned and gave me a blank stare. I stood up when I saw Mrs. Leland enter the bathroom beside Mr. Johnson's office and walked over to him.

"Come on, Pete. Fess up, you like me."

He looked away. "No, I don't."

"Ah, you can speak. Sure, you do."

"No, I don't. Shut up and go back to your seat, girl." He made girl sound like a dirty word.

I lowered my face until we met eye to eye. "Girl, huh? I could show you how much a girl I am. Or more likely, how much of a boy you're not."

His Adam's apple rolled up and down.

Nervous, are we? Good.

I pressed a hand to his chest. *Thump, thump, thumpity thump.* His heart began beating faster. I brought my lips beside his right ear.

"It's good to be nervous of me. I'm not human. Okay, I look like a human teenage girl, thanks to some higher being. I am, in reality, a demon. You know, hellspawn and fires of Hell."

"There are no such things as demons," he mumbled. "Angels, either. Dad says that's nothing but church hogwash."

"Pete, there are. Do you know why you kissed me? It's due to a spell I put on you."

"No such things as spells. I don't know why I kissed you. Maybe for a second, I went crazy."

"That's such a reasonable explanation. Be honest. You don't buy what you just said. I can smell the indecision, how confused you are. It doesn't matter—all those kids in the gymnasium think it's your teenage hormones working. Even that best bud of a creep, Woods, thinks you like me. I bet they even gossiped about us at lunch."

"No, no, no. I went mental, nothing else."

"Pete and Cressie sitting in a tree, kissing like—"

"Stop it, stop it, stop it!" he cried, covering his ears.

"Planto is puer cado in diligo mihi."

I drew away.

Pete shivered, dropped his hands, and looked at me with big puppy-dog eyes. His Adam's apple slid up and down like an elevator that didn't know which way to travel. The boy had no control. His lust and love rose in a cloud.

He stilled. His gaze met mine, and he stood, yanking me against him.

Oh yeah!

His kiss drew my breath from me as his teeth nibbled at my bottom lip. His heart pounded.

Oh yeah. The boy could kiss.

We broke apart when I heard the toilet flush. I wiped the wetness from my mouth and went back to my seat. Breathing heavy, Pete stared at me, heat and puzzlement warring in his eyes.

"As I said, Pete, it's a spell. I can take it off you, too." I snapped my fingers.

He flinched. "God!"

I winced. "Please, keep some names to yourself. That hurts the ears."

We kept quiet when Mrs. Leland left the bathroom and went back to the office to resume her typing.

Confusion darkened Pete's eyes as he whispered, "You're really an actual d-e-m-o-n?"

I moved away. "Wow, you can spell. Yes, that's what I am."

"What kind?"

"What?"

"Were you a human being who died or something else?"

I sniffed. "I was never human, despite what this body says."

"How old are you?"

"Eons old."

"Eons...what does that mean?"

"Hell's bells, you are a dunce, aren't you? Eon means more years than you can count. It goes beyond thousands of years."

"Give me something here."

"In astronomy, it's considered a billion years just for one eon. Since before the Creator formed this world and the rest of the universe."

"You—"

"—are older than you? I'm the older person in this relationship."

"There is nothing between us. Understand?"

"Oh, but there will be...again. A few words in Latin, and you're mine. Until I grow bored with you."

His face whitened.

Glad we got that straightened out.

He didn't look at me, and I crossed my legs and hummed under my breath. Until Mrs. Leland came over to us, her glasses perched at the edge of her nose.

"All right, you two, the last bell of the day will ring in a few minutes. Mr. Johnson gave me the schedules for the classes you will be taking, plus other papers for your parents to read and fill out. Let's get the two of you back to the gym."

We tottered after her, and I whispered the love spell in Pete's ear. He took my hand; Mrs. Leland never noticed.

I dropped Pete's hand when we got to the gym, where I joined Harper and Jake. Pete followed me, but I shook my head and, with my chin, indicated a glowering Brian Woods stomping his way. The jerk reminded me of a huge, clumsy gorilla. He just needed a monkey grinder's hat. I snickered.

Harper asked, "Are you all right? You put a spell on Pete, didn't you?"

I sat down and began stuffing the papers Mrs. Leland gave me into my bookbag. "He's just a great diversion. It's boring. Until the battle begins, a girl's gotta keep herself out of trouble."

I watched Brian jaw at Pete, who shrugged and stared down at the floor. I wanted to go over and turn Brian into a toad or something that fitted his nature.

Harper hissed. "No!"

I blinked at her. "What? What did you think I was going to do?"

"Either punch Brian Woods in his fat nose or use magic on him. I believe more of the latter with you."

"All right, I'll behave, Harper." *For now, anyway.* I frowned. "First time he does something to you or Jake, or even Pete, he'll be sorry." The promise hung in the air.

I took a deep breath. I had never been able to breathe on my own before. I'd always been in someone else's body, and it was their lungs that took in air. These were *my* lungs. They made breathing such a novel thing to do. Humans are so blasé with the mundane, minuscule stuff they're able to do.

Once the apocalypse blows over, I figured I would be sent back to Hell. Heaven wasn't getting rid of the Pit anytime soon, and I doubted I would be allowed back into Heaven. I plan to make sure I have some leverage if Lucifer still ruled there. The Prince of Lies would be angry with me being on Heaven's side for the big event. Getting Brian Woods' soul might make things easier for me. It might not keep me out of Tartarus completely, but with a human soul to bargain with, I might only be stuck there for a short time.

Some woman I didn't recognize stood behind the podium. Mr. Johnson was nowhere to be seen. The same went for Mrs. Johnson.

The bell rang, and the regular Dogwood High students' noise grew louder as they headed for the school buses outside.

"Hello, Moon Ridge students. I am Mrs. Perkins, and I teach twelfth grade Government, which some of you will be taking from me. I want you to all line up in four lines at the gym doors, and there must be no pushing or shoving; all single file in an orderly manner."

Bodies surged toward the doors, oblivious to her instructions. I let the tide sweep me along with Harper and Jake. Neither Pete nor Brian was near us. But when I felt a hand take mine, I glanced aside and saw a grinning Pete. Way, way back, an angry Brian banged his way through students.

I said, "Didn't you drive yourself here?

"No, my father dropped me off. He told me to take the bus home."

"You do know Brian rides the same bus as us."

"You can do things to him. I'm not worried."

Not worried? Thank goodness Harper or Jake didn't hear Pete. I think they would freak out that he knew my secret.

Pete tightened his grip as we halted behind Jake. "I am not letting you go."

Brian got in another line, not at the end, but closer to us than I liked. He made a threatening slice across the throat with his hand. With the grin on his face, the boy looked even more like a gorilla.

What would happen if I made him a real-life ape? Would his parents notice if I did?

"Go ahead, Cresil. Then everyone will know about magic and demons."

"Who? What?" I looked at Pete, but he just smiled, and Harper appeared too busy talking to Jake. Anyway, it sounded male. Much older than Pete or Jake.

"You know that Brian Woods is the perfect patsy, a brainless idiot anybody can control."

Horrified, I watched a large shadow appear right beside Brian: Baal. Some of the students must have sensed the evil as they shuddered and broke away from the line.

Brian looked uneasy.

A shadowy tentacle whipped from the shadow and hooked onto the boy's shoulder. Brian twitched the shoulder. His eyes widened and sweat beaded on his forehead. He moaned.

I screamed. "Brian Woods, get out of there!"

Harper called out. "Cresil, what's going on?"

A teacher grabbed my shoulder. "What's wrong?"

I pointed to the shadow. The shadow no one else but I saw. "It's going to possess Brian Woods."

"Young lady, please stop with the dramatics," said the teacher after she glanced at Brian. "There is nothing wrong."

The shadow slipped inside Brian's meat suit. Brian's eyes gleamed black as oil before they blipped back to Brian's watery brown.

"Too late," I said, "Brian's a puppet now."

The teacher looked confused. "What's too late? There's nothing there. What's this about puppets? Are you pulling a prank?"

I crawled into Pete's arms, shudders passing through me.

"It's too late for all of us."

Chapter Twenty-Five—Harper

Cresil sat at the front of the bus and refused to budge. She wouldn't say why. She only dragged Pete into the spot next to her. Jake and I took the seat behind them. Other Moon Ridge students filed onboard, surging past us to different locations on the bus.

One of them, Tyree, halted to give Pete a funny look as he looked at Cresil, then Pete, as if he couldn't believe what he saw. He was forced to continue on in another surge of students heading to the back of the bus.

Brian Woods lumbered onto the bus. He paused and leaned past Pete until his face hung inches from Cresil's. I was about to call the bus driver, thinking Brian was about to bully her when he spoke with a deep voice I didn't recognize.

"Cresil, you do not smell like a spirit separate from your meat suit. How did this happen?"

Pete said, "Brian? What's up with your voice?"

Cresil said, "That's not Brian. Baal's the puppeteer now." She sounded frightened.

Brian grinned at Pete, straightening before he turned to Jake and me. His eyes gleamed dark as night and the skin of his face shifted into a caricature of Baal's demonic ugliness. A second later, Brian's mug returned.

"Hello, Harper." His eyes flicked to Jake as he continued using the creepy voice. "I cannot wait to have this fool use his mojo on me," he drew closer, "because I am going to shred his flesh into many little pieces and send his soul to Hell by express mail." His attention whipped back to Cresil. "As for you, Cresil, deciding to slum it? Sleeping with the enemy? Is this loser mortal boy worth it?"

Pete said, "Why are you being a butthead, Brian? You've always been before, but not on this level of weirdness."

Baal snickered. "Brian no longer has control of this fleshy prison. He is locked in his mind, screaming like a baby. He lets you dumbass mortals think he's all big and tough, but the wimp is puissant. Exactly like you, Peter Jameson. You cried the night your mama died at the hospital. Your daddy slapped you and told you to be a man. Though he's no man, he let his own daddy kick the shit out of him as a kid. As for Grandpa, he scammed the public and that is how you guys got all that money. Grandpa sure cries like a baby in Hell."

His face grew hard as stone and he spouted, "As I watched, I heard an eagle that was flying in mid-air call out in a loud voice. The star was given the key to the shaft of the Abyss. When he opened the Abyss, smoke rose from it like the smoke from a gigantic furnace. The sun and the sky were darkened by the smoke from the Abyss. And out of the smoke locusts came down upon the Earth and were given power like that of scorpions of the Earth. They were told not to harm the grass of the Earth or any plant or tree, but only those people who did not have the seal of God upon their foreheads. They were not given power to kill them, but only to torture them for five months. And the agony they suffered was like that of the sting of a scorpion when it strikes a man. During those days, men will seek death, but will not find it; they will long to die, but death will elude them. The locusts looked like horses prepared for battle. On their heads they wore something like crowns of gold, and their faces resembled human faces. Their hair was like women's hair, and their teeth were like lion's teeth. They had breastplates like breastplates of iron, and the sound of their wings was like the thundering of many horses and chariots rushing into battle. They had tails and stings like scorpions, and in their tails, they had the power to torment people for five months. They had as king over them, the angel of the Abyss, whose name in Hebrew is Abaddon, and in Greek Apollyon. The first woe is past; two other woes are yet to come."

Pete's forehead furrowed. "What is all that crap?" He may have sounded tough, but you could hear the fear in his voice.

The demon laughed. "Nothing important to you. Just about the end of the world, scripture in your stupid Bible. But I wouldn't worry when that happens—your soul will be down in Hell by then." He saluted with his hand. "Have a great day!" The voice sounded like's Brian's again.

He tramped to the back of the bus. Students squirmed away, letting him sit by himself. He just sat there with a grin that did not reach his eyes.

I hissed. "What's all that about?"

Cresil turned to peek at Pete, but he stared ahead as the bus pulled away. She fumbled with her book bag's zipper, keeping her voice low.

"Baal controls Brian Woods." She stopped touching the zipper. "He now has another portal. Brian's the new portal. Demons will soon be marching into this dimension from Hell." Her gaze met mine. "I suspect though, he will call up another low-caste demon so he can switch places and let it be the sacrifice when the portal is opened. He wants to march by Lucifer's side when Hell comes knocking at Heaven's gate."

She went quiet as the bus made its first stop. Tyree and a couple other kids rushed off without a word to anyone. Tyree jack-rabbited down the street without a backward glance as the bus pulled away.

Jake said, "Get off at my street. We need to tell Sotuknang. Are you with us, Pete?"

Pete didn't look at Jake. "Do you think I am going to go with you? I've been smooching with a lame demon, and Brian has gone demonic postal on me and threatening to send my soul to Hell."

Jake reached over the back of the bus seat and snatched Pete by the coat sleeve. "Do you think Baal will believe you're with us or not, just by not getting off where I live?"

"I just wanted a flunky. Before, the only friend I had was Brian, though I was more his flunky. I'm not getting off at your stop. I don't want that thing wearing Brian like a new set of clothes hunting my butt down. We're parting ways, so I can scatter back to my house and lock myself in. I'm not getting involved in all this supernatural junk. Demon girl's not worth my life."

He shut up and leaned his head back, closing his eyes.

Cresil turned her head from him and stared through the window. Her dusky skin had paled and she didn't look well. She looked back at me, and I caught sight of a single tear dribbling down her cheek.

"I'm sorry about Pete," I said.

She scrubbed at the tear. "I was only using the little drip to relieve boredom, nothing more."

"Cres.. ."

"Look, Harper, get over the Pete and me episode. It's dead."

"All right, nothing more on the subject." I stared back at Brian. He crossed one leg over the other and appeared to be whistling a tune. Others seated near him didn't take their eyes off him. "What about Baal?"

Cresil didn't sneak a peek back at him. "Like any demon, he could be exorcised."

"Can you do that?"

"That's just my suggestion. I'm a low-class demon, sorry, but that's not in my job description. Another demon lord, Lucifer himself, angels, God, they can do it, but not something that scuttles beneath Baal's feet. Maybe Jake's mother could do it. Or you can convince a priest. Hell's bells, I can't believe I said anything about a priest."

Jake said, "We're coming to my street."

Cresil bit her bottom lip. "I bet Sotuknang can do something about Baal. He's an archangel."

I rose when Jake did. Cresil got to her feet, but not before she punched Pete in the shoulder.

He opened his eyes. "Wha...what the..." Obviously, fear didn't stop him from drifting off.

Cresil said, "We're at Jake's street, whiner, just in case you decide to join us."

He jumped to his feet and slung his bookbag over a shoulder. "We're parting ways here. I don't want to get off at my usual spot as that's where wacko Brian lives, too."

"Whatever," replied Cresil, sounding as if she didn't care what he did.

I understood. Cresil liked him. Pete only showed her his true colors, which was only about Pete. I felt sorry for her.

The bus pulled over to the bus stop, and the four of us filed out into the aisle and off it, joined by a few others. As the bus pulled away, we caught sight of Baal in Brian's body heading for the front of the bus. The bus driver did not slow down. The next stop was two blocks away.

Pete's forehead gleamed with sweat. "Thank God, she didn't stop and let him off the bus. I gotta scatter and get home. Lock the doors and the windows, add protection." He looked at Cresil. "Would holy water work? Or a cross or garlic?"

"Garlic's for vampires, you dummy," remarked Cresil, stomping past him. "And I am not telling you if the other two things work or not. After all, I'm only a lame demon."

Jake slung his bag over a shoulder. "Come on, Pete. There's no one home at your place. If you think just locking all the doors and windows at your house will keep that monster out, you're stupid. Baal can dump the body and slip through the walls as a spirit."

Pete clutched his bookbag strap like a lifeline. "He's not getting in. I didn't invite him."

Cresil grabbed him by the back of his neck. He tried to get away, but he couldn't. She used demonic strength on him. "Look, dork, Baal will storm your castle by dumping Brian Woods' body like Jake said and take yours instead to keep the portal open. That's bogus what I said about the vampires anyway. Garlic doesn't do anything." She took her hands away as if touching him bothered her and she marched away, Jake and I sped up to keep up with her.

Pete tottered after us. "Are you saying vampires are real?"

Cresil didn't answer him.

I let out a sigh of relief when we made it to Jake's house without incident.

Jake opened the unlocked door, and we filed in, even Pete. Mrs. Hewitt strolled into the living room, wiping her hands on a dishtowel.

Her eyebrows furrowed. "Why is that boy here?"

Jake replied, "Pete?"

She tossed the towel to the coffee table. "Who else would I be asking about? I'd rather have a demon in my house than that ingrate. I didn't mean that crack about you, Cresil."

Cresil headed toward the kitchen. "None taken, Mrs. Hewitt. Are there any of your cookies today? Maybe cream soda, too? I need a fix—bad."

"There's a fresh batch of pumpkin cookies I made earlier on a plate on the table in the kitchen but no cream soda. I do have milk and orange juice. I went to the store when I woke up this morning, sensing you all might come here after school. I would hurry about those cookies. Sotuknang just sat down when I plated them."

Cresil hastened into the kitchen.

Pete crossed back to the front door. "Guess I need to leave."

Jake grabbed him by the shoulder. "Hold it, Pete. Mom, I think this is the safest place for him. He didn't want to come here, but he's changed his mind. "

"Safe from what—his...oh no." She grew pale. "It's Baal, isn't it?"

Pete's eyes widened as he backed away from the door, looking terrified. "Is he here?"

"No, he's not," said Mrs. Hewitt. "He's possessing someone you boys know, isn't he?"

Pete asked, "How does she know that?"

Jake said, "Remember how I always tried to blow off my mother being psychic? She's the real deal."

Pete narrowed his eyes. "She's supposed to be a phony. Dad thinks she's crazy."

"No, she's not. You heard her say she woke up to a feeling that we would all be coming here after school, not just me. Why she went to the store."

Pete opened his mouth when Mrs. Hewitt said, "Pete, your mother said to knock it off. That it wasn't your fault, she died from cancer, and that your father had no right to tell you to grow up and be a man. Don't worry about Chloe, either; the woman doesn't have anything between her ears. All her talk about sending you to military school is just that: talk."

Pete stared at her dumbfounded. Then he narrowed his eyes again. "You could have gotten that anywhere. I've seen a show on TV that said psychics learn all about people so they can cheat them."

"Your mother just told me you used to wet your bed, but she hid it from your father, so your father wouldn't whoop your bottom." Mrs. Hewitt flashed him a look of pity.

Jake stared at Pete. "Did you really wet your bed?"

Pete flushed. "Not my fault." He frowned. "No, I didn't. Only losers wet their—"

"Knock it off, Pete," I said. "It's out, and none of us will tattle about it in school."

Mrs. Hewitt sighed. "Jake, take Pete to the kitchen and join Cresil and Sotuknang before they eat up all the cookies. Pete, the man's not human either. He's an archangel, so watch your manners around him." She shook a finger at Pete. "No cussing especially!"

Jake dropped a hand on Pete's shoulder. "I'm sorry, Pete. I'm sure it wasn't your fault. Let's grab a cookie or two. Mom's pumpkin cookies are super, especially with milk."

Mrs. Hewitt and I sat on the couch.

"Tell me what happened, but only after you call your mother to let her know where you're at first," said Mrs. Hewitt, handing over her phone. "Here's my house phone. I know you have a cell but save it. Tell her I invited you and Cresil to visit."

I made the call; Mom answered on the first ring.

"Good afternoon, Moon Ridge Real Estate. How may I help you?"

"Mom, it's me, Harper. I'm over at the Hewitt's."

"Oh. How was school today for you and Cresil? She's not at home alone, is she?"

"She's with me. And before you ask, we didn't get any homework tonight. It was more about getting assimilated into the new high school, things like that. We even brought some papers home for you to read and sign."

"I'll be home later than usual tonight. I have to show a house to this couple—the old Brennan farm. But I can pick up some pizza on the way home for dinner."

"Don't worry about getting any pizza. Mrs. Hewitt invited us to dinner here. Get yourself something nice for your dinner. Cres and I will be home about eight if that's okay with you."

"If it's no bother for Mrs. Hewitt, that's fine with me. See you both at eight. Love you."

"Love you, Mom."

"Tell Cressie the same for me."

The phone call ended with a click on her end. I gave the receiver to Mrs. Hewitt, who put it back in the cradle of the telephone

"Looks like Cresil and I will be staying for dinner."

"I have a pot roast and potatoes in the oven. Now, what happened?"

"Baal possessed Brian Woods."

Lines furrowed in her forehead. "Isn't that boy a worse bully than Pete Jameson ever was?"

Voices rising in pitch from the kitchen reached our ears stopped me from answering, so we went to check it out.

Chapter Twenty-Six—Harper

Mrs. Hewitt and I found Sotuknang, the boys, and Cresil eating cookies and downing glasses of milk. Loud laughter came from Cresil and the boys, Sotuknang spilled some milk on himself.

Do archangels eat and drink? I guess they do, same as demons.

Sotuknang waved his hand, crumbs from the cookie he held dropping on the table. "Mrs. Hewitt, these are divine. Mind you, being an archangel, I haven't had much in the way of human food, but this tops the three other things I have eaten in my millennium."

"Only three kinds of food in all that time, huh?" said Cresil with a snicker. "You need to get out."

Mrs. Hewitt walked over to the cabinets and took out a glass. "Sotuknang, have they told you what happened at school today?"

"No." He looked at Jake. "Tell me."

His eyes glowed, and I knew that he already knew.

"Baal possessed Brian Woods," blurted Cresil. "Like you didn't know already. Omniscient much?"

Sotuknang shook his head. "The little demon is right. I should have said something, but the children were so happy, eating the cookies and having fun."

Pete broke in. "Hey, I'm not a child!?" He cocked his head. "Are you truly an angel? Where are your wings? I don't see any wings or halo."

Sotuknang said, "Yes, I am an archangel. I started teaching Jacob, so he will be able to use his magic to fight Baal. Once, I took him somewhere to teach him live, but most have been in his dreams while he slept. He needed a crash course in being a sorcerer since we do not have much time." He frowned. "As for your friend, I knew the demon lord needed another possessed human for that open portal, just not who. I am sorry."

He looked at Cresil.

She dropped what remained of her cookie on the plate on the table in front of her. "Hell's bells, why are you looking at me, Sotuknang? I haven't been in Baal's back pocket—well, look at me! To him, I'm Hell's turncoat. He won't give me the latest news. You know Lucifer wouldn't spill the beans to me, either."

I broke in. "What are we going to do about it?"

Sotuknang stood. "You will do nothing. I will be the one to do something."

Pete stopped munching. "Are you going to kill Brian? Because of the demon inside him? Hey, he may not have been the nicest friend I had, but he's human, possessed or not. Aren't you Heavenly do-gooders supposed to help the innocent? Not that Brian's all that innocent, but he still deserves help." Cookie bits flew out of his mouth.

Sotuknang nodded. "Yes, angels are supposed to help the innocent. Bad or not, the mortal boy does warrant that."

A sword appeared. He bowed to us and vanished in a blaze of light.

Mrs. Hewitt heaved herself down in the chair Sotuknang vacated. "We should have stopped him. I just had another vision. He's in danger."

Pete threw down his cookie. "I don't know about you guys, but I am going over to Brian's house. Not that I don't think your angel buddy will hurt Brian, but I'm not taking chances." He stood. "Brian's human so he needs help. Am I right? He shouldn't become demon fodder."

Great, now he wants to play hero when earlier he was scared of Baal in Brian. Out loud, I said, "Pete's right. No matter how much of a bully Brian has been, he's a hundred times better than a demon."

Jake rose and took my hand, kissing me on the cheek. "You're the best."

Cresil shoved the last of the cookies in her mouth and got to her feet. "What?" she asked, crumbs spitting out of her mouth, "I need fuel to fight Baal."

Pete shrugged and slung an arm around Cresil's shoulder. "You're not too bad for a demon or even as a human, Cressie. Even if you're a slob when eating."

She shrugged his arm off. "Let's get it straight, monkey boy. Only in that human school or by Harper's mother will I allow myself to be called Cressie. Call me Cresil. Stop with the digs about how I eat—I've only been human since yesterday. Otherwise, I might turn you into the braying jack ass you act like."

Jake laughed. "Hee haw."

Pete didn't look pleased, but as we piled out of the house, he trailed us like a lost puppy. Everyone crammed inside Mrs. Hewitt's bright yellow station wagon. If we wanted to let Baal know we were coming, the car would do the trick.

She zipped the car back out of the driveway and into the street, barely missing an old green sedan that screeched to a halt. Not even checking to see if the other vehicle or the old man and woman inside it were fine, Mrs. Hewitt shoved the shift stick again and spurted down the street, leaving smoke in their face.

I glanced out the back window and at their startled faces.

Jake leaned over to whisper. "Don't worry; she'll get us there safe and sound."

Cresil scrunched against me on the other side, mumbling, "She's going wipe us out before I can use this body for all sorts of things."

Upfront and seat-belted in, Pete gripped the strap above the passenger door, stumbling over a prayer.

Mrs. Hewitt drove to the street where Brian's house stood. She punched the brake and squealed the car to a stop. People rush past us, screaming.

Mrs. Hewitt rolled down her window and asked, "What's going on?"

A man paused, huffing and puffing, and he thumbed back where he ran from. "It's happening at the Woods' house. Brian Woods is acting more like a monster than he usually does. What I mean is, he turned into a monster for real. There is a glowing man with wings, and he's battling it out with the boy, like a monster movie of the week. Both of them are up in mid-air." He took off.

Mrs. Hewitt said, "I saw this in a vision after Sotuknang left us." She rolled her car close to the curb and shut off the engine.

We all piled out.

The man was right. Between flashes of something bright that hit other homes in the neighborhood, we saw the "glowing man with wings" and the "monster" duking it in the front yard of what remained of Brian's house. I hoped Brian's parents had escaped or weren't home.

Sotuknang swung his sword, but Baal ducked and swung a clawed paw to knock it out of his hand. The blade twirled over and over as it flew at us. Cresil grabbed Pete and dropped with him to the asphalt, and it missed their heads by inches. It kept going, slicing some branches from some trees, and winging out of the neighborhood.

"Are you all right?" asked Cresil.

Pete sat up and dusted himself off. "Yeah. Thanks for saving me, Cressie, sorry, I mean, Cresil."

He climbed to his feet and stuck out a hand to help her up. She let him, but she didn't have time to dust off when Jake yelled.

"Look at the sky."

Mrs. Hewitt and I looked up and we both gasped. Gigantic, black clouds rolled across it.

Mrs. Hewitt said, "Get back inside the car. We're leaving."

Jake began walking away. "I'm not leaving Sotuknang."

Mrs. Hewitt screamed, "Jake, no! Get back here!"

He ignored her.

Her face drained of blood, and she had a tight grip on the door handle. She didn't move but yelled one more time. "Jake, please come back. He's an archangel; he can take care of himself."

I looked at Cresil. A grimace passed over her features.

"Yeah, yeah, send the dumb demon after your boyfriend."

"I didn't say anything."

"You don't have to. It's there, in your eyes. In the way your hands clenched into fists." She gently pushed Mrs. Hewitt aside and opened the car door, pulling up the back seat.

"Get in, Harper. You too, Pete."

I stared after Jake's diminishing form, indecisive. Cresil snapped her fingers, and I found myself in the back seat. Pete stood toe-to-toe with her.

"You think I'm chicken or something, letting you take off after Jake?"

She shook her head. "No, but I don't need help. I have magic. Now, get in."

The pair stared at each other.

Pete shrugged, then crawled in. He said with a snarl at me, "Nothing from you. She might have just zapped me in here as she did you, but more likely, she would have turned me into a hamster in a cage. I am not taking chances with her." He stared at her. "But damn, isn't she fantastic?"

Mrs. Hewitt didn't argue. Tears in her eyes and lines of defeat in her face, she slipped into the driver's seat.

Cresil slammed the door shut, then jogged after Jake.

Chapter Twenty-Seven–Cresil

I must be a fool. I could have used my magic and brought Jake back that way. Except when I tried, I couldn't. The only thing to do was go after him. Dumb, considering my power may be dead. As for Jake, I sensed a significant surge in his powers when he left us.

I almost ran into him.

Jake stood at the edge of the front lawn of the house next door to the battlefield. Rubble littered the grass. I hoped whoever lived in it escaped. I shot feelers to see if anyone lay beneath the destruction, but I didn't detect any bodies, wounded or dead.

I touched Jake's shoulder. "Jake?"

He glanced over his shoulder. I saw the worry in his eyes. "I think Sotuknang is losing."

"What?"

The archangel had lost his sword, and only had his archangel mojo. That might not count much in a war against one of Lucifer's best dark angels.

Baal must have shucked Brian's body because I didn't see the teenager anywhere. He struck out and hacked off half of

Sotuknang's wing on the archangel's left side. Light dripped like blood down to the ground.

Unlike what mortals believed, angel wings are not feathers but made of light. Angels are composed of energy—the same goes for spirits of mortals who passed away. Even us demons, though we're a much darker type of energy.

Another slash of Baal's claws and Sotuknang's other wing dropped to the ground. The demon snatched Sotuknang by the throat. Bit into it.

The archangel held sadness in his gaze as he looked at us.

Tears sprang to my eyes.

"No!" yelled Jake, his eyes lighting up, and he tossed fireballs at Baal.

The demon evaded them, then with a grin he twisted Sotuknang's head, tearing it from the neck. He chewed at the Sotuknang's face and began to burn like a glowing lamp. Blobs of light splattered Baal's face and he gave us a gleeful look.

"Bastard!" yelled Jake.

I snagged Jake by his T-shirt before he bounded off. "Oh no, you don't." I snapped the fingers of my free hand and chanted, "Fax is letalis tergum ut telum Harper."

He whipped around; horror etched in his face. "No, I need to kill the—" The boy sorcerer vanished in a flash of light.

Baal stood in my face, angel light dripping from his claws and face. The rest of him no longer lit up like a torch. He dropped what remained of Sotuknang, like it was nothing more than trash.

"Hello, traitorous imp." He giggled and licked all the light off, one claw at a time.

Angel blood is poisonous to demons. Well, most demons. Only very few could handle it. I thought Baal was low enough on the demonic hierarchy not to have immunity.

I guessed wrong.

"The archangel tasted good. I'm sending what's left of him to Hell for Lucifer's meal." He clicked his claws, and the remains of the archangel faded away.

"But he is one of Lucifer's brothers. Lucifer was an archangel once, as you were an angel once. Meaning that's cannibalism."

"You think the Dark One cares? He has done so many terrible things in his long demonic life that cannibalism is nothing." He planted his face back in mine. "It will be nothing for me to eat the face of a fellow fallen one, especially one with the stigma of mortal about her. What is God going to do, damn me to Hell? Wait, He already did that!" He guffawed.

I sweated, my heart pounding like a drummer beating away on drums. I'd never felt more human, more mortal.

Baal lifted a strand of my hair. He took a sniff.

"Mmmmmmm...Smells like flowers."

"It's from shampoo. The stuff has a floral scent. It's nothing that great, just some cheap stuff."

"Oh, but it is good. Edible, I bet." He yanked on the hair, ripping strands from my head. Tears blurred my vision.

"That hurts!"

He didn't apologize, just shoved it in his mouth. I wiped the wetness from my eyes and watched the fiend eat. Yuck! Who eats hair?

"The taste is not up to the smell, but it is okay." He stepped closer. "Wonder how the rest of you tastes. Besides, I will free your demon self from this frail flesh. Send its shiftless apparition back to Hell."

I backstepped. "I don't want to be set free. I like this body."

Lines grooved in his forehead. "You're a demon, for Lucifer's sake. Not some dirt-eating hairless ape."

I kept walking backward, hoping I didn't trip. "You eat me, and I might be gone forever. The archangel claimed that maybe God Himself might be behind this mortal shell. I don't know what happens to me if you kill this body. I might explode like pop rocks in your mouth. There have never been any rules for this before."

Shoulders hunched and eyes narrowed, Baal bent his knees. "Like that bothers me, prissy lowlife imp."

Hell's bells, he's going to tackle me like a football player.

He flashed a big grin.

He heard me!

"Of course, I heard your thoughts, Cresil. You are such a fool. Ever wondered why you ended up a lower-form fallen angel after the Fall, hairless-ape lover?"

"Because I followed Lucifer like a fool?"

"No. You have forgotten your past. You were devoted to Our Father and the rest of the angelic pantheon. Then, Gabriel accused you of being a traitor. Remember that?"

It's been eons, but yes, I remembered that time before the Fall from Grace. It seemed that Gabriel's horn had turned up missing. All the angels believed me guilty, except one. I remembered only Sotuknang had defended my innocence. *Look what happened to him; why didn't God stop Baal?*

Something clicked. "I'm betting you took Gabriel's horn. Or even Lucifer. Blamed the likeliest choice: me."

"You are right, insignificant patsy. I did it," he hissed. "Lucifer was too busy, preparing for the rebellion." Baal pounced and grabbed me by the rest of my hair and hauled me nose to nose with him. "I liked you, but you never saw me. You were such a pretty little thing, all glowing. Friendly to all," he snarled, spittle flying from his mouth, "except to me."

My heart pounded. I always seem to upset the bullies.

He flashed that creepy smile again. "You had no choice, but to join Lucifer's rebels. After all, the horn was missing and God was about to banish you to the mortal world, wings clipped. Once we were in the Pit, you were once again on a lower level than me. And still, you found ways to ignore me and not have anything to do with me." A long, green tongue slid out like a frog's aiming for a fly and tickled my face, slid across my lips. "Love my kiss, Cresil? Wait until my mouth is taking chunks out of you."

"Yuck. You thought I'd want to be with something like you?"

His tongue slurped back in, Brian's jaws unhinged and expanded, and I looked into a deep chasm ringed by sharp, glistening fangs. I remember how the Pit looked: a giant mouth of some leviathan. Baal's opened mouth looked just like that, on a smaller scale, but no less terrifying.

"Leave her alone."

Baal snapped his mouth shut and swiveled his head around, his body following after. The brute jerked me by my hair around. Tears erupted from the pain.

Jake held a staff. *Where did he get that?* He pointed at us, mumbled something, and an enormous ball of ice zeroed from it.

Frantic, I wrenched my hair free, strands left in Baal's paw, and leaped aside, landing on what remained of the grass. Pain sparked through my left side. *Damn this mortal form, so easy to bruise and break*!

The ice ball stuck Baal, and he became an instant ice statue. Brian's body had split from him and dropped unconscious to the ground.

Okay, he still inhabited Brian's body. No wonder I didn't see Brian unconscious anywhere. He must have tucked the kid under his form to keep the portal open.

Pete appeared out of nowhere, dashed over, and helped Jake grab Brian.

Pete groaned. "Dang, he's heavy."

Jake mumbled something, and Brian lifted up a couple of feet off the ground. "This should make him easier to transport, so, shut up and let's get him and us back to the car. The ice spell won't hold Baal for long." Jake turned to me. "Can you make it on your own?"

I climbed to my feet. "Yeah, pretty sure I can."

Harper climbed out of the car when we came upon it. Jake and Pete loaded the still-unconscious Brian into the back behind the front seat.

A roar shook the air. *Baal must have become unfrozen.*

Pete got in up front on the passenger side while Harper inched back inside behind his seat. Jake forced himself in beside Harper as I took up to her right, and we sandwiched the poor girl between us. Mrs. Hewitt started the car, but it didn't take, so she retried a few times until the engine finally kicked in.

Mrs. Hewitt made a screeching U-turn.

I looked out the back window and saw substantial black smoke roaring like a freight train not far behind the vehicle.

"Faster," I said with a shriek.

Mrs. Hewitt replied, "I'm going as fast as this old car can go."

Jake cried out, pointing. "Look, there's our house, Mom."

That's when the car stopped. I don't mean the engine died, but stopped just a few yards from the Hewitt house, still running. It shook, softly at first, then shuddered violently as if from an earthquake. Thrown, I found myself on the laps of Harper and Jake.

Mrs. Hewitt screamed as the steering wheel ripped from her hands and tore itself out of the dashboard. It flew over her head and into the backseat, zeroing on Jake.

"Nocto," said Jake.

It spun past him, and the glass of the passenger window shattered. The dials went crazy, thin red hands spinning around.

Jake and Pete opened their doors, and they tumbled out. Mrs. Hewitt leaped from the driver's side while Harper got out. The doors slammed shut, trapping me and the unconscious Brian inside as I couldn't get any to open for me, by magic or normal means.

Baal wanted me in here.

Jake pointed his staff at the back door to my right, and his magic got it open.

I tumbled out, hitting the pavement. The passenger door up front made a cracking noise and it cleaved from its hinges to fly off into the air, narrowly missing Pete and Jake. With Harper's help, Pete and Jake ran to the back of the station wagon to yank the unconscious Brian out.

Once we had him lying on the street, we watched in shock as the car rose into the air, flying like an arrow at the massive oak tree in the front yard. Black smoke rode it, and for a second, we saw a terrifying face in its midst. The impact was loud, and people hiding in their homes rushed out.

Tears rolled down Mrs. Hewitt's cheeks. "My car."

"At least you still have your house," said Pete.

At that moment, a deafening noise filled the air, and a row of tremors rolled through the house. The vibrations grew worse and starting with the roof, the whole house dropped. A giant hole appeared below, and every bit of the building, backyard, and even the lawn, trees out front, and what remained of the car spiraled down it.

Mrs. Hewitt screamed. "My house! My whole life got sucked down that hole." She clenched her hands into fists and started bawling.

Jake drew her into his arms.

"Time to head for my house," said Harper.

It would have been easier if I could have magicked all of us to the Doyle house, as Brian remained blacked out. But when I tried, a few sparks crackled, and then, only a thin gray smoke rose from my fingertips. I tried a couple more attempts, and still nothing. I felt like a defused bomb. "I bet my magic was sucked out of the air when the house collapsed, or maybe Baal took it away from me at the other place. Then again, once we're at your house, Harper, and time has passed, it might return to me."

I didn't let on to the others how this worried me. Maybe I had become an entirely magicless mortal, which only left Jake in the hocus-pocus department. But even though he admitted he could use the transporting spell; he wasn't good enough to do it for all of us.

Harper and I each took one of Mrs. Hewitt's arms. The woman's shoulders slumped, and her face seemed dispirited.

I ached for her.

Jake did the spell he used earlier on Brian and the unconscious boy lifted a few feet off the ground. Fear kept us quiet as we headed to Harper's.

I looked back over my shoulder, but I didn't see anything, not black smoke, shadows, or a solid shape. That didn't mean Baal stopped following us, just nothing I could discern.

Harper called out, "There's my house."

Relief flooded me. *We're home.*

I let go of Mrs. Hewitt and froze. Now, why did I think of Harper's place as home? I would ponder that later; right now, there were more important worries.

Harper slipped out the house key nestled in her pocket. Before she could insert the key, the front door swung open, and her mother popped her head out, lines furrowing her forehead and puzzlement in her eyes.

"Harper, what's going on? Why does Jake's mother look upset? I see you have Jake and some other—is that Pete Jameson?" That's when she saw Brian slowly lowering to the ground. "How, how...what's going on here?"

To say Aunt Clara was freaked out, was an understatement.

Harper drew her mother out onto the porch, so Jake and Pete could carry Brian inside. I hurried Mrs. Hewitt indoors before rejoining Harper and her mom.

Mrs. Doyle crossed her arms. "Harper, what's going on? I saw that kid in the air. In the air!"

I peered at the growing shadows at the edge of the front lawn. The night would soon be here. With darkness and having eaten archangel powers, Baal's abilities would be double trouble for us

Harper urged her mother inside. "Mom, I can't tell you right now. Let's get inside and make sure everything is locked up and made safe. We'll answer all of your questions afterward."

I knew that Harper had never wanted her mother involved in all of this, but it looked like what she wanted and what happened no longer mattered. I closed the door and set all the locks, including sliding the deadbolt home. I said a spell to add an invisible dome of protection over the house. I crossed over to the couch, where the guys had laid Brian.

Jake looked at me. "Cresil, help me check all the windows and the back door. I'll need to set up a protection spell to back up yours. I'm glad Sotuknang taught me that and enough other spells before Baal killed him."

"Sure."

Jake and I ran through the house, making sure all the windows were closed and locked, the same for the back door. Jake used his magic to coat all the doors and windows with the most potent protection spell he knew to keep demons out and added more protection weight to mine.

Sotuknang had taught him well. It'd been smart of him to teach Jake in his dreams. I'd just wished he had survived long enough to get the boy into the best sorcerer shape, magically. But we will take what we have.

"I can't promise that Baal and his bunch won't get in as he will know a spell to defuse both of our combined magic, considering he ate some of Sotuknang's archangel powers," I said, "but at least this is better than nothing at all."

"I hope it works, Cresil," said Jake.

He sprinted downstairs to grab a blanket and pillow from the hall closet.

I entered the bathroom upstairs to gather some supplies for Brian, including a towel, washcloth, a bucket full of cool water, and a bottle of painkillers for the headache I'm sure he'll have when he wakes up.

I got back to a quiet living room, the only noise coming from the ceiling fan's whirling blades. The atmosphere hung heavy. Even though Harper, her mother, and Pete weren't psychic like Mrs. Hewitt or had powers like Jake or me, I knew they felt it. It grew more palpable as I brought what I gathered and dumped it all on the coffee table, setting the bucket of water on the floor beside the couch.

Mrs. Hewitt sunk like a pile of crumpled clothes in a chair in the corner and began crying again. Her face became blotchy and tear-stained, her hair a messy crow's nest. Jake crouched at her side and placed his hand on her shoulder, whispered something to her, but she ignored him. He shook his head at the rest of us, at a loss.

Aunt Clara sat on the corner of the chaise chair, fiddling with a glass filled one-fourth with iced tea. Harper looked down at her, and she looked up at her daughter with frightened eyes.

"Tell me, Harper. What's going on? What's wrong with that boy? I can tell he's unconscious, but why isn't anyone making a 911 call? How in blazes did he float in the air? Why is Jake's mother here and why is she crying? Tell me the truth."

Chapter Twenty-Eight–Harper

I trembled, unsure of what I should tell Mom, and I glanced at Cresil. She nodded. I knew what she meant by that: tell her.

I borrowed a chair from the kitchen, placed it next to hers and sat down. Not stopping, I told her everything, from the moment my friends and I had called up a demon to the destruction of Mrs. Hewitt's house and the imminent end of the world.

She didn't say a word, just listened. No judgment calls in her eyes, condemning me for the demon summoning to not letting her in on what we had been doing since then to the start of World War Hell. Most teens don't tell their parents the many secrets they keep, but I admit this blew having unprotected sex, getting into drugs, or drinking, out of the water. She didn't blink nor show any reaction, so I worried about how she was taking this.

When I finished, she stared down at her glass, lifted it, and downed the rest of the tea. Still saying nothing, she rose out of the chair, glass in hand, tottered a couple of steps, shivered, and the glass fell from nerveless fingers. It hit one pointed side of the coffee table and shattered, the pieces scattering on the carpet. She didn't move, just stared down at the mess.

"Mom." I pulled her to me and hugged her. "I'm sorry."

Her body seemed small in my arms.

Drawing away, I saw the tears tumbling out of her eyes and down her cheeks. Through the gleam of the wetness in her eyes, I saw the betrayal. I'd hurt her—badly.

"Mom, it's underhanded of me, not telling you."

She wiped the tears with her hand. Her lips pursed, and her face tightened as she pulled away. "I'm your mother. I hope I have always been there for you, at least I thought so." She swept a look at Cresil, returning to me. "I mean, using some demon to bespell me into thinking she's a niece of mine. How could you?"

She believed Cresil was a demon, meaning she believed me. I should have told her earlier. "I know, I know. It was Sotuknang who did the spell, and he was an archangel. But I wanted to keep you out of all this for your safety." Tears blinded me. "Lives were already lost, and maybe I'm close to becoming an adult, but I'm not! All of this is way above my head."

Mom touched one of the tears on my eyelashes. She drew me close and kissed both of my eyes before smoothing my hair back and looking into my gaze.

She said, "Maybe it's partly my fault."

"Let's forget blaming either of us. Let's start fresh," I said. "As fresh as long as we have with an apocalypse hanging over our heads."

The hurt and upset no longer shone in her eyes. Instead, I saw love. "I love you, kitten."

She called me by what she used when I was little. My heart clenched. We hugged.

She tucked a strand of my hair behind my ear and kissed my cheek. "I wish we could go back, and you could be a typical teenager before you reach adulthood and learn life is not always fair. Hell is forcing the unfairness down your throat."

"It's all right, Mom."

"No, it's not. But I promise to stand by you in this mess to the end." She turned to Mrs. Hewitt, who finally had stopped crying and now hovered over Brian, bathing his face with a damp cloth. He still hadn't moved.

"Pansy?"

Mrs. Hewitt looked. "Yes, Clara?"

"I'm going to take Harper upstairs to tell her something."

Jake's mother nodded. "Go right ahead. It's about time you told her." She nodded at Jake standing next to her. "We'll be fine here. Jake and Cresil have this place warded, so you should be safe up there."

Mom gave Mrs. Hewitt a funny look, but she led me upstairs and I wondered what she needed to tell me that, for some reason, she couldn't tell me in front of the others. Unless she still had qualms about Cresil and worried about the demon overhearing. Except what didn't she want anyone else to hear?

We entered Mom's bedroom. She closed the door and waved her hand at the bed. "Sit."

I perched on the edge of the mattress. "What can't you tell me—"

"—in front of the others? Because I am not sure how you'll take this, never mind anyone else."

Okay, maybe this wasn't about Cresil.

She took a deep breath, let it out, and sat beside me, diving straight into her story.

"I was the wallflower in high school—no guy asked me out. It was the same in college. When I came back home and got the Moon Ridge Realty job, it hit me that maybe I might end up a spinster, never marrying. My best friends, Pansy Hewitt and Sally Wimley, worked to get me blind dates, but honestly, none of those guys sparked anything in me to try a second date. The few that interested me, I never heard from again. Who wanted to take chances with a mousy, bookish girl who wore wire-framed glasses almost bigger than her face? It's what I began to believe. Anyway, one day, this good-looking man walks into the real estate office. The sun shone its light through the window behind him, and I swore it looked like a halo around his head, his whole body, to be honest. He had a twinkle in his blue eyes. I think I fell head over heels for him at that moment."

I whispered, "Dad?"

"Yes, that was your father. John Brand claimed to be looking for a house, as his company had transferred him to Roanoke. I showed him several, but he picked this one, even paid cash for it. That shocked me, but I'd become so besotted by that time, I ignored it, thinking he had been saving for a long time." She paused, took another breath, and let it out, and continued. "Anyway, he asked me if I cared to join him to celebrate. I agreed, telling him it would have to be after work. He left, but he returned as I was locking the door and took me to this lovely restaurant in Roanoke. We had wine, and it went to my head as I listened to him talk, not hearing any of the words.

We saw more of each other after that, and before I knew it, he swept me off my feet with a proposal, and we had a beautiful wedding at St. Thomas Catholic Church. Everyone felt happy for me, even Pansy, although she did act strange around him."

"What do you mean?"

"She kept looking at him funny at the reception; she'd been like that from day one when I first introduced him to her. It appeared something about him bothered her, something she wanted to say, but she never did. She even looked like she'd been about to say something as we hugged each other goodbye when John and I left for our honeymoon, but she didn't.

Something did seem different about your father on our wedding night at the bed and breakfast we stayed at, but I ignored it. I mean, he made me happy, did nothing wrong, even in his lovemaking. Besides, I'd never been so happy in my life, even those long times he supposedly went on the road for his job in Roanoke." She looked at me. "A job with no Christmas parties, where I never met the boss or any coworkers, heck, never saw the paycheck, just money he showered on me to pay the bills. Then one day, he never returned from one of those trips. When I checked up on the job, I found it never existed in Roanoke or all of Virginia. Not even in the United States or anywhere else in the world. Two days later, I found out I was pregnant with you."

I didn't understand where she was going with this. Okay, my father was a dirtbag. He probably had several wives in different towns or something. I had resigned myself long ago that I would never see him in my life. After hearing this, I didn't care if I ever saw him. But what brought on this story from Mom?

I must have had a confused look on my face, for my mother quit talking and gently touched me.

"Honey, your father wasn't human."

What? I didn't understand. "What did you just say?" I crossed my arms and peered into her face. "Are you sure you're my mother and not some pod person from another world?"

She shook her head. "I'm human. But your father wasn't."

I squeaked the words out. "What was he, and how did you find this out?"

I wanted to take back the question. I didn't want or need to know. Mom was human. So, was I—right?

I jumped up and moved over to her dresser, touching and picking up a knick-knack here and there. All the time, growing up and thinking I didn't feel like others. Of course, especially by middle school, a lot of kids thought that. We wondered if we were adopted, if our parents came from another planet or might be super spies from an enemy country planted in daily American life.

What kid didn't feel like they didn't belong? But my situation, I needed to know.

I repeated when she didn't answer me, joining her on the bed. "Tell me."

She swept me into her arms. "Oh baby, if I could tell you he was an ordinary man, I would. But seven years after he disappeared, he returned."

My breath caught and Mom let me go and resumed her story.

"You were in school that day. I hadn't gone to work as I had this nasty headache that wouldn't go away. My cheek was on my pillow as I laid in bed, letting the painkiller take effect, when I heard the front door open and close. I sat up, scared, thinking someone had gotten into the house. Funny thing, I knew I'd set the locks on both the front and back doors before I went to lay down. I got to my feet, looking around for something to use as a weapon. That's when John walked into the bedroom.

"Hello, Clara?" he'd said as if he hadn't been away for seven years. He walked over to me. I backed away. I mean, this man dared to come back. Where had he been all this time? Had his wife dumped him? Or had he been involved in something criminal and was being investigated? So many possible reasons flashed across my mind. As for him managing to open the door, I had changed all the locks when he disappeared seven years before, so any key he still had wouldn't work. I just never thought of the impossible. I mean,

I don't believe in things supernatural. Harper, you know I don't even watch horror movies and all those stories about Moon Ridge; I never paid much attention to them, as to me they're nothing more than folklore. I even ignored about Pansy claiming to be psychic, making it easy to remain her friend. Everything I watched, and did, was grounded in reality."

She hitched a sob and shuddered. "But the man I'd married those years ago, the father of my child, took me by my shoulders and told me everything." Her shudders grew worse. "I'd been sleeping with an angel. Not an 'It's a Wonderful Life' type of angel, but one that lives by the sword, a warrior angel—an archangel.

"He told me that they had sent him to impregnate me, a Daughter of Eve, as he called me. Not to care for me, or anything like that, but because you needed to be born. Except he claimed he fell in love with me, the bastard."

My mother looked at me. Anger flared in her eyes, and she no longer cried. "He wanted me to know this, that you were all part of some destined prophecy, a special Nephilim. That he never meant to hurt me or fall in love with me. As if being an archangel gave him the right."

My father was an archangel?

I thought back to St. Thomas Catholic Church's Catechism classes. How many archangels are there? Six, no, seven, or eight? Michael, Gabriel, Raphael, Raguel, Azrael, Uriel and Jerahmeel, if I remembered right. Which one is my father? But Sotuknang claimed to be an archangel, and he's not in any archangel mythology I've heard. So, maybe it is much more than eight. How many archangels existed in Heaven?

"Mom, I don't have angelic abilities," I pointed out. "I have been nothing but ordinary all of my life."

"There was the one instance."

I frowned. "When was that? I don't remember anything."

"You had just turned one year old." Mom snatched a tissue from a square cardboard box on the bedstead and wiped at the tear stains on her cheeks. "I'd just put you to bed after a birthday celebration I'd given you. You had your first piece of cake and ice cream and loved the stuffed teddy bear I gave you. You clutched it to you after I put you down for a nap. I closed your door and turned to walk away when I heard something coming from your bedroom. I went back in." She took my hand. "You weren't in your crib. I found you floating a few feet above it, still clutching the bear and surrounded by an orb of light. It scared me, and I screamed. You woke up and started crying. The light popped, and you floated back down. I told myself it had been my imagination, that I had heard you crying and that's why I reentered your bedroom. I convinced myself enough to forget it, as you never did anything like that again. Then your father returned."

But I hadn't done anything like that since—at least nothing I could remember. *And yet, you never felt like you belonged.*

If I had angel powers, why hadn't they revealed themselves to me? Maybe I could have stopped all this mess, prevented my friends from summoning Baal. Had my father done something so I couldn't use them? Had he thought to train me later?

I asked, "Mom, what happened to my father after he told you his secret?"

She twisted the tissue. "I called him mad, and that if he needed to make up some story to cover his absence, saying he's an archangel was not the one to tell. He kept insisting. I realized he believed what he said. I opened my mouth to suggest maybe he needed to see a shrink when the memory of you in a floating, glowing orb came back to me. That's when I knew he told the truth about himself. I became frightened and yelled at him to leave and never return. He said he wouldn't leave us, but I retorted that I didn't want him near me and not at all near my daughter."

"I'm sorry, he'd said, and tried to pull me to him.

I fought back. Told him to keep his hands off me. Aren't angels supposed to be holy and above the needs of mortals— like sex? I doubt John is your real name, so which archangel are you?"

But he pleaded. Told me his name was Michael. That he didn't expect to love me. I'd never had any feelings for any mortal, he said. I only served my Father in Heaven, he said. Then he said he could never understand why He cared for his mortals, got down on his knees and grabbed my hands, and said I made him understand."

"He kissed my hands. I was uneasy, because feelings that I thought long dead arose, and I yanked my hands away. I screamed at him to go away!"

"He stood, tears in his eyes, and bowed to me. Said, he'd leave me, and you, his Nephilim child. That maybe one day I could forgive him."

Mom blinked back tears. "That's when light enveloped him, and he became a large glowing orb that passed through the ceiling."

It hit me. "My last name was never Doyle."

"Doyle is my maiden name. I figured our marriage was fake, that signing a name not his to the marriage certificate never made it real. I never filed for divorce, and I just let people assume I had. I let them believe I'd taken back my maiden name and, angry with him, let you use it. I did research what Brand meant as I wondered why he used it." Her eyebrows furrowed together. "Funny thing, I found it meant sword, fiery torch, or a beacon. Archangels are warrior angels and use swords."

So...the Archangel Michael's my father?

If I remembered my Catechism classes right, he opposed Lucifer and saved souls at death. The latter made him become a father of a child of prophecy to battle the apocalypse understandable. Not that it made him more sympathetic in what he had done concerning my mother and me.

The prophet Daniel (12: 1) called him "Michael the great prince who shall rise at the time of the end.

I jumped up from the bed. Why did I have that thought?

Mom stood. "Harper, what's wrong? If what I just told you makes you hate me in any way or upset, tell me."

"No, no." I took a breath. "Let's get downstairs and join the others. They need to know the truth about me."

She nodded. "All right."

But the walls shook. One side of a shelf on the wall loosened, and all the little statues on it crashed to the floor, some breaking. A giant roar came from outside, causing the house to shake again.

"Oh no, Baal's here," I said.

"Harper, maybe those are tremors from an earthquake."

"No, Baal's doing this. Let's get downstairs."

The both of us ran out of her bedroom and down the stairs.

Chapter Twenty-Nine—Harper

Jake stood at one of the two windows in the living room. He had lifted the blind and was peering out. Dropping the blind, he whipped around when Mom and I flew off the last step and over to the couch where Brian had regained consciousness and sat up, groaning.

Everyone else kept their eyes on him as more caterwauling erupted from outside.

After all, he had been possessed. No demon took up residence now, but who's to say that Baal didn't have control of him?

"Why am I here?" Brian demanded, not even keeping his voice down. "What joke are you creeps jerking on me?" He got off the couch and winced at the clamor coming from outside. "What's making all that racket out there? My head's pounding enough."

"We're not pulling anything on you, Brian," I replied, "that 'racket' as you call it, is coming from a demon that possessed you."

"Cut the crap about demons and possessions," snarled Brian. "You gotta do better than that to try and fool me."

Jake snapped, "Like we want to yank your chain, Brian Woods. Get over yourself and keep quiet."

"Why should I?"

I crossed my arms. "Unless you want to wait until the demon just outside my house is in your face. Or worse, wait until Baal decides to reuse your flesh. Hate to tell you this, but you might be the big bad in high school, but that thing out there has you outclassed." I rejoined Mom where she trembled.

Another roar, this time the house shook as it did earlier. Brian stumbled over to join Pete, Mrs. Hewitt, Mom, and me huddling against the wall as far as we could get from the front part of the house.

Pete inched away when Brian squeezed next to him. "Woods, you should know what it is. Don't tell me you can't remember it used your body for its apartment."

"What are you jabbing about, Jameson?"

"I think the demon wants its rental back."

"A demon? Are you on drugs or something, like the other fruitcakes here? About time to quit the Brian/Pete duo, 'cause I don't hang out with flakes."

Cresil said, "That thing out there wants to jump-start Armageddon, and it needs your body back so it can open a portal to allow hordes of demons to enter our world. How do I know? I'm a demon myself."

Brian stared at her like she'd grown two heads. "Damn, you're a fricking headcase, girl. Don't see what Jameson sees in you."

I saw Cresil open her mouth to cuss Brian out or maybe do something with her magic, when something large and heavy hit the front of the house. It caused the drywall to rain a cloud of dust down on us from the ceiling.

Pete whitened and pressed against the wall, as if hoping he could do a chameleon and hide within it.

"That's not good," said Jake.

Cresil retorted, "You think? Baal keeps that up, and this house will go the way yours did."

A loud bam at the door, and the drywall beside it cracked. Mom and Mrs. Hewitt bolted for the kitchen. Brian fled after them, crying.

I remained.

"Big baby," retorted Cresil. She shook her head when Pete followed close behind the other boy. "There goes my hero." She stressed the last word with sarcasm before joining Jake.

Both she and Jake raised their hands, balls of lightning flickering in their palms, his colored purple, hers red. All of a sudden, it grew quiet. Silent enough that you could hear our breathing and the whirring of the ceiling fan still working. I was surprised that our electricity still worked, after all, Baal had taken it away from this house before and brought it back so my mother never knew about it.

The pounding went crazy, and suddenly, the door busted off its hinges and hit the floor of the entryway with a crash. A large shadow stood in the doorway.

Jake threw his ball while Cresil tossed hers, then we all crowded together at the kitchen entrance. This way, we could escape. The balls fizzled out before they even hit the dark thing.

Brian screamed from the kitchen. "Don't invite it in."

Cresil called out, "That's for vampires, you dolt. And too late, Baal crashed his way in."

The shadow shimmered, doing something like a television picture shorting out. Tendrils of black smoke zeroed past us into the kitchen and hooked Brian, yanking him off his feet and onto his back. His head bounced hard against the floor as it drew him back into the living room and toward it.

Cresil stuck out her hands, more of her red lightning sparking from the fingertips.

It struck air, missing Baal as he streamlined into Brian's mouth. The boy's mouth snapped shut.

Brian stood, his eyes black as pitch, and he spoke in a deep voice. "Cresil, you were always a lousy shot."

Cresil guided Jake and me toward the kitchen. "You got your body; now get out of this house and leave these people alone."

Baal flashed an evil grin. "Oh, I am leaving. Another time, I would have brought this house down and killed everyone in here. Punt kicked all the souls to Hell. But I got a to-do list to get working on, like opening a portal and bringing over an army. I'll have plenty of time for massacre and pillaging, fun stuff like that once I check the first things off my list."

I asked, "How can you be such a terrible monster?"

"It comes naturally to me." He dropped the grin, and a frown passed over his face and he sniffed. "What's that disgusting aroma I smell?" He stepped closer. "The stink of the Holy is in this place. But it can't be."

I clenched my hands at my side and nodded. "Yes, it can be, Hell breath."

His nostrils flared and he took several more whiffs. He narrowed his eyes. "Hell's bells, Nephilim. I should have realized the truth about you before. You are a child of a Seraph and just not any kind of angel, but an archangel."

He bent his head to one side as if listening, then speaking out loud, just not to us. "Yes, my lord. Ah, the prophecy. I understand. Which archangel fathered her? Could it be that namby-pamby Gabriel? Maybe Uriel or...yes, it had to be Michael."

He returned his black gaze to us. "My lord Lucifer doesn't want me to worry about you, for now, Nephilim. We need that portal open first. He even has another low-caste demon waiting to shove into this costume of flesh I'm wearing." He bared sharp teeth in a terrible smile. "But don't you worry your pretty head, once the army marches over to this plane of existence, I'll be back for you and traitorous Cresil. I always wanted a Nephilim to play with and Big L says I have first dibs on you." He danced a jig to the center of the living room, stopped, and bowed. "Until we meet again, I've got a body to sacrifice, and murder and mayhem to pursue. Busy, busy, busy." He snapped his fingers. "Oh, I almost forgot. Need to forward time to two days before Halloween, or the portal won't work." He spoke some strange language I knew wasn't Latin and felt the air turn odd as waves filtered through it.

Baal had just moved us forward in time.

Then he vanished.

Chapter Thirty—Cresil

I knew where Baal would go to open the portal. I convinced Jake and Harper to check on their mothers, who were wise and remained in the kitchen. Once they did, I snapped my fingers and dissipated, but not before I put the front door back up and locked the mortals inside the house to keep them safe. I added more safeguard sigils to make sure nothing demonic could get inside.

Besides, this way, Harper and Jake couldn't come after me, not right away, as those sigils would also keep them from getting out. Hoping Sotuknang hadn't got far enough along in teaching Jake on breaking my sigils, I knew sooner or later, he would figure a way to trip them magically.

My molecules reassembled, and I stood down the street from the burned-out house where Harper and her friends first summoned Baal. The whiff of pumpkins and dead leaves on the autumn breeze wafted to my nostrils. Homes in the neighborhood had been decorated with monsters, ghosts and other Halloweeny things.

Of course, the opening of the portal coincided with two days from Samhain. It's always better to do such magic on Samhain or Beltane, as it gives an extra kick to keep the portal open. Even two days early still had power due to the closeness of the special day.

The only problem would not be just the wrecked building, but the whole neighborhood would be sucked into Hell when Brian's body became torn apart, destroying the demon inside it and the portal would remain open for however long Lucifer wanted. I closed my eyes, pain riveting through me. *Many people will die, their souls lost forever to the Pit.*

For the first time in my long life, I cared. I had mortals I loved and wanted to save. I couldn't let that happen, even if that meant the end of me. It would never make up for all the terrible things I had done over the eons, but that didn't matter. Harper, Jake, Mrs. Hewitt, Aunt Clara, even Pete, all the good people on this planet deserved it. Even the bad ones should get a chance to change. Nobody would if Lucifer and his demons went toe-to-toe against Heaven.

I ran down the street, ignoring a wave from an old man in a coat raking leaves and kids dressed in their Halloween costumes already, playing in their yards, even though trick-or-treat wasn't until two nights from now.

The sound of my tennis shoes slapping the cement of the street filled my ears. It made me nervous. Had Baal or Lucifer heard it? Maybe I should just teleport all the way. *They know you're coming, fool, no matter how you're doing it. Probably hoping you will.*

I slowed at the edge of the yard of the burned-out house and stepped onto the overgrown, dead grass. I tiptoed through dandelions and other weeds, whispering a few words of magic to take away any sound I might make. Licking my lips, I looked up at a window. Becoming invisible, I peered through the window into the room I recognized as the one I'd first appeared in a year ago. The walls were nothing more than a blackened skeleton of the building and the floor was stained with rubbed in ash and debris.

Brian—or Baal—stood in the middle of the room. In a triangle painted in blood on the floor beside him reared a snake made of black shadow.

Lucifer.

He had placed three black, lit candles at each point. For this ritual to work, it had to be the blood of an innocent. No scratch that, I knew it was blood, human blood of a dead virgin. I looked around and saw a pair of children's tennis shoes peeping through the doorway that led into another room.

Sadness filled inside me. Then anger.

I would stop these beasts from bringing in more of their kind into the mortal realm. No more children would die.

I became solid again. "Ego accerso a mucro." With my words, a sword appeared in my hand. As if I still had my angel wings from my days when I resided in Heaven, I flew through the glass of the window, landing on the floor in a crouch, becoming visible once more.

Baal smiled. "About time you showed up. Lucifer and I were waiting for you. Now the party can start."

I stood. "What are you talking about, hellspawn?"

He chuckled. "If I'm a hellspawn, what does that make you? You never do think, do you? If I slit the throat of this body to open the portal, I would lose a living body to possess since I need a lower caste demon to possess it for it to work. No, I plan to use your new frame as my new home."

"Excuse me, you get in my body, and you will still lose." I glared at Lucifer. "You too, Lucifer."

The smoke became a shadow person. "No, I won't, Cresil. Baal, you are mistaken. Instead of using that foolish demon in the dead child's body and putting it into the teen you're wearing, use Cresil. What she is now will amplify the power to keep the portal open much better." Lucifer's chuckle was enough to scratch glass.

A whisper came from behind me. I smelled a foul stench. Whipping around, I swung my sword.

Twin orbs of glowing darkness looking out of the dead child's eyes. The dress was torn and filthy, and the corpse dragged one foot. Had it already been broken when Baal took her or caused when she might've fought to escape? Or did the monster snap the leg bone on purpose? It didn't matter. I had to stop the demon inside.

The child rushed me, and I swung my sword again, but the metal grew ice cold. "Hell's bells!" I cried out, dropping it.

The child's body slammed into me, knocking me off my feet, and my head banged against the ground.

I lay there, stunned.

Something squirmed its way inside me, passing through skin, muscle, and bone. The demon squeezed its way inside my brain. The body it'd been using dropped in a tangle of loose limbs.

"God!" I cried out, grabbing my head as I rolled onto my knees.

Its screams ricocheted in my head. Good! The sneak hated me using God's name, and I felt it clawing at my soul. Strangely enough, the word no longer bothered me.

"We will have none of that, turncoat," growled Baal, zapping me.

Agony rippled through my skin as I hit the floor flat on my side, tears blurring my sight. A man's voice flowed out of my mouth. It too, screamed, as if in pain.

"Why am I in this body, Baal? You promised I would be in the army."

Even though the demon controlled my body and speech, the stupid twit hadn't locked me away in the brain, and I saw everything. I even knew who the dark spirit happened to be: Pete's grandfather.

Baal approached and dropped to one knee, picking up my sword. I watched him caress the blade, a loving glint in his eyes. He stared into my eyes at the both of us. From the triangle, Lucifer waited. His red eyes flashed.

Baal shook his massive head. "No, foolish Samuel Jameson, you were never meant to join us. Only the pure original Fallen will make up the Legion. The rest of you are nothing more than our tortured damned." He raised the blade. "Samuel, you are being honored for a special purpose." He caressed my face. "As for you, Cresil, Lucifer and I knew you would be something special to manipulate.

Unique, a demon, one of the original Fallen, made into a living being of flesh. Lucifer decided your body would be the perfect vessel to hold the demon inside, that you would make the best sacrifice to keep the portal open to allow Lucifer and his Legion to enter this world, and...I finally get to destroy you." He flashed a cannibal grin.

Samuel's screams echoed in my head as Baal brought the blade down and sword met my throat.

I remained silent, not want to give Baal any satisfaction.

He pressed hard to work the metal to cut through muscle to the bone.

Samuel finally stopped yelling as my head parted from my shoulders and rolled away. I floated up to what remained of the ceiling, unseen by Baal. I watched as a portal formed where the triangle on the floor had been, made of whirling red and black, a foul stench wafting from it.

"Welcome, my lord Lucifer. This world awaits your conquering legion." Baal's voice held dark joy in it."

Lucifer became a vision of Darklight and stepped aside as the first demon came through.

A shadow at first, it morphed into a sort of flesh. Terrifying, eight tentacles with claws at the ends whipped out and snapped at the air. One of them snatched my human head and brought it up to his maw full of needle-sharp teeth and swallowed. It went after the rest of my body.

I hoped it choked on me.

It didn't, only burped and moved on as another fiend entered the mortal realm.

The Devil stood before Baal. The demon lord knelt before him, his head bent as he stared straight down at the ground. Baal's fear filled the room, pungent from his sweat. Sweat? Demons never sweated. And yet, like aggressive piss and tangy with sheer terror, it filled the area like unforgotten nightmares. But the Devil chose to ignore Baal and stared at the vortex in front of him instead.

"Come forth, my evil things," Lucifer said in a booming voice. "I'm hungry for souls and the power they will give me to breach Heaven."

He turned back to Baal and smiled, reached inside the demon lord and ripped a screaming Brian from him. The dark angel opened his mouth wider than Brian's head and bit it off. He tossed the headless body to the demons that began fighting over who got what parts, if any.

Lucifer belched. "I needed that snack."

The terrifying sounds from the devils faded as I ascended through the ceiling and up, up, up, until I heard nothing more.

Chapter Thirty-One—Harper

Jake gasped, clutching his chest. "She's gone."

Frightened, I knew the answer as I felt it too, but I still asked, "Jake, who's gone?"

He straightened and looked at me, his eyes full of anguish. "Cresil. She's dead."

Pete grabbed Jake by the T-shirt. "Cresil's a demon. There's no way that she can die. Right?"

Mrs. Hewitt scraped her chair back from the kitchen table to pour another cup of coffee, pausing mid-way to close her eyes. Her nostrils flared, then she reopened her eyes to look at us. "Cresil was made into a living, breathing person. Jake's right. She has passed over." Tears rolled down her cheeks, and she left her cup by the coffee pot, returning to her chair.

Pete wrapped his arms around himself. "How did it happen?"

Jake stared at the back door. "Her body's been sacrificed." He faced us. "That means the portal's open."

Pete's face paled, and he dropped into a nearby chair. "No, it can't be," he said in shock.

I sat next to my mother. "I thought they planned to use Brian's body."

Jake replied, "They used her instead and Brian was used as food for the demonic." He looked strained. "The image of a sword slashing through Cresil's neck and her head rolling flashed in my mind. The portal is open, and we are all screwed."

A member of the three who was needed when the apocalypse began is gone. Yes, Cresil drove me nuts at first. But once you got to know her, for a demon, she wasn't half bad.

Alive, she had been becoming human.

We'd found ourselves locked in, which meant she'd sneaked out to try and save Brian, stop it all. She became my cousin to fool my mother, but as she'd been an original Fallen angel and my father being Michael, it meant she really was my cousin.

I began to cry.

Jake drew me into his arms. "It's all right, Harper."

"No, it's not," I said, gulping,

"We all knew it might happen. No, it did happen. We can't help Cresil, but we can do something about her death. We have to stop the apocalypse from destroying the earth." He laid a finger under my chin and lifted it. "Maybe we're short one, but there's still two of us left."

Mom handed me a tissue, and I wiped my face.

That stupid prophecy.

Both Sotuknang and Cresil died for it. Possibly Brian, and who knew who else already had and will soon.

"The two of you aren't going anywhere," my mother said. "You're both only teenagers. Revelation, be damned! Let Michael and his angels battle those devils."

Michael.

Now that it concerned her child, my mother chose to ignore that my father was connected to it, too. That he might be destroyed by the demons.

I glanced at Mrs. Hewitt, but I saw nothing in her gaze. No fear for Jake or anything else. I wondered what her spirit guides told her.

Pete had been quiet. Did I see fear in his eyes? I could say he was a coward, but I realized he was only seventeen, like Jake and me.

I stepped away from Jake. "Mom, I'm half archangel—a Nephilim. Besides, this is my world, with millions of teenagers, plus adults and children, none with a drop of angel in them. I don't like it, but I guess it might have to be up to me."

Mom's eyes flashed with anger. "I don't care. Your father chose to lie to me about who and what he was. He didn't stay around to help raise you. You're *my* daughter. I don't think Heaven has much to say about you or Jake giving your lives. Only me as your mother and Pansy as Jake's have the right."

Jake broke in, "But—"

Mrs. Hewitt had retrieved her cup and washed it, setting it in the drying rack. "Mrs. Doyle is right, Jake. You both are too young to become warriors."

Jake sputtered. "Excuse me, but you allowed Sotuknang to teach me. Remember, Mom? If Harper is half angel, I bet she has powers." He looked at me. "Am I right?"

"I guess. Mom did say I became an orb once."

"What?"

"I was a baby then. But I bet I can do more than that now." I looked at Mom. "If Mom would get over that my father's an archangel and let us get in contact with him, maybe I can find out what I can do."

"Absolutely not!" said Mom.

"Hello?" The voice was eerie and soft. It chimed like bells. A tall, glowing figure stood in the middle of the room. "I am the angel Baruch. Michael and the other archangels are getting ready for battle. The demon army is here in Moon Ridge, and they wish to contain it and not let it spread out to the rest of the mortal realm."

Mom clenched her hands. "Michael couldn't come himself to tell us this?"

The figure bowed its head. At least, I assumed that was its head.

"Yes, Madame, he is God's warrior and has to lead the others. But he sent me to make sure you all stay here. He does not want you or his daughter to come to harm. Nor does he wish that for the sorcerer foretold about, either. He said to tell you, Madame, that being with you taught him how to be human and to care." It drew closer, its light giving off heat. "That he loves you."

The figure vanished. None of us said anything for a few minutes.

Pete spoke first. "That was an angel? Kinda cool. Well, not cool at all, with demonic armies and the apocalypse. Or losing Cresil." He plopped down in a chair. "We're going to die, aren't we?"

Confusion flittered across Mom's face.

Mrs. Hewitt patted her on the shoulder and said, "Men. Even if they are archangels."

Jake spoke. "I don't care what that angel says. Harper and I are part of stopping this. Something tells me if we stay here, Lucifer and his bunch will ream a big one to the archangels."

Before anyone could stop him, he snapped his fingers, and the back door flew open. He ran out into the night. I bit my lip as I looked at my mother.

"I'm sorry, Mom, but I'm going with Jake. Relock the back door behind me."

"Harper."

I paused at the doorway.

My mother crossed over to me and hugged me. I heard sniffles and felt wetness on my cheek.

Mom was crying.

I hated leaving Mom and Mrs. Hewitt, but Jake was right. He and I needed to end the apocalypse, not the archangels. Too bad, Cresil no longer existed. I didn't know how that changed the equation in Lucifer's favor, but it didn't matter. If Jake and I didn't attempt, well, as some little green alien in a science fiction movie always said, that one had to try or not. We needed to do this, forget trying.

I whispered in her ear, rubbing my cheek against her wet one. "I'm scared. My stomach's spinning around like some washing machine and my heart's slamming away. I want to stay here, be cuddled by you, and feel as safe for as long as I can, but we both know it's not an option for me."

Mom gave me a teary-eyed smile and wiped my cheek. "I know. But only a bad mother would let her child go out into a situation like this. A mother is supposed to protect her daughter."

I shook my head. "You're not a bad mother. It's not your fault."

"I wish it were someone else who had to do this. Not my daughter."

"No, you don't. You wouldn't wish this on anyone."

"Not on my son, either." Mrs. Hewitt joined us. She looked defeated. "It appears no one thought to ask the mothers of these teenagers for permission. The living are just pieces on a chessboard."

Pete rose from his seat for the first time. "You guys can't go. Why do you and Jake have to do this thing? It's dumb." His face gleamed pale, and his eyes were wild, his body shaking.

"Take care of Pete," I told Mom and Mrs. Hewitt. Pete would be safe with them. Not that I believed Pete would offer to help. Anyway, he's just human.

Before any of them decided to stop me, I stepped outside. The door slammed shut behind me, the locks resetting themselves as if by unseen hands or by magic. Jake stood before me, his hand raised and muttering underneath his breath.

"Jake," I said.

He nodded at me. "Let's go."

"Where are we going?"

"Can't you feel it?"

He was right. Misery, fear, and all the darkness flowed to me, and I fell to my knees. I covered my ears as screams of many of those who had just died pressed against my eardrums. It felt awful, the worst thing I could imagine. My heart banged away like a rocker's drum as fear had its way with me. It must be the archangel in me.

Run! Go back indoors, back to Mom. You won't escape evil's wrath forever, but you can for a little while.

Jake stuck out his hand. "It's okay, Harper. I almost ran back in. But we can't."

I untangled my body and took his hand, let him help me to my feet and into his arms. He held me tight. His lips felt soft, warm, and safe on mine. Except that's an illusion as nothing was safe, not even us. I still heard the dying. We had to help those still alive, to keep their souls out of harm's way.

I squeezed Jake's hand. "Let's do it."

Jake spoke the chant. "Take nos quo everto es." A warm glow covered us, and we stood inside a giant orb. It rose into the air, and before I had time to adjust, it zapped west. Jake and I fell into a tumble of arms and legs. He apologized. "I'm still getting the hang of this sorcerer thing."

The orb deposited us on the ground, just outside the town's only library, and dissipated. Looking around, we saw nothing. Neither living person nor thing shared the area, nor did we hear or see any of the demons.

There were smashed windows in most of the buildings on Main Street. Vehicles clustered along the street. Some of them had crashed into others, but not one of them held bodies, living or dead. The only sound came from a few crows flying or perched on streetlights or roofs.

The library's door creaked open. A head stuck out. I recognized Mrs. Gimble, the head librarian.

"You two!" she hissed. "Come inside. Quick."

We hastened up the wooden steps with as much stealth as we could manage. I winced at each little sound our footsteps made. I'm sure any demons hanging around heard.

We ducked inside, and Mrs. Gimble shut the door behind us with a click, and she set the locks. Back in the shadowy corners of the shadowy room, people huddled together.

"There are others in here," I said.

Mrs. Gimble nodded. "Some patrons were here when those, those, oh, I don't know what they are, anyway out of nowhere they came, striking at people, animals, and birds. I allowed in those who made it inside before the black smoke things headed for the front door. Helped by a couple of library aides, we quickly locked every door and window. Any cracks we stuffed with cloth, hoping that kept them out. I mean, they looked like smoke, for goodness sake! The power died, so we've had no lights since then. We huddled in here, but that didn't stop us from hearing awful screams and the sounds the creatures made coming from outside." She shuddered. "The sounds...they made my skin crawl, and I clapped my hands over my ears, hoping that would keep them out. It didn't work. It reminded me of drunken revelers who'd gotten out of hand at a Halloween carnival one time." She grimaced. "No, no much worse than that."

Jake said, "I remember this building has a basement. Can we get downstairs to it? All of us?"

"Certainly," said Mrs. Gimble, turning to the others and pointed at a door near the drinking fountain. "Everyone, head through that door. The stairs will lead you down to the basement."

She didn't question Jake's orders. I'm sure if this happened before the apocalypse, Mrs. Gimble would have taken umbrage at some teenager telling an adult what to do, but the circumstances had upset her.

There weren't as many people with us as I imagined as an LED candle lit up and revealed about fifteen bodies. I recognize Pete's father, Pete's stepmother, Mrs. June—who lived down the street from Mom and me—along with three families, two teenagers from school I didn't hang out with, and Stacey Brown. Stacey looked disheveled, a few rips in her frilly blouse and mud-splattered jeans. Her usually neat hair looked as if rats had nested in it while what skin showed gleamed as pale as her bloodless lips. She stared at me, but she didn't even act like she knew Jake or me, just wandered around, stopping once in a while to tremble. Not that long ago, I might have felt satisfaction at the stuck-up queen bee brought low, but no one, not even she, deserved all of this.

"What's going on out there?" demanded Mr. Jameson. "We only stopped here for my wife to check out a book. This woman won't let me or her leave. What is going on out there? My son is at home, alone."

I spoke. "No, Pete's not, Mr. Jameson. He's at my house, with Jake's mother and mine. As for why Mrs. Gimble won't let you leave, there are demons out there."

Chloe Jameson giggled. "Demons? Posh! Is this a Halloween prank a couple of nights early? Do you stupid kids and this person think we are fools to believe that? What are these demons doing—stealing souls? I bet some of you teenagers are behind all that fracas going on outside for the past couple of hours. Pete can take care of himself, but my poor little chihuahua, Poofy, is at home alone, too. No doubt my baby's fretting."

Mr. Jameson snarled. "You left that mangy cur in the house when I said stick her out in the backyard when we left to come here? If I find any of that fleabag's poop in the house, I'll kick it out!"

"Poofy will get fleas if I'd put her outside when we left the house. She hates it outside anyway." Mrs. Jameson started tearing up.

Mr. Jameson shook a finger at her. "If that mutt leaves one piece of evidence on the rug, I'll—"

Jake looked grim as he broke in. "Neither Mrs. Gimble nor Harper nor I have lied about demons. They're real and they're out there, destroying Moon Ridge. Anyone Mrs. Gimble allowed inside will tell you the same thing. Nobody is getting out of here because that might alert those demons that there are people in here."

Mr. Jameson huffed and folded his arms as he glared at Jake. "You're Jake Hewitt. You and my son hang around together. I also know you're the son of that crazy lady who thinks she talks to the spirit world, as she calls it. I can see that the apple doesn't fall far from that pathetic tree. Demons. Right."

Tall as the older man, Jake stared back. "Well, my mother is right. You don't have any right to talk about my mother like that."

"Kinda late defending her, aren't you? I remembered you and Pete laughing about her 'craziness.' last summer at my house."

I stepped in front of Jake before he said something he might regret later. When things got back to normal, then he and Mr. Jameson could hash it out.

I said, "Sir, look, whatever you think about Mrs. Hewitt or not, there are demons."

Mr. Jameson stared down his nose at me. I could see the distaste in his eyes and along the tight lines of his mouth.

"Who the hell are you?"

"Harper Doyle." I took a deep breath and added as an afterthought, "Sir."

He didn't say anything else, but he grabbed his wife by the arm and towed her over to the locked front door.

"Mr. Jameson, you shouldn't leave," I said. "It doesn't matter if you believe it's demons or people making those sounds you've been hearing, but something bad is happening out there. Head downstairs to the basement where you have more of a chance to stay safe."

He stopped, his wife stumbling against him. The noise from outside the building sounded terrifying. A strange voice whispered from the other side of the door, and Mrs. Jameson's face went pale beneath her makeup.

"Maybe they're right, Rick. Maybe we shouldn't leave this building." The woman tried to free her arm from his grasp, but she proved unsuccessful. "Whoever, whatever...just whispered, sounds scary."

He turned on her with a snarl. "Don't you care about that worthless dog at home? The one you whined and bitched about when you first saw it in the pet store in Richmond months ago."

Her eyes grew big and shiny with tears as she whimpered. "You got Poofy for me."

He dropped her arm. "Personally, if there are demons, I hope they found her and ate the little rat."

Still crying, Mrs. Jameson grew angry. She stomped past him and with one hand on the knob and her other one at the lock, she screamed at him.

"Poofy means more to me than you or that rotten kid of yours! I will not let anything eat my dog, and I'm leaving here to get to her. Poofy and I will stay locked inside that house—and that means neither you nor that brat is welcome to hide out in it—until what is happening is over or the Marines come rolling in. Then I will pack all of my stuff and leave this rat trap of a town with my dog and go back to New York City."

He sneered. "Go right ahead. I hope some demon has its way with you."

I watched with horror as his wife turned the lock and twisted the knob. The door swung open. Several breaths hitched and the smell of fear rose in the room. I brushed by Mr. Jameson to stop her as Jake muttered Latin beneath his breath.

Mrs. Jameson giggled and turned around to stand in the open doorway, looking at everyone.

"See? I know I'll get home safe and sound."

Just as my right hand almost reached her, black smoke swooshed in, caught her around the middle like a hook, and dragged her outside before she could scream. The others in the room did it for her, shrieks filling the room, and running footsteps slapped against the floor as people scattered to hide.

Mr. Jameson stood there; his lower jaw dropped.

I shook my fist at him. "See? Demons."

I ran through the doorway, Jake right behind me. The door slammed shut behind us, its locks clicking into place. Most likely, that's Mr. Jameson, believing us now. What a coward. He didn't care about his wife or what had occurred to her, just worried about himself.

Jake and I tiptoed around the building, searching the area, hoping we would find Mrs. Jameson still alive. We found no sign of the woman, black smoke, or shadows. We did find books lying on the ground, but not a sign of who left them. A shrill screech filled the air and the books rose into the air and flew at us.

Jake chanted, "Libri volatilis obviam nos, reverto ut vestri quietus locus iterum."

The books halted in mid-air, though a few spines got close enough to touch the tip of our noses. They dropped back to the ground.

"That was fabulous, Jake." I gave him a thumb's up.

He grinned at me. "I am beginning to love being a sorcerer. It's sweet being a magical superhero."

"A superhero, huh? Getting a little above ourselves?"

"Isn't this just sickening? Aren't you two a little too old to be playing house?" Several voices said it at the same time.

We broke apart to find Mrs. Jameson standing in front of us, no longer alive. Her skin had turned gray, and her eyes shone dark as night, while her carefully styled hair hung ragged and dirty and her dress in tatters. Several things had crowded inside her body.

Jake lifted his hands, readying himself.

With her lips shaping into a shark's smile, the demon-possessed woman shook a finger. "We'll have none of your tricks, little magic boy. Try it, and we promise to snap your pretty little girlfriend's neck. You might be faster and stop us, but again, we might have the faster sleight of hand. Are you going to pull a Houdini on us now?"

Jake fisted both of his hands, but he lowered them to his sides.

The corpse laughed.

"Now, was that hard to do?" They flicked her eyes at me and drew closer.

I gulped and would have backed away, but her hand flew out and seized me by my arm. The grip tightened, and painted nails cut into my skin, bringing up blood. Tears welled up in my eyes.

"Please."

The demons snickered. "Please, please, please. Please what? Please don't hurt me? Please don't eat me? Or please don't possess me?" They let me go, and pressing a hand over the bleeding cut, I staggered over to Jake and stood by him. "Don't worry, little girl, we don't want to possess you. That's old hat with you. Though you look delicious, and we bet the archangel in you tastes good with ketchup." They crooked the dead woman's neck and a long serpentine tongue slipped out, slurping its way around the dead woman's painted lips.

"What are you?" demanded Jake.

The tongue slithered back inside. The chilling smile still hung on the lips. "We are Legion, for we are many." The voices blasted out of her mouth. "Well, a few of the demon army anyway. It has been a long while since we inhabited a body. This flesh pleases us, although the slut fought us when we came to her. She fell to her knees and cried, begging us to let her go, to let her and her little dog leave this town." It snickered, actually a lot of snickers. "We told her we would let her go free. The dumb bitch, we stretched the truth. As we filled her body, we set her free all right. We ate her soul all up, and now she'll never have to worry about a thing anymore. At least, not until we deposit her tattered entity in Hell. We promised ourselves to get her doggie later. Haven't had a dog in eons." The face grew ugly and gnashed teeth.

"Harper, get back indoors," ordered Jake. When he saw the indecision in my eyes, he pushed me away. "Go!"

I bolted and he rushed at the head woman. I wanted to stay and help, but I did what he wanted instead. Besides, what could I do?

Supposedly, I was this Nephilim, a part-archangel, part-human hybrid. I had shown a small portion of powers when I was a baby. But I haven't done anything since then. I didn't get any sense of power within me, not one crackle, and yet, I could feel the evil demons. But that was it.

Jake had magic, and even Cresil had her demon abilities.

Me? I'm nothing but a weak human who can only feel when the demonic is near. Looks like I didn't inherit much from my archangel father.

I knocked on the door. It didn't open. Maybe everyone was down in the basement, which meant I wouldn't be getting inside. I heard locks clicking, and the door opened a crack, a single brown eye peeking out.

"Who are you?" It was Mrs. Gimble's voice.

"It's me, Harper, Mrs. Gimble. Let me in."

"How do I know you're you?"

"Don't you think if I were a demon, I wouldn't be polite and ask? I would bust my way inside."

"Get in." She opened the door and got out of the way.

I slipped inside, and she shut the door behind me, setting the locks again. As if that would keep demons out if they wanted in. I wished I could make sigils appear on the building like Jake could.

We clattered down the stairs to the basement, stepping off the last step onto a cement floor. Out of nowhere appeared glowing orbs, spitting fire. I skidded, losing traction, and fell on my buttocks.

The orbs changed into six tall shadows with red eyes. A low keening noise filled the air. I touched my ears with my fingers and realized the sound caused them to bleed. The keening grew shriller, and I slapped my hands over my ears. It didn't work.

Dizziness overcame me and the bleeding worsened, piping through my fingers. I yelped, but a high-pitched sound came out of my mouth. I thrust out my hands and everything became bright light.

The keening turned into screams.

My vision cleared, and the bleeding had stopped, the dizziness gone. Where the shadow things had been, only six piles of ashes remained.

What happened? I stared down at my hand and found my fingertips glowing. Confused, I lifted them to my nose and took a sniff. A sweet odor touched my nostrils. The confusion grew. Had I done that to the shadows? How?

Close your eyes.

What? "Who said that?"

The voice came again. "Close your eyes, Nephilim, and search within. Believe in yourself and the power you hold."

I looked all around but saw no one. An angel?

"Yes."

"Why aren't you guys whomping the demons?"

"Because the time is not right for us to do so. Besides, I know you inside and out, and I believe in you and Jake. Now you need to get back to Jake and save him. You both need to get your mothers and Pete out of Moon Ridge, plus the others still alive and unpossessed, and go warn the rest of the world."

Suddenly, I recognized the voice. "Cresil? Is that you?"

No answer. A hiss, then it replied. "Yeah, it's me. I hoped you wouldn't realize it."

"We thought that Baal killed you."

"He did. Well, my human body anyway. I am now back where I started: Heaven."

"You're talking to me from Heaven?"

"Later, after we prevent Armageddon, we need to talk. We don't have time for that now. Can you get back to Jake and help him. The longer we both jibber-jabber, the easier we make it for those demon spirits in Mrs. Jameson to harm him."

"But...."

"Go. You have the power."

"Cresil..."

Silence. It appeared she'd left me.

I stood and saw people huddling in the back of the basement, scared. One of them was Mr. Jameson. Lucky for them, the demons had wanted me. Not Mrs. Gimble, though. I understood. Something evil managed to get inside and possess her. Maybe it'd knocked at the door, and she thought it was Jake and me.

Anyway, I didn't find her anywhere so she must have been burned by the angelic light I gave off. Otherwise, those demonic things wouldn't have gotten in here. I told those people to head back upstairs with me, and before I opened the door to go out, I told them to wait for both Jake and me to come back and get them.

Stepping outside, I closed the door. The dark spirits inside Mrs. Jameson's corpse had Jake by his arms, forced to the ground and unconscious. Mrs. Jameson's mouth hung wide open, unnaturally big.

"Hey!" I yelled. "Don't you dare eat him!"

Legion turned to look at me, but they kept their grip on Jake. The demons sniffed with Mrs. Jameson's nose, wrinkling it a second later as if they smelled a foul odor.

"Nephilim. An archangel's get, too. Disgusting. We don't understand how we did not see what you are. We don't understand why any archangel wants to slum with mortals. All this God's sons mixing with human women are unnatural."

I retorted, "And you possessing a body you don't have a right to, is?"

"There are ethics, and there are ethics."

I tried to make myself look more threatening. "Let go of Jake, and maybe I won't burn you pitiful souls, but let you slink back to Hell."

"I don't think so, archangel breed." They lowered their obscene mouth to Jake's head. He struggled harder, but he couldn't break free.

Anger burned like a fever inside me. I couldn't stop myself even if I wanted; I lifted my hands, and hot, bright light blazed from the fingertips.

The screaming of many voices reached my ears. The light vanished, and I saw the smoking, blackened body of Mrs. Jameson barely able to crawl away, the shrieking coming from a mouth with its lower jaw falling to the ground.

Jake pressed his back against a wall, his eyes big and round with shock and maybe even terror.

Mrs. Jameson's body rose in the air and hung there. It bumped several times, spun around, and finally, the evil spirits left the body, which plopped to the ground, silent and still, before it disintegrated into ashes.

The evil spirits ascended to the sky like a giant swarm of bugs.

They became one gigantic obscene face looking down on us. Spine-chilling laughter spilled from the face's mouth.

"All you did, Nephilim, was furnace blast the dead body. Most of us survived. You only got rid a third of the army." The mouth grinned. "The apocalypse is still on time."

They dissipated.

I needed to figure out the power inside me.

Jake joined me, looking apprehensive. "Was all that power inside you all this time?"

I nodded. "I think so. It took my anger to bring it out. My fear earlier also made it come out, when six demons attacked in the library." I glanced at the empty sky. "It still isn't enough to get rid of all of the demons loose on Earth."

"I hope you never get angry with me. I don't want you going nuclear on me if you ever figure out your power."

"I would never do that, Jake." I looked into his eyes. "Never."

He nodded. "I believe you. What about getting those still alive in the library out of here? If there are any alive, you did mention demons."

"There are people in there."

Human screams followed by unearthly roars and laughter came from far away. Chills skittered up my spine. Jake looked at me. "That must be where the main part of Hell's army is."

I nodded.

How can I stop that? I only killed a smidgen of that legion of demons earlier. Do I expect to be able to eradicate the whole mass, including Lucifer and Baal, with only Jake's assistance?

"I'm scared, Jake." I shivered. "I can't do this. How can I stop a giant army along with Lucifer? I have no training or understanding of this power inside me. I don't know how to bring it forth or even how to use it. I think I got lucky with that smaller piece of the Legion." I looked at him. "I'm only a teenager. I only want to worry about what college I'd like to go to when I graduate, worry about passing my math class, and get asked to the prom. Not this apocalypse crap."

He took my hands. "I'm sorry if I acted scared of you earlier. I'd like this to be nothing more than a nightmare, but it's not. I believe you'll get the hang of what you can do. Maybe if we run into one of those angels, you can ask how to control them."

"I could have destroyed you along with Mrs. Jameson's body."

Tenderness shone in his eyes. "But you didn't."

He kissed me, and I returned it, feeling the soft gentleness of his lips. I wanted to keep kissing him. He made me feel better—and safe, too. Except, we weren't really secure, not with demons marching through Moon Ridge and the end of our world hanging over us.

Where are Cresil and those damn angels? Everything flushing down the toilet and God seeming to not care about the innocents living here.

I withdrew, though I still held his hands. "Cresil came to me."

"Wait a moment. Cresil's alive?"

"No, Baal used her for the sacrifice, so her body is no more. She's in Heaven. She became what she was before the Fall. I assume that meant an angel. At least, that's what she told me, through sort of angel radio?"

"Why aren't the angels coming down here and doing something about these demons?"

I shrugged and stared down at the ground, digging in the dirt with the toe of my tennis shoe. "I like to know that, too."

His grip on my hands tightened.

Wincing, I looked back at him. "Jake, you're hurting me."

He released my hands. "I'm sorry, Harper. I'm angry. People are dying, or demons are taking them over, and Heaven isn't doing squat about it."

"You're wrong, wizard boy."

Jake and I spun around to see a bright, sizable ball of light hovering. I recognized Cresil's snarky voice.

"Cresil!"

"Yes, in the spirit."

The light pulsed, growing so bright that it hurt the eyes. The light dimmed until it disappeared, except for two wings made of light behind the translucent figure standing there. I approached it. The being touched me with hands cold as ice. It didn't matter. Cresil was with us. Heart pounding, I began to cry even as I smiled.

"Cresil, it's good to see you," said Jake.

"It is great to see the both of you again. I am here to tell you that Heaven hasn't abandoned this town or the rest of Earth."

Jake asked, "What are they planning to do?"

She didn't reply. Instead, she cocked her head to the side as if listening to someone we couldn't see. "Okay." Cresil's voice was low. "Of course, I understand." She turned back to us. "I had rebelled with Lucifer and the others against God and Heaven. The angels have long memories. They wanted me to prove myself that I'm ready to be allowed back into Heaven for good."

I glowered. "But you proved you're not bad after all, so you should be forgiven. What kind of angels are they? Holier-than-thou types?" I propped my hands on my hips. "If they were so good, then why send the Archangel Michael down to Earth to seduce my mother? I'm not an immaculate conception, that's for sure."

A smile lit up Cresil's pale, ghostly face and she shook her head. "That rejoinder should have come from my lips, not yours, Harper." She chuckled.

"Well, it's true. I think they should let you back in the fold."

"I understand the other angels' reasoning. After all, I've been a naughty demon for centuries." Cresil paused and, with a puzzled look in her eyes, looked up. Her smile dropped, but it returned in glowing fashion, and she nodded. She looked at us, laughing with delight and clapping her hands. "God has declared that I will be allowed back into Heaven. He feels that I've proven myself enough."

She hugged me, then Jake. Her touch felt warm and not cold. Her glow returned in brilliance times ten as she stepped back. We covered our eyes but couldn't do anything about the blast of the unbearable heat.

Suddenly, it became cool again. When we took our hands away, we saw Cresil no longer with us. They had recalled her to Heaven.

Harper, you need to get those still alive in this town out of here. Tell them to get in their vehicles and head for Charlottesville. Cresil's voice filled my head.

"Charlottesville?" I repeated.

Jake looked all around. "Charlottesville? What about Charlottesville, Cresil?"

I'd forgotten that his powers enabled him to hear her talk in my head when she was a demon. I guess it hadn't changed since she became an angel. "Shush, Jake. Go ahead, Cresil."

That is the safest haven for now. Not for long, though. Half of Hell's army has already marched south, toward Roanoke, and those innocent souls they don't take, the demons will destroy. They'll keep on going, heading south and west. The belief here is they will be making their way north and east soon enough. More and more demons are spilling out of the portal, and they are joining those already here.

"Cresil?"

She didn't reply, which meant she'd stopped using the celestial radio to my head.

I took Jake's hand. "Come on, let's get those in the library and then search for other survivors. We need to get them out of town and headed for Charlottesville."

We headed back to the library. It took some effort to convince those inside that it would be in their best interests to escape to Charlottesville, maybe even farther. One woman wanted to head for Roanoke as her mother lived there, but we told her that going west was dangerous with some demons already massing that way and leave it to us to try and help her mother and others.

Everybody fled to their vehicles parked in the library's parking lot or along Main Street. Trucks and cars zoomed out of town, dust and smoke from their exhausts the only proof of their escape.

I hoped none of the demons would stop them.

Mr. Jameson didn't say anything when he found out what happened to his wife.

We followed him to his SUV, the only one left in the library's parking lot. He paused after opening the driver's door and stared at us. "I always believed she loved that little mongrel more than she loved me." He shook his head. "No, I doubt she loved me. Her days as a model were ending, and I represented a safety net for her."

Mr. Jameson climbed in, unlocking all the car's doors. "Well, get in. My son's at your place, so we'll stop to pick him and both of your mothers up before fleeing Moon Ridge." He grimaced as he swept his gaze around. "I've always hated this town. But Dad left all of his assets to me, adding a stipulation in his will that in order for me to receive them, I could never move away. It looks like the demons thumb their noses at his stipulation, and I get to scram out of Moon Ridge anyway."

I said, "Thanks, Mr. Jameson. Just go get Pete, Mom, and Jake's mother. Jake and I need to find who else may be still alive here and get them to leave."

The sun had lowered in the sky.

I glanced at my watch and saw it was late afternoon. Lucky for us, we hadn't run into any demons, although it didn't mean they weren't around.

Not saying anything else to us, Mr. Jameson drove away. I prayed he would get to my house and get Mom and the others out of town. I took a chance my phone still worked and made a call. Lucky for me, it rang, and someone picked up.

Her voice came over the phone. "Harper, where are you?"

"Listen, as I can't be sure how long my phone will work. Mr. Jameson is coming to get his son, plus you and Mrs. Hewitt. He's taking you to Charlottesville."

"What?"

I gripped the phone tighter. "Cresil is now an angel, which she was long ago. She said to get the survivors in this town out of here. Jake and I are staying here to search for any others and get them out of here."

"No, once Rick Jameson gets here, we are coming to get the two of you!"

I wanted to say yes to her. I didn't though.

"No. Jake and I are part of all of this, remember? Now Cresil is an angel, it is up to us and her to stop what is happening."

She pleaded. "Harper, you may have angel powers, but unlike an angel, you're not immortal, and you can die. Please, don't do this."

Did my mother think I had delusions of superherodom? I wanted to listen to her. I wanted her to hold me and tell me it's only a bad dream like she used to when I was a little girl and woke up in the middle of the night screaming or crying. I wanted her to say monsters did not exist.

But I kept hearing Cresil's voice in my head. I couldn't let her down. Not the whole world, not my mother, not even my archangel daddy, not even Jake, who I cared about. Cresil.

Not only had she become my best friend, but she'd become a sister to me.

I fought back the tears and the fear. "Mom, I'm sorry. I'd like to go with you, but neither Jake nor I can. Maybe, just maybe, we can give the devils their due with our combined abilities, at least until Heaven comes to the rescue."

My phone died. It still had three bars, so I guess it was due to Hell's interference. I imagined Mom's unhappy face, blotched from tears, maybe still speaking into her phone that might have gone dead, too.

Jake found a motorcycle, the key still in the ignition. I wondered what happened to the owner, but checking the nearby building got us nothing. Maybe he was possessed or ended up murdered by some of the Legion.

I shuddered, but I still climbed behind Jake as he admitted he owned a motorcycle once until his mother made him get rid of it. She felt he would die riding it due to a vision she had. I just hoped that today was not the day.

But we couldn't be sure if his magic or my angelic powers could teleport us. We stopped along the way on various streets, found people that hadn't left already, told them to head to Charlottesville, then kept riding through town, and finding most of it deserted.

Either many had already left, or the demons took them. We found no sign of any dead. That meant those became human steeds for the Legion to ride and control like puppets.

A half-hour later, we arrived at the edge of downtown.

Unfortunately, a crowd of demons waited for us.

Chapter Thirty-Two—Harper

I had never seen so many shadows, tall, short, all of the things with red eyes. They darkened the town even though night was still an hour away. Out of the wave of darkness, a massive, ugly demon in the flesh stepped forward.

"Baal," I whispered.

The face flashed a grin of sharp teeth. "Ah, little Nephilim, it's so good to see you again."

Jake spoke. "Why don't you and the others give up and go back to Hell."

Amusement flickered over Baal's face as he arched a brow. "But I was thinking about moving here. Earth has such great real estate."

He dropped the grin, and his jaws expanded. Not his voice, but Brian's flowed out of the mouth. "Help me, guys. I'm in him. He ate my soul. I know I've always been a jerk, but the stuff this monster does I wouldn't do. Ever." He began bawling. "Please, please, please. I want my mother and father."

The body stiffened, and Baal shrunk the jaws back to normal, his eyes dark as ink. "I had to shut that whiney baby up. Mmmmmm...maybe it's time to send this boy's soul to

Hell. I never told him his mother and father are down there already; I'm sure they'll welcome him with open arms. They need help to push that giant boulder I've got them trying to roll up the side of a cliff." He guffawed.

To our horror, he murmured, "Tribuo mihi meus mucro," and a glowing orb appeared on the end of a tentacle.

Jake threw out a hand. "Absentis!"

The orb flew out of Baal's grip.

"Stupid brat!" Snarled Baal.

Baal became a long column of black smoke rising until it became a gigantic mass.

Jake muttered, "Addo Vepres Silva nobis." One minute a ghostly Brian kneeled beneath Baal. The next he kneeled next to us. The spirit bawled like the kids he used to beat up.

"Come on, you jerk," I said, gritting my teeth. "For such a big and tough bully, you are nothing but a wimp when a real beast shows up."

He sneered at me as he wiped away his tears. It didn't work, as the waterworks kept raining out of his eyes. "Who are you to call me a wimp?"

A roar filled the air.

Brian looked over his shoulder, and the blood drained out of his face, and he dropped the sneer.

"That's it," he said. "I am getting out of here."

Brian's ghost floated from the area, leaving us to face the demon horde. I doubted he would have been of use to us anyway.

The shadows had combined into one gigantic mass of shadows and tentacles. I wondered if we could defeat it. Jake may be a sorcerer and I, a Nephilim, but I wasn't sure how long we could handle the Hell beast and not lose. I couldn't be sure my powers would work, either.

Jake whispered something under his breath that I couldn't hear, and two plasma balls appeared above his hands, sparking. He threw them at the creature as it stalked toward us. The balls soared through it and kept going until both punched into the side of a building.

Boom. The building sunk into itself.

The thing kept coming.

Jake made more plasma balls and tossed them, along with stakes of lightning bolts, at it. None stopped the creature in its tracks.

Instead, the monstrous fiend roared, shaking the earth. Parts of buildings fell all around us. The ground cracked to reveal holes of molten heat. Suddenly, as if something invisible pulled the rug from beneath his feet, Jake was flipped on to his back.

Moon Ridge, and us, were doomed. Virginia was doomed. The world was doomed.

My stomach rippling with cold fear, I fought to center myself. Do a Zen thing and bring out the Nephilim within me. I closed my eyes and thought of nothing. An iridescent spark lit one corner of my mind. It rose until it was in line with my third eye and filled me until I became the light.

Chapter Thirty-Three—Jake

I lay on the ground, the wind knocked out of me. In horror, I saw the demonic monster above me, roaring and waving its tentacles. I needed to get up. I needed to draw my magic and start hitting at it again. Except waves of dizziness struck when I lifted my head. Fighting the waves, I rolled over onto my stomach, then to my knees and hands.

That's when I saw Harper.

Her head was flung back, and her arms stretched wide, columns of iridescent light snaking from her eyes and fingertips. The glow edged the outline of her entire body until she shone iridescent herself.

She's gorgeous!

The dizziness decreased, but a headache still pounded behind my eyes, and I climbed to my feet.

The shadow thing had left me and whipped a tentacle at one column of the light. It gave off an unholy howl as the tentacle was engulfed in flames. Using another tentacle, it slapped at the fire to put it out, but it must have hurt as it whimpered. The giant broke into pieces and dropped to the ground, once more the demon army, Lucifer in front, Baal beside him.

Lucifer's eyes glowed hellfire red.

"Get Michael's get!" ground Lucifer "Tear her limb from limb. I want nothing left, except her tattered soul that I will drag to Hell and leave it there for some Hell hounds to gnaw for a thousand years."

I ran, stumbling but keeping to my feet. I thrust out my hands, and with a few choice words in Latin, magic shot from the fingertips.

Both Lucifer and Baal laughed and ducked the magic. It struck the first two lines of demons, obliterating their black smokiness.

Baal shifted from shadow to some butt-ugly visage not unlike Lucifer's. He had a head between bulbous shoulders connected to a stocky frame. A sword that shone like black oil in one tentacle, he lunged at me.

Harper appeared beside me. No longer looking human, only iridescent light with heat radiating off, so hot I had to back away. Tentacles of light spiraled from her and captured Baal.

He shrieked to the others. "You bunch of lazy fiends, get this Nephilim off me before she goes nuclear."

Lucifer just smiled. "No, let's see how well Baal can handle my brother's child."

Baal flash Lucifer a look of betrayal.

That's when orbs of brilliant light appeared in the sky above, driving back the darkness. These orbs flew down at the demon army, slashing through it. Demon cries filled the air. The sound of a horn rang. I never saw it or the being who blew it.

The angels had finally arrived.

They swooped upon the demon army. Sounds of battle, along with screams and shouts, filled the air.

Harper and I didn't have time to check it out. She still held Baal in her grip, but her light seemed to be dimming.

I still had my magic, and I tossed balls of it at him. Both of us fought with what we had.

Another fiend joined at Baal's side, and it glowed with a dark light, wings made of the same light outstretched from its back. It gripped a long sword of red in one hand. Its eyes shone red and fierce.

Harper spoke. "Lucifer."

Where before he had been ugly, now the devil had terrible beauty. Beautiful or not, the rotting corruptness wafting from him said otherwise.

Lucifer sneered. "Need help, Baal? It appears that Michael's brat and the human boy who cares for her are thrashing you."

"I am glad you have not abandoned me, my lord. They are yours. Only you should be allowed to cut their souls free and send them to Hell."

"Coward," spat Lucifer. But with joy in his eyes, Lucifer raised his sword. I made two balls of crackling power, and they floated inches above the palms of my hands. I doubted that they would be able to take down this fallen archangel, but maybe this would give Harper and me time to escape.

I'm here, Jake, said Harper in my head. Our powers joined together.

I felt hers join mine—mighty and hot. The noise of battle all became silent. Only the sound of my plasma balls, the thump, thump of Lucifer's footfalls, and the low growl issuing from him filled the air. My heart pounded, and my mouth went dry. I could smell the fear as I sweated.

"Leave them be, brother."

A commanding voice came from behind Lucifer and Baal. I noticed for the first time that all the demons and angels were no longer there. Who'd won?

A grand orb of radiant light appeared behind Lucifer, shifting into a tall, glowing figure with golden eyes.

Baal snarled and lifted his sword high, turning and stampeding at the interloper. That's when everything froze, including Baal. I looked at Harper and saw that she had returned to human form. She clasped my hand. We could still move.

To our misfortunes, so could Lucifer. He still held his massive sword.

He laughed. "You know that old trick doesn't work on me, Michael."

Harper stiffened. "It's my father," she whispered, edging closer to me.

Baal vanished.

Michael's light dimmed and I caught glimpses of a face with dark blue eyes, long, flowing hair the same golden blond as Harper's, it's figure wearing a robe. As the light began to power down, I could see where Harper received most of her looks. I squeezed her hand.

"It doesn't matter if he stays to get to know you or leaves," I said. "You'll always have me. Always."

We glanced at each other. Harper smiled.

I wanted to kiss her at that moment but knew I couldn't as this would be a dumb time. But I promised myself there would be later.

If we make it through this alive.

Stupid inner monologue.

We waited to see what the archangel and his demon brother would do. And speaking of angels, where was Cresil all this time?

"Lucifer, why don't you go back to Hell. It's not time yet for the end of this mortal realm or for you to lead an army into Heaven, if ever."

"Did you think after all this time, I would listen to you, big bro?"

Michael looked sad. "No, you never did obey. When Our Father told you to step down from your little revolution and apologize, did you? No, you spat at Him, laughed, and said something about better reigning in some black hole than being a little cherub at his feet. Our Father knew you would never quit trying to take over Heaven, so he gave you your wish and let you fall into the realm He created from the vision in your mind. He also allowed your followers not willing to lay down arms to fall with you into the Pit."

He glanced at us. "Harper and Jake, get out of here. This is between Lucifer and me. We have unfinished business."

Michael glared at Lucifer. "This is something I should have done right the first time."

Lucifer sneered. "That's right, little girl. Do as Daddy orders. Otherwise, he might drop you in some pit as Our Father did."

A sword of light appeared in Michael's hand.

Lucifer swung first, and Michael slashed out with his. *Clang.* Blade against blade sang out loud, the sounds discordant.

"Come on, Harper." I yanked on her hand. "Let's get out of here."

We took off at a run.

Behind us, the sounds of their fighting rang in the air as the screech of something terrible.

We made it to the other side of town in silence. Not one demon attacked, nor did we see an angel, not a single human, animal, or bird, either. Moon Ridge had become a ghost town, bedraggled, graying, and empty, but without ghosts. What human life had perished, demons had delivered their souls to Hell.

Maybe if Michael won, he could have the good ones sent to Heaven.

Harper thumped down on a park bench in a park with dying grass and trees stripped bare of leaves. Paper and other pieces of trash littered the ground.

"What are we going to do, Jake?"

I held out my hand, and she let me assist her to her feet. "We need to leave town until we hear that Hell has lost for good. Since we never saw Cresil again, I guess all that prophecy crap was nothing more than nonsense."

"Your boyfriend is telling it straight, Nephilim. Except you're not going anywhere."

Out of nowhere, before Harper or I could move, a column of black smoke surrounded her and when it dissipated, I saw Mayor Jones, Harper's neck in a chokehold and his other arm circling her chest, trapping both of her arms. She struggled but couldn't get free.

He had black eyes.

It wasn't the mayor, but Baal using his body.

Baal warned, "We're sorta family, little Nephilim. I'm kind of a cousin to Lucifer, and he's a brother of Michael, and you're Michael's kid. Family or not, move again, and I'll snap your neck."

If I used my magic, Baal might be faster and snap her neck before I zapped him. I've never felt more impotent. Useless.

Chapter Thirty-Four—Harper

Baal held me, his hold tightening as Jake drew closer. Colors dimmed my sight as the air to my lungs was cut off. I remembered Mom's warning about me being mortal, even with archangel blood coursing through my veins.

Baal warned, "Not so fast, hairless ape. It won't take much for me to tear her head from her neck, even in this pathetic monkey suit. Nothing else, I will magick up a knife and slit her throat before you shoot plasma balls at me. Maybe Hell lost the war, and Lucifer might be back in the Pit, but I can still get my revenge." He leaned over to lick my cheek. "Kissing cousins," he whispered to me.

Sickened, I shuddered.

Frustration in his eyes, Jake didn't move.

Baal loosened the grip on my neck a bit, but he still kept a good hold. I wished I could do something. Kick back and strike a kneecap or stomp on a foot. I couldn't. I tried my power, but nothing happened.

Bal giggled. "Is your power cell dead, little girl? It sucks being not like your papa, doesn't it?"

Jake said, "Look, Baal, let Harper go and take me instead. Her magic vanished after Michael showed up, and she is nothing more than a puny human. I have my powers, but she isn't a threat to you or any other demon."

"Mmmmmm. Sounds attractive, except I know you're fibbing. Harper is a Nephilim, daughter of a son of God and a Daughter of Eve. I can smell the odious power within her. I think she used it up until it recharges. I'll let her go for a price. I'll shed this fat guy's skin and use yours instead."

I squeaked. "No, Jake. If he possesses you with your magic, he won't need a bunch of demons."

Baal squeezed my neck again. Colorful balls of light danced in my vision.

Jake called out, "Baal, stop. Kill her, and there's nothing left to stop me from whamming your ugly puss to Hell and beyond."

Baal loosened the hold on my throat. "How shall we do this? Ah, I know."

His hand dropped from me, and he sent me flying to Jake's arms with a shove to my back.

"Are you okay?" Jake touched my bruised neck gingerly, and not waiting for an answer, thrust me behind him. He threw out his arm and opened his mouth to say the incantation.

"Secus velox. Immobile."

Nothing happened. The air stilled, and it seemed nothing moved, not even Jake as he stood still as a statue.

I touched him.

And recoiled. Jake was a real statue!

I caught Mayor Jones walking toward me. Except, his body wobbled like a bowl of jelly. The body crashed to the ground, and Baal stood in the spot, one of his massive cloven hooves on the back of Mayor Jones. He looked down at the man like he would at a disgusting insect.

"Thanks for the use of your body, good mayor, but now I do not need it. The boy will fit me fine, like a new suit of clothes. What should I do to you? Yes, I got it!"

The mayor shrank until he was a cockroach.

Baal lifted a hoof and squashed it. What remained stuck on the bottom of Baal's hoof, and the demon tore it from there and stuck the mess in his mouth.

"Yum. The mayor found his spot in life, right in my belly." The demon giggled. "His puny soul adds to my power."

He looked at Jake, and called out, "Haud diutius a statua."

Jake became a living, breathing person again, taking a deep breath. He glared at Baal. "You're not getting me."

Baal stalked us. "Want to bet? You may be a powerful sorcerer, but I struck down your teacher before you learned all you should know. You are still beyond your potential. Let me in, and I promise I will use that capability well." He paused and cocked his monstrous head. "Hells bells, I might be able to take on old Lucifer himself and rule in Hell. Forget that—and rule this sad sack realm. Afterward, I can claim Heaven." He looked around with disdain. "When I do finally get to reign in Heaven, one last thing will be to get rid of this planet of hairless apes." He shrugged. "Obliteration seems too good for it, but that's what will happen."

He took a step. "Unus." A second step. "Duos." He broke into a run. Just as he opened his mouth, a boom cracked the air, and something zoomed down from above. It slammed into the demon, and both rolled and rolled, going past us and hitting the side of a nearby building.

The wall collapsed in.

Jake muttered, "A orbis of tutela inter nos, supremus nos quod sub nos. Apocalypse tutela."

A loud humming surrounded us and even above and beneath our feet. "What did you just do?"

"A circle of protection. We're going to need it. It might give us time for your powers to rev back up." He kissed me before he turned.

I watched as Baal stood and shook himself like a dog after a bath. He prodded the other with a clawed toe and snickered.

"You were easy to knock out."

The other form rose until it hovered over the demon. It glowed so brightly that I couldn't make out any of its features. Not my father, as this had a smaller form.

"It's not my father. Whoever it is, I hope he or she whoops Baal's butt, but after it does and before it heads back to those Heavenly gates, I am going to demand they let us see Cresil one last time." I frowned. "Where is my father?"

I stopped talking when the angel shot a bolt of light at Baal, who dodged it like a ballerina twirling on his tippy toes.

"Is that all you got, you piece of light?" shouted Baal. A big, black ball appeared in his tentacle, and he tossed it up and down as he eyed the angel in the air. "Why don't you come down here and take me on without all that flying crap?"

The angel floated down and touched the ground.

Baal chuckled.

"I bet you never bowled. I remembered you pansies in Heaven as too good to relax and play around. Might not be what God ordains, right?" He brought his arm back and leaned over and rolled it across the grass.

It streaked for the angel, but the angel rocketed up. The ball shot up into the air after it.

Baal propped a shoulder against a tree. "Okay, bowling balls can't do that, but then it's not a bowling ball. It's an imp. And it's going to rid me of you. Then I can get back to the business in hand before you poked your angelic nose in."

He sent that parting shot and headed toward us. "Michael should have exorcised me back to Hell for good. He sent the others down there, but I escaped. It shows how stupid and pathic angels really are."

He reached out for us, but something surged and shocked him. "Ouch." He grew red-faced as he grunted and tried to shift but couldn't move a muscle.

Jake said, "I think the angel placed the demon under a dome of angel magic."

I pointed out. "Long as it holds the monster. Otherwise, there'll be one pissed off demon if he gets free."

Baal began pounding at the invisible wall of whatever kept him imprisoned. He yelled with a roar. "When I get out of here, I'm going to bash the two fleshies to a pulp."

"You're not doing anything to them, Baal."

I asked, "Cresil?"

"I'm the angel."

I looked up and saw her with the black ball in her hands.

"Want do you want, Pansy?" asked Baal with a snarl. "You sound damn familiar."

"Of course, I sound familiar, dumbass. I'm Cresil."

"You mean the little punk demon who became a real girl? You're dead."

"I decided to join the good guys. Heaven made me an offer I couldn't refuse."

Baal laughed. "What's that? Become a fruitcake?"

"Remember how you used to knock me around? Well, those days are over. Now it's my turn. I'm sending you back to Hell on a one-way ticket."

Cresil threw the imp at Baal. It screeched when it hit the demon in his chest, exploding, but when the smoke cleared, the demon lord stood in one piece, morphed into his shadowy form, and rushed Cresil. She flew backward, but he kept barreling at her.

A sword of light appeared in her hand. Baal magicked up his own made of hellfire after changing to a more solid shape.

Both thrust their weapons at each other. The blades sang, but not in a good way as our ears bled from the sound. Neither paid attention to us, so I snatched Jake's hand, and we bolted. We needed a place to hide.

"Jake, let's head for my house."

We found the motorcycle still intact. Jake slung his leg over it and dug for the key in his jean pocket. Lucky for us, it hadn't fallen out. He stuck it in the ignition, turned it, and the engine roared to life. I crawled behind him and wrapped both of my arms around his middle. The cycle's wheels rolled down the street.

A loud boom filled the air. Flashes of lightning sizzled across the night sky. I could feel the heat all the way here. Another flare sizzled, this time much closer.

I yelled at Jake above the roar of his bike. "We need to hurry. Cresil and Baal are making one hell of a storm."

I wondered about Cresil. Was she all right? I didn't think about it anymore as Jake made the bike race faster. Buildings, trees, lawns, playgrounds, and telephone poles all merged into one long multicolored line. I grew dizzy from the changes, and everything seemed to be spinning out of control as I hooked my hands together at Jacob's belt buckle and pressed my cheek against his back, hanging on for life.

My back grew hot. I peeked over my shoulder and saw a lightning bolt had struck the street only seconds after we passed that spot. A chunk of asphalt gone, replaced by a hole. More bolts struck the asphalt.

I tapped Jake on the right shoulder and yelled over the wind. "Whoever is doing that is getting closer."

The wind tossed back his answer. "I know."

He revved the motorcycle a little faster.

One bolt hit the street right in front of us, and the motorcycle skidded on its side. It crashed against a telephone pole, but not before Jake muttered something under his breath, and we both vanished. We reappeared and landed on a bunch of pumpkins outside of Moon Ridge market.

We rose from the smashed pumpkins, pieces of pulp and seeds on our clothing, faces, and hair. I fished as much as I could get off me, but we decided to head inside the place, having no time to clean.

Lightning bolts fell out of the sky like bombs, detonating on contact with the ground. We made it to the market but found the front double doors locked.

Jake chanted, "Patefacio ianua."

The door lock clicked, and one of the doors slid open. We dove inside. The door slid shut, locking behind us.

Lights off, the place seemed creepy. Walking between shelves full of canned food, I thought shadows in corners moved.

Jake had magic.

I hoped my angelic powers had finally returned as I sensed the evil. I grabbed a broom hanging from a shelf just in case. If nothing else, I can ram it into an eye or two or three or more with the stick part.

"Phasmatis tentati!" Baal's voice bellowed everywhere in the store.

Shadows erupted, shooting from corners, behind the checkouts, and snaking along the floor from the back of the building.

I whirled around, and my broom passed through three shadows. Toilet paper and paper towels rained down as Jake shoved me toward the meat section. I bolted, stumbling, managing a quick peek over a shoulder, and saw that all of the shadows had merged into one giant worm that slithered along the linoleum.

When we made it to the meat section, Jake rummaged among the packaged meats. He tossed each one aside, making a mess in the cases.

I asked, "What are you doing? That worm thing is not far behind."

He frowned. "One of the things Sotuknang did teach me was how to make an army of beasts from meat."

"Excuse me, an army of cows and chickens will stop the shadow creature?"

He paused and looked at me, an eyebrow arched. "No, I will not be magicking up cows and chickens. Sotuknang taught me to make lions, wolves, and tigers."

A loud crash resounded. Heart pounding more than it already was, I stared uneasily at the area from where I believed it'd come.

Okay, that's not far from us. My heart pounded harder.

Baal is going to win this war. He must have done something to Cresil. My father may have gotten Lucifer back to Hell, but he didn't stop Baal.

Or maybe Lucifer killed my father.

Jake had several packages of ground meat scattered on the floor and knelt before them, chanting. Another crash. My heart now in my throat, I whipped around, ready to bring out my inner Nephilim.

Shelves full of stuff flew up as whatever caused them to do so barreled like a train out of control toward us.

I screamed. "Jake. Whatever you're going to do, I would do it now."

Roars and snarls filled the air.

I turned and saw the lion. It stood close enough for me to feel the heat coming off its body. It moved closer, and I pressed back into a glass case full of meat. The lion sniffed. I didn't think it was for the steaks and chicken pieces in the case behind me either.

Jake yelled, "Tentatio vermis!"

The lion roared and leaped past me, nearly knocking me over. Other beasts joined it: four lions, several wolves, and five tigers. They dove into the earthquake of shelves that had just reached us.

The worm reared up, screeching. It knocked aside several of the animals Jake had conjured. But they got back up and charged it again. The lion that earlier had sniffed me had its jaws enclosed over a hunk of flesh, just close to what might be the thing's head. The monster swung back and forth, trying to shake it, and two attached wolves flew off.

The other animals darted in, swiped with claws, and slipped out of the way when the worm fell, trying to crush them. The lion didn't get away in time but got crushed. The wolves let go and loped away.

The monster reared up again. It opened a mouth and swallowed the dead lion.

What remained of Jake's magic animals cornered the worm by the freezer section. One tiger got close enough to leap and sink its fangs into the flesh, pulling until the top part ripped off. The striped cat landed on the floor and spat out the head with what looked like disgust.

The worm's body wiggled wildly. Its bodiless head screamed; the loud sound was horrible to hear. It hurt our ears and both Jake and I fell to the floor.

The remaining lions, wolves and last tiger fell on their sides, screaming.

A gray mist appeared where the head of the worm had been. When it dissipated, there was a new head. Did the original worm do what flatworms do and regenerate?

An unearthly howl arose. It came from one of the wolves. The piece the tiger bit off attached to the canine.

Jake said, "That thing is eating the wolf!"

God, he was right. The thing ate so fast that within seconds the only part left of the wolf was its tail. That went quickly, too. The piece began growing until a second worm hovered there.

I may not be psychic like Mrs. Hewitt, but I didn't see a future for us. Or the magicked animals, either. The worms attacked and absorbed the animals into their flesh. Then the worms merged into one worm, doubled in size.

A hypersonic shrill filled the building, a few more shelves fell, and the glass in the meat case and the nearby refrigerators shattered into glittering pieces.

Jake muttered another bit of Latin. An invisible bubble enveloped us so we wouldn't get cut.

I saw a hot, bright glow hover in the air in front of the demon worm.

"What?" asked Jake, not looking. "Another demon appeared?"

"Remember when the archangels came to battle Baal and his army? They all had that same glow, and when they spoke most of the time, it carried a shrill tone, too. It's an angel, but I can't see if it's familiar."

The angel touched the ground and morphed into an iridescent figure, a shining sword in its hands.

"It's Cresil."

The monstrous worm twisted and turned, dodging Cresil's sword. Cresil darted after it and raised the blade, slashing downwards to cut into the worm's flesh.

Smoke rose from the area as the monster squealed. It swung around to snap at Cresil's head, but she yanked her sword out and flew out of the way. The worm crashed into the meat case, the packages of meat flinging everywhere.

"Let's get out of here," said Jake. "Protectio no more." His hold on my hand tightened as the shield vanished, and we bolted for the front of the store. Just as we reached the doors, Baal appeared, blocking our escape.

"Hello. kiddies. Cousin Baal is back to play with you." His eye went dead. "That damned Cresil did not banish me back to Hell. Heaven sent a shoddy worker in what should have been an archangel's job."

He drew closer.

We stood there like frightened rabbits before the headlights of an oncoming eighteen-wheeler, potential roadkill.

Jake pushed me behind him and snapped his fingers. Sparks sizzled from them. "What Cresil didn't finish, I will." He whispered to me. "I'm getting you out of here."

I felt my power revving up. "No, Jake—"

"Transporto Harper domus."

I found myself about two blocks away from the store.

Jake was still back in the store, maybe battling Baal, maybe dead. He knew I had my own powers, that I could help him knock Baal back on his rear end. To save those powers for the fight ahead, I ran back to the store. The night made the buildings appear as silent shadowy sentries. Shadows appeared in front of me, morphing into different figures. I didn't see familiar red eyes, but that didn't mean they weren't demons.

They wavered back and forth in bizarre shadow play, and their arms elongated, reaching out for me. I backstepped a few steps, but the arms distended even further. The things seemed like caricatures of people. They began to speak.

"Harper Doyle, come to us. Let us touch you." The voices seemed off, cartoonish.

I demanded, "What do you want?"

They dragged out my name in a strange extended way. "Harrrrperrrr."

Instead of scaring me, they made me upset. The things were in my way of getting back to Jake. "Tell me who you are."

"They're spirits of some mortals in this town that I killed and collected their souls. I didn't send the souls to Hell yet." Baal stomped from around the back of the building to stand on the sidewalk where the shadows drifted. He patted one of the shadows on the top, and the thing mewed like a kitten, rubbing against him like a well-fed cat. "Told them if they found you, I might give them back their bodies."

He laughed as if that was a funny joke.

I doubted he would return them to their bodies.

"Free them."

He laughed again.

A sliver of fear coated my anger, but I dared not let him know that.

"Baal, free them of their bondage to you. If you don't—"

He finished with a jeer, "—you'll strike me down? Ah yes, a Nephilim. The bastard child of Archangel Michael, but what I have seen of your puny angelic powers doesn't scare me, little one. I plan to add your soul to my motley collection. You'll soon be a marionette dancing to my tune."

I clenched my fists. "First, I'm not the illegitimate child of my parents. My father married my mother. I bet that is something you can't admit to."

He clapped his hands, looking delighted. "Oh, how nice." He did a little jig, staring straight up. "Hear that? What goes around comes around, and it will certainly smack you in your halo, Michael. You may have been the one to kick me over the edge into Hell, but it will be me using your daughter to smite the wings off your Heavenly body. You'll be kissing my toes when I reign in Heaven."

My anger dimmed. Uneasiness crept into me. I still couldn't figure out how to bring up my powers on command.

Anger and fear do that for me, although a third time they had come on command, but I wished I had more time to figure them out. I had tried a couple of times, but zilch.

"Why don't you make it easy on yourself and come over here." Baal extended a tentacle.

"She's not going anywhere with you."

Jake stood to the left of Baal, a long wooden staff in his right hand, and he aimed it at Baal's head. Above him, Cresil hovered, pointing her sword at the demon.

I grinned. Things appeared to be looking up.

"Ego expello vos Baal, tergum ut Abyssus," chanted Jake.

A bolt of white lightning blasted from the end of the staff, zeroing in on the demon. It struck him with a loud explosion, sparkling smoke blinding him from our sight. When the smoke dissipated, he still stood there amidst a blackened circle of broken cement.

"Guess your magic isn't as strong as you thought, untried sorcerer. You still need more training before you can achieve the power to defeat a demon like me." Baal giggled.

Jake shook his head. "It should have worked. You should be now toasting your toes in the fires of Hell."

A gust of violent wind slammed into Jake and sent him flying into the side of a nearby building. He slid down the building's side to the ground and didn't get up. His staff had broken in half.

"Jake!" I screamed.

Cresil called out, "Baal, let's finished this."

Baal opened his hands wide and out of the blue, another sword appeared in his hand. The demon fell into a stance, the weapon gripped in one hand, and one leg stretched out behind him.

Cresil said, "Darklight. How did you get Lucifer's battle sword?"

Baal whipped the sword back and forth, and vibration came from it in several booming notes. "I picked it up when Michael kicked the dark lord's butt back to Hell. He didn't see it lying on the ground. I figured when the time was right, I would use it over my own weapon." Baal added, "I guess the time is right. Once I strike you down, Cresil, I am hoping Michael himself will appear. He'll have to fight me when he sees I have his Nephilim daughter." He crooked a finger on his free hand and said, "Come on, turncoat. I'm in the mood for angel food cake."

Chapter Thirty-Five—Cresil

Memories of being bullied by this creep and that he dared to harm my friends made my volatile nature flare. I dive-bombed down, screaming. Once my feet touched the ground, I swung my sword, and it met Baal's with a clang loud enough to hurt mortal ears.

His eyes glowered with hate. He snarled and kicked out a cloven hoof, sending me crashing into some trash cans. Trash flowed over me and the ground. My sword flew out of my hand and hit the ground a few feet away.

Dirty and upset, I crawled to my knees and felt pain from one of my wings, the one on my right. I tried to flap it, but pain spiraled through me as light dripped like blood to the sidewalk.

I grimaced. It didn't matter. My hand against a wall of a building, I climbed to my feet. Not able to fly and get the sword, I called it to me. "Addo meus mucro volo."

Nothing happened. *Well, angel donkeys.* I tried again, this time using a transporting spell to take me to the sword. I needed to hurry.

Baal stalked me, Darklight gripped tight, and a shit-eating grin plastered on his face. "Transport mihi ut meus mucro."

I still stood in the same spot. *The spell didn't work.*

Baal broke into a run. He held his sword high. Yeah, I'm dead meat. The demon would be feasting on a slice of angel cake.

The bastard grinned as he thrust Darklight into and through me, jamming it into the brick of the building behind me. I stumbled away as he grunted and pulled it back out.

I tripped and fell in the street. Standing, I saw that I had bloody scrapes on my knees and the palms of my hands. *This can't be happening; I'm not flesh.* Yet, I saw the wound in my middle bleeding red, not light. I hobbled to where my sword lay. I just hoped I would get to it before Baal came at me. Being flesh meant that even with my sword, there was a rather good chance Baal would kill me.

Angel feathers.

Chapter Thirty-Six—Harper

I scurried over to Jake and, digging a hand underneath one armpit and snaking the other around his side, I pulled him over to the side of the building and sat him up.

Jake was like dead weight. He grew aware as his eyes fluttered open, and he scrambled to his feet with my assistance. I led him to a nearby gas station and convenience store. Luckily, it had been left unlocked, and we entered.

Able to do it himself, Jake limped over to a big box and sat down. He looked at me. "Where's my staff?"

"You mean that stick of wood you had? It spilled into pieces when you hit the side of that building."

He glanced down at his hands. "Nothing's broken. Baal's right. I'm no sorcerer, only a boy pretending he could save the world."

I used some paper towels and a big bottle of purified water I found and wiped at his face's blood and dirt. "Jake, you're a good sorcerer. It's just you never got to finish your training. Baal knew that when he butchered Sotuknang."

He gave me a halfhearted grin. It hurt to see him like this. Even if what might be between us fizzled out if we stopped the demons, he would always be my friend. I took his hand and gave it a gentle squeeze.

"I'm sorry, Jake. I wish I could turn back time and save Sotuknang. Maybe that's one of my angel abilities. I don't know, or might never know, since I can't flip the switch to make them work when I need them." Standing, I tossed the dirty paper towels in a trashcan. "If I could figure out how to bring them forth without being angry, maybe we could stop what's happening."

Jake jumped to his feet. "Sit. Maybe if you stay quiet and do something like yoga, you can find a way.

"What do you mean?"

He pointed at the box. "Sit. Humor me if nothing else."

I sat.

When I opened my mouth again, Jake shook a finger at me and gave me a look. I sighed and settled in, closing my eyes, and trying to empty my mind to everything. It was difficult at first, as one resonance butted into my Zen state. Thud. Thud. Thud. It filled me like an eternal hum.

Then revelation hit me. It came from my heart. As it kept beating, it started to slow down. Lowed by it, the blackness behind my eyelids changed to red and, within seconds, to different sparkling colors. They danced like sprites, skating in my vision. I wanted to open my eyes, but I couldn't. My lids had grown like heavyweights. A flash of bright light and I stood in nothingness.

"Hello?" I called out, my voice echoing. "Is anyone here?"

"Do you expect someone to be in this place, Nephilim?"

I saw Sotuknang sitting with his legs crossed in mid-air, sucking on half of an orange. Done with it, he tossed it aside, and it vanished. He grinned.

"Things are no longer needed. They just become nothing. Very ecological, wouldn't you say?"

I finally found my voice, and all I could do was sputter like a nincompoop. "Ah, but, but, you're—"

He finished for me. "Dead? Not technically. Not an archangel, either, not anymore. Maybe I am just an illusion in your mind. Something to help you summon your powers."

"How do I switch them on?"

He pointed at me. "You're asking me? I didn't know enough to keep Baal from blasting me from existence. I couldn't complete Jake's training. And you think I can let you in on your secret? I'm a loser of an archangel. Heck, Sotuknang's not my real name. Just something the Hopi called me the first time one of their shamans saw me in a vision in a sweat lodge. Just as Michael is not your daddy's true name, either. No mortal can say our real names. It's too alien for your tongues."

"So, I'm not going to find my powers? This is all a waste of my time. I mean, after all as you said, I'm talking to something not real in my head."

He cocked his head to one side. "Did I say you wouldn't bring them forth? No, I'm just not the one to help you. Only you can unlock the door that holds it all in." He stretched. "I've got to go now. Ta ta." He blinked out.

Maybe he'd never been there, and I had been talking to myself. Maybe I needed a shrink. Or maybe...

I floated through the nothingness as I spied a black speck in the distance. It never got closer no matter how much I traveled. I began to think it never would when I realized my self-defeating attitude. Maybe that was part of me unlocking the door. I needed to get over my defeatist attitude.

I closed my eyes and muttered beneath my breath. "I am right in front of it."

When I reopened my eyes, I found my nose against a large black door. I took a step back and leaning over to peer close, I saw a tiny keyhole. It had no key inserted in it.

Why was this done to me if I wasn't mean to have my powers? Somehow, I didn't believe anyone did it, but me.

As a baby, I did it. Later, twice I did it, but through fear and anger. Then I had managed to use them a fourth time, without anger or fear. I'm ready now to free them so Baal could be sent back to Hell.

How?

A different male voice spoke in my head. "*You need Cresil to merge within you again. Together, you will free your powers and banish Baal for good.*"

Huh? "Who said that? Did you get in my head and hear my thoughts?"

"*I am the one who beget you. My daughter, it has been foreseen that you will stop the end of the world, but only if you share yourself with Cresil.*"

"Cresil and I are both happy to be shed of each other."

"*My daughter, you must do so. There is no other way. You must hurry, as Cresil is losing to Baal. If the demon strikes the next blow, he will end her existence. The prophecy won't be worth a plum nickel. Do it.*"

"Prophecy, drophecy," I muttered. "Absentee father for most of my life and now he thinks he can order me around."

"*What?*"

"Nothing."

"*Knock it off and repeat after me. Cresil, come to me. I summon thee to resume the quarters of my body.*" He sounded aggravated.

"Okay, here's goes." I called out, "Cresil, come to me. I summon thee to resume the quarters of my body."

At first, nothing happened. Just as I tried it again, I felt something tugging like at the end of a fishing line from me to it.

Cresil didn't want to merge with me again.

I understood how she felt, but still, I closed my eyes and chanted, "I summon thee, Cresil," repeating over and over.

Something slammed into me. I opened my eyes, gasping. Jake held my head in his lap.

"What's wrong?" he asked.

"Cresil is in possession of me again."

He spit out, "What?"

"Not my idea. My father suggested it."

He looked startled. "What? I told you to do the yoga thing to free your powers, not let her back inside you."

Cresil sounded piss. "*Don't tell me I'm possessing your body again?*"

"Yes, you are, Cresil."

"*Why?*"

"Because my father ordered me to do it. Something about all this concerning not just me, but you, too, the both of us combined, to unlock my Nephilim inner self. I just can't be a superhero by myself. I needed my trusty sidekick."

"Great! Just what I wanted to be: a part of you and a sidekick to boot. Here I thought I graduated to angel status, but instead, I get sent back to demon detention."

I let Jake assist me to my feet. "I'm sure once Baal is banished, Heaven will set you free of me again. I don't think it is set in stone that it's a lifetime partnership. Now, concentrate, help me make some kind of metaphysical key to unlock my inner Nephilim."

Cresil sighed. *"Whatever."*

Something surged within me: a current that rollercoasted through my nerves to my brain. Another blinding light exploded in my vision, and I felt myself falling away.

Cresil shrieked in my head.

****

I awoke to find myself on my back.

Jake kneeled over me, concern in his eyes.

"Harper?" he asked, sounding unsure. "Or Cresil?"

"I'm here, Jake."

"Thank God." He kissed me.

Had it all been some hallucination?

"Let me shove your hallucination up your you know what."

I struggled to sit up. "I'm okay. No dream though."

"I would say not."

Strange, but I didn't have a headache or any other pain, but I felt invigorated.

"Well, since I am stuck in your skin, do a test to see if it works."

I crossed over to a freezer. "Jake, I am going inside this freezer. Lock me in."

"No, I'm not doing that."

"Jake. I need to see if I can blast it open or something like that. I need to do a test trial." I climbed inside.

"I don't like this."

He shut the door. A loud snap of the lock echoed, locking me in. I put my hands against the door and concentrated.

An anxious Cresil paced inside me.

I ignored her and felt a charging in my skin like a thousand ants. A large ball of pure light zapped from my fingertips and punched into the door. *Boom.* The door fell off its hinges and crashed to the floor.

That felt pretty cool. I actually power fisted the freezer door. I was a super hero.

"Don't get cocky. A freezer door is one thing, but Baal is a major something else."

I placed a hand on a hip. "This is advice coming from someone who once was the demon of impurity and laziness."

"Look, can't a girl be forgiven for that? I'm one of the good guys now."

I stepped onto the door and into the store.

Jake grinned. "You did it," he said and hugged me. "Guess I got a superhero girlfriend now."

"Hey, a girl's got to keep up with her sorcerer boyfriend."

"Hey, you two, knock it off. I helped some."

Jake and I ignored her and kissed. She muttered something else in my head. Finally, when she grew quiet, I withdrew from Jake and seized his hand.

I grinned. "Let's go dispatch Baal back to Lucifer with our regards."

"Yes, so I can get Michael or somebody from Heaven to get me out of you," said Cresil.

As Jake and I headed for the front door, I asked, "You don't want to save the world, Cresil?"

"Yes, I want to. I want to kick some demon butt. But I am tired of sharing the rent."

We walked out into the waning sunlight. We had been through this all night. It was dawn, but to the thickening darkness smudging the sky like an infestation, it seemed more like night still. That's when I realized the darkness came from zillions of flies and shadows. Shadows that were lost souls Baal had collected.

Baal stood among them as a gigantic shadow with tentacles.

He sniffed. "Ah, I smell a Nephilim with her powers awakened. I can still slit your pretty little neck." He turned to Jake. "As for you, half-done sorcerer, the next time I will fry your brains out, and not just slam them against some building. I am not repeating that mistake again."

He took a couple of steps closer. "Nephilim, I plan to strangle your soul and eat it before I rip Cresil to shreds. Yes, I know the little bimbo is inside you."

I felt Cresil struggling, so I let her take over.

She shouted through our mouth. "Baal, you're such a braggart. Think you can take on both me *and* Harper? That's where you will screw up. Two are better than one."

Baal replied, "Cresil, you are too lazy to do squat. I don't think being an angel again will make much difference. Now put the Nephilim back on."

"Oh no, I am no longer that demon. I let you and Lucifer lead me like an adoring puppy and what has it ever gotten me? A hole in Hell fit only for the lowest lost souls. All I got out of the Fall was rejection and being put down by fiends like you. Why did I ever listen to you guys?"

"Easy. You were one of the youngest angels. It didn't take much to lead you astray, ready to rebel at the drop of a halo. You wanted to get rid of your wings, 'cause you believed Lucifer's words about 'better to reign in Hell than serve in Heaven.' You just didn't get it that Lucifer would do the reigning; the rest of us would be nobility and suckers. Guess who is one of those suckers?"

Cresil steamed. I knew she wanted to strut up to him and punch him.

So Baal wouldn't hear me, I thought at Cresil. *Don't listen to him, Cresil. It's what he wants. He'll blast my body. That includes you in the bargain.*

"*You're right,*" she agreed. "*I acted no better than a rebellious teen when Lucifer convinced me to be a follower and not a free thinker.*" Cresil shook our head and stuck my chin out at Baal. "You're not getting me to snap at you, Baal. You won't win, either. Harper, Jake, and I will bust you back to Hell. God is right to trust in his mortals. They won't let a Hell on Earth happen anytime soon."

"Hells bells, you sound as if you admire these hairless apes."

"Better than many I met in both Hell and Heaven."

Cresil quieted and I was in control once more. That's when I saw the orb, so bright it nearly blinded me.

Baal flash a cannibal-sharp grin. "Hello, Michael."

Chapter Thirty-Seven—Harper

The ball of light shifted into a man dressed in jeans, a chambray shirt, and a pair of army boots. He had long blonde hair tied back in a ponytail. He carried a shining sword with intricate symbols etched into the blade.

Dad.

Except he didn't feel like a dad, more like Michael, the head archangel who led the hierarchy of Heavenly Host. Not real like the fathers my friends had, but more like the President of the United States—untouchable.

He approached me. Though he appeared like an older human man, I saw his not quite human, glowing golden eyes.

"Harper..." He stretched out a hand.

I put up a hand. "It's all right, Michael."

His forehead furrowed. "I did not mean this to end like this for you. I didn't mean to hurt Clara or you. You have to understand; not being human, that made it beyond my comprehension. I did it on orders from God."

"Yeah, yeah, let's put all this stuff on hold. Don't we have a world to save and Armageddon to stop?"

For a second, the glow in his eyes vanished to show two very human blue eyes full of frustration. The glowing ones returned. "Yes, of course."

He turned to Jake and threw something at him. Jake caught a staff made of red colored wood, covered in symbols. "That is the staff of Moses, sorcerer. Use it wisely."

Jake stared at it. "This belonged to Moses?"

Michael shrugged. "Moses was a simple man who believed in simple things. I felt one who is a great wielder of magic deserved a staff that parted the Red Sea." He smiled sadly. "Sotuknang would be proud of you today." He turned to me. "Cresil, it's time to fuse your powers with Harper's."

I could feel Cresil grinning. "*Let's give that demon some Heavenly clout.*"

My powers grew white-hot; Cresil had joined hers to mine. We had become like a nuclear reactor. That scared me for a minute, but I swore I felt an invisible hand in mine.

"*We can do it together, Harper. Like sisters.*"

We stared at Baal. He showed neither fear nor concern. Instead, his tentacles hit the ground like whips. One by one, black smoke appeared and dotted various spots around Baal and the ghosts. The smoke became sixty demons of all shapes and sizes.

Baal licked his ugly lips and snickered.

Michael said, "No honor, I see. The bully can't fight his own battles, but he must have a gang to back him up. I am sorry I did not seal the portal after tossing Lucifer in."

"Did you think I would take you on with insects and some ghosts? Of course, I summoned some soldiers from Hell." He wiggled his heavy hairless brows like worms. "As demons, we never play fair."

Michael shook his head, "You never played fair as an angel, either."

"Come on, Dad, we can do it."

Shocked, I realized I had called Michael 'Dad' and glanced aside at his face.

He didn't look at me, just kept his eyes on the demons, his face like stone.

Okay, so he's not my father at this moment. He might not be when we won.

I focused on the demons.

"He's focusing on Baal."

I didn't answer Cresil, just drew in a breath.

Michael yelled, "Charge!" and ran with his sword upraised. Cresil and I together formed a lightning ball between my curved fingers and ran.

We met the demons.

Jake zapped with his new staff, screaming in Latin.

The flies surrounded us, biting. Michael flashed a white light, and all the flies became crispy nothings. Good, that's one problem down.

I toss lightning ball after ball at demons and ghosts. At first, I didn't want to harm the spirits. It wasn't their fault what the demons had done to them.

When one of them punched me in the stomach with an ectoplasmic fist, I decided all's fair in war.

Most of the ghosts fled when they realized Baal had his hands full to keep controlling them. The few that stayed proved easy to exorcise. With just demons left, I switched Cresil's and my focus to shooting power through my hands and turning them into yucky goop. We sent their actual forms streamlined back to Hell.

I ended up being careless. As finally the last of Baal's minions was vanquished, I heard a noise behind me. I pivoted around. The blade of Baal's sword hung inches from my face. No time to get out of the way. No time to make a lightning ball and shove it at him. My life flashed before my eyes.

"Harper!" Michael leaped and knocked Baal to the ground. No longer in human form, Michael became pure light, with wings of light sprouting from his back. Instead of the blue eyes, I saw the glowing golden ones, anger blazing in them. He lowered his sword but did not take his eyes off the demon, pointing the tip at Baal's chest.

I hitched my breath, and my heart pounded. Instead of him sticking it in, he carved an odd symbol with the tip, right over where the heart would be if Baal had one.

"Come, Harper, join me. Jake and Cresil, too. I would like to cut this bastard into pieces for threatening you, Harper, but the world comes first. The time to stop the end of the world is now."

Cresil and I joined him, Jake, right behind. Michael laid a glowing hand over mine and I felt as if I lost a part of me. Cresil, in her angelic form, stood on the other side of me. We formed a circle around Baal.

Michael chanted as he kneeled and held his sword like a cross before him. "Ego expello vos tergum ut Abyssus, nunquam ut reverto hic." The sword's symbol glowed with light. He said, "Point your hands at Baal and repeat what I just said."

Baal's eyes widened, and he screamed. "No!" He pleaded as Michael continued to chant, even crawled onto his knees and begged. It was to no avail as Michael ignored him, and the four of us chanted. A ring of white fire surrounded Baal. He fell to his side and lay there, screaming.

The fire blazed higher.

I didn't feel any heat off it, only iciness.

It engulfed Baal. His screaming grew shriller, then died.

Michael lowered his sword, and the fire vanished.

Baal was gone, too.

Michael saw me. "We returned Baal to the Pit, and the fire has sealed the portal for good."

I could feel a difference about Moon Ridge. It was cleaner, like spring had arrived.

We had won.

Michael took a step toward me and held out his hand. Not sure if he came to me as Michael or my father, as his eyes still glowed even though he'd changed to his human form. I went into Jake's arms and shook my head at the archangel.

"I will leave you then." For a second, it looked like he sagged, but then, he held himself ramrod straight.

Jake asked, "What about Moon Ridge, the people?"

Michael said, "Once they realize the demons are gone, they will come back. The same for the rest of this state. As for those souls Baal stole and did not stay to fight, there are no bodies to return them to, so I will find them and shepherd them to Heaven." He looked at Cresil. "It's time to leave. We are no longer needed here. I'll let you say goodbye to your friends, but only for a few minutes."

A flutter of wings and Michael left in a sprinkle of glittering light. Had I been stupid to show my fear of him? I might never see my father again. My only memories will be of him fighting like a warrior and banishing a demon.

I wanted more than that. I wanted a father who would help me with homework, who hugged me, and was there at the dinner table.

But I wouldn't get that with the Archangel Michael.

A jingle of bells chimed. I turned to Cresil.

She sighed and shrugged her shoulders. She had a 'what can I do as it goes with the territory' look splashed across her face.

"I am being called home." She hugged me. "I will miss you, Harper. Okay, I don't miss you and I joined together. But I feel we have become good friends." She cocked her head. "Actually, sisters."

I choked back tears. "Yes, we're BFFs. Feel free to visit anytime."

Cresil withdrew, gave Jake a quick hug, and shook her head. "I don't know if they will let me."

She vanished before our eyes until only her sad little smile remained. It dissipated. I took Jake's hand.

"Let's go to my house and wait there for my mother and yours to return."

Jake gave a quirky grin. "Knowing my mother, she probably already has them on their way back, as she read tea leaves or her Tarot cards and found out a couple of hours ago that we won."

I laughed as we rode the motorcycle down the street.

"I don't need cards to see the future. Demon-free is all I ask for." I leaned against his warmth as we walked down the street.

I wished my future had my father in it, too. But that would be too much to ask.

Chapter Thirty-Eight—Harper

As soon as Jake and I made it home, the front door swung open, and both Mrs. Hewitt and Mom came out. Mom barreled down the porch steps and to me, grabbing me in a hug, sobbing. She managed to tell me Mr. Jameson never took Mrs. Hewitt and her to Charlottesville as Mom decided to drive them in her car.

Mrs. Hewitt and Jake hugged each other, too.

"Thank God, you're safe," Mom said, drawing back and wiping at her tears. "The power came back on and the news on our TV talked about how rescue crews are coming to Moon Ridge to find out what happened and look for any survivors who hadn't manage to get out since we'd gotten the worst of it. The governor even spoke about asking for FEMA's help. Which the President and the U.S. government granted pretty quick."

"It's over, Mrs. Doyle," said Jake.

"Are you sure?"

I nodded. "We're sure."

She sighed. "Pansy had her cards out on her lap while I drove us to Charlottesville. Just as we got there and we parked in a diner's parking lot, she told me to turn around.

She told me the cards let her know it would soon be over and the demons sent back to Hell. She had tears in her eyes when she said the cards also communicated you two would be safe." She frowned. "Where's Cresil?"

Jake said, "She is an angel, and Heaven called her back, after she helped us defeat the demons."

I licked my lips as I thought about how to tell her about my father. "Mom?"

"Yes." She peered at me. "Is there something else?"

Nervous, I fidgeted, shoving my hands in my jean's back pockets. "My father fought with us."

No emotions flickered across her face, though her body stiffened. I wish she would say something. Even if she just said she didn't want to hear anything about him.

She shifted. "I assume as the Archangel Michael?"

"Yes, as the archangel." I stared down at my shoes, not wanting to see her face as I added, "He was great with that sword of his. And he helped us exorcise Baal and Lucifer back to Hell. If it weren't for him, I don't think we would have gotten rid of the demons, no matter the foretelling about Cresil, Jake, and me."

"I see."

It still hurt her to talk about him. I wondered if the lies about him and his true purpose with her and me might always twist her heart with pain. I took her hands.

A single tear escaped one of her eyes and slid down her cheek. For a moment, she appeared older than her age.

I wrapped her in my arms. "Don't worry about him, Mom. You have me. We made it this far without him in our lives, and we can exist to the end of our days without him." I drew back. "I suspect with me being a Nephilim whose powers work, I'll run into him here and there. But I doubt it will be to take me out to dinner or whatever fathers and daughters do together."

She rubbed her eyes. Then she reached out to tuck a loose strand of hair behind my right ear. "Oh, honey, I am so sorry that you don't have an ordinary father. You deserve one."

Jake snorted. "Ordinary fathers can be absent, too, you know. I haven't seen my deadbeat dad since he took off when I was a baby. We know why Harper's isn't around. What's my mortal father's excuse?"

My mother patted him on the shoulder. "I'm sorry for you, too, Jake." She placed an arm around each of our shoulders and led us toward the house. Mrs. Hewitt had already gone in. "Let's get inside. I have soda we picked up in Charlottesville, and how about I make us some sandwiches? I might be able to dig up a bag of chips in the pantry. Pansy bought an apple pie at that diner before we left. Does that sound good to the both of you?"

Jake said, "Sounds great to me. I just realized I am famished. Demon bashing is ravenous work."

I laid my head against Mom's shoulder. "It sure is."

****

That night, I sat at my desk in my room. I stared dreamily ahead, not reading the book I'd taken from my bookcase.

Earlier, the four of us sat down to a dinner of tuna sandwiches, chips, soda, and slices of apple pie. The best supper I'd ever had.

"Jake, you're right. Demon slaying does bring an edge to this tuna sandwich," I mumbled around a mouthful of bread, tuna, tomato, and chipotle mayo.

He just grinned before he took a swig of his soda. Later after dinner, we sat on the porch steps and enjoyed the early evening. Since their house had been destroyed, Mom allowed Mrs. Hewitt and Jake to stay with us. Mrs. Hewitt got the extra bedroom, and Jake would sleep on the couch.

I broke out of my daydreaming, looked down at the open book on my desk, and grimaced. Soon, Jake and I would be heading back to Dogwood High, in a month, after Thanksgiving. I thought we might need more time before we did.

Mom pointed out that Jake and I needed normalcy in our lives right now. All the kids that survived what happened in Moon Ridge whose parents returned would need that.

"Look at those towns hit by tornados and hurricanes in the news," Mom said. "They work hard to get back to normalcy, and Moon Ridge will, too."

Things would be interesting around here with all the rescue crews, FEMA, and investigating teams trying to determine what caused the destruction. I felt sure that Mrs. Hewitt and Mom might let up enough for Jake and me to check things out. Maybe make sure no one discovers any paranormal evidence. What supernatural happens in Moon Ridge stays in Moon Ridge.

Someone cleared their throat behind me. Had Mom come in without me hearing her? I turned around in my seat.

Not my mother.

My father stood there, not in all his angelic glory, but in human form. His hands stuffed in pants pockets, he scuffed a booted foot.

I stood. "Hi, Dad, or do I call you Michael?"

"You can call me...Dad."

"I see you're not in archangel mode. I wasn't sure about calling you Dad yet."

"No, I thought that this would be more comfortable for you." He cleared his throat. "I prefer it myself."

I grew suspicious. "Is this about Nephilim work?"

He whipped his head up. "Can't a man stop by to see his daughter?"

I stood and approached him. "Of course, you can. I just thought that with you being an archangel and me part of some divine plan, that Daddy and his little girl stuff had a different set of priorities."

He reached out a hand, then dropped it.

I stared into his eyes—human blue—and saw the insecurity in them. Big, bad Archangel Michael felt unsure about his kid, maybe even scared.

Honestly, I didn't know how I felt about him. I mean, he didn't have a nine-to-five job like other fathers. He was a hero, I guess, but not like a soldier or policeman or firefighter. No, he fought demons and maybe even other angels. I'd been human all my life until I learned otherwise.

I looked at his face and saw his eyes shining, but not from being an angel.

Is he crying?

I walked up to him and touched one of his arms. "Dad, it's okay to love me. I think I love you, too."

He hugged me, and I hugged him back, neither of us saying a word. A loud gasp broke the stillness.

We both turned and saw Mom standing inside the room, one of her hands pressed against the wall while the other covered the spot over her heart.

It hit me. He had done the archangel thing and hadn't entered our house the usual way.

Dad moved away from me. "Clara."

She didn't answer, just stared at me.

I grew uncomfortable.

"Uh, Mom, Dad came to visit me."

She glared at him. "I hope you aren't here to take her away and go fight some nasty demons. She's still under the age of eighteen and in my custody. When you left, you never said otherwise." Her hands became fists. "Once was enough. Take her again, and I'll fight you tooth and nail."

He shook his head. "I'm not here as an archangel or to take her away from you, but as her father."

She blew out a breath, though she still clenched her fists. "You could have come by to talk to me first about visitation rights."

His lips had a wry twist. "I figured you would have slammed the door in my face. If I had appeared in your front room, I could imagine what you would have done. You always had a great right hook." He smiled. "You look great. Blue always did look heavenly on you." Redness splashed across his cheeks and the back of his neck.

Do archangels blush? I saw the way he looked at her. I don't think heavenly had anything to do with how she looked.

A flash of understanding came over me. *He loved her.* Maybe in the beginning, it had been all about getting a child for the coming apocalypse, but I think it turned into something else for him.

I turned to look at Mom and caught something in her eyes, too. She still loved him. No matter all the pain and hurt he caused her, she never had fallen out of love with him.

Interesting. Maybe there was a chance for me to get them back together again. I knew it wouldn't be easy. I'm sure Heaven had its plans for Michael, but kids I knew had fathers fighting wars in foreign countries they didn't see for a long time. We could work around his job schedule. It would just be a little more complicated than the norm, that's all.

I piped up. "Hey, Mom, got anything left of that apple pie Mrs. Hewitt bought?"

She blinked. "Uh, yes, we do."

I grabbed Dad's hand. "Come on, Dad, Mrs. Hewitt bought this great apple pie. We have soda, too."

He followed Mom and me out of the room and downstairs to the kitchen. The tension between them hovered like a thick wall of stone that began to crumble.

Stopping the end of the world was easy, but getting your parents back together, especially when one isn't human, that's not so simple. But I'm a Nephilim, and I bet I might be able to pull it off.

Maybe I could hack this archangel for a father thing yet.

Just as I moved to follow them into the kitchen, a knock came at the front door. *Now, who's that?* I crossed over to it and pulled it open.

Cresil stood on the porch. Instead of looking angelic, she looked like an ordinary human girl. Dressed in jeans and a hot pink T-shirt with 'Where are my minions?' splashed across it; she wore black sneakers, too. She had her dark brown hair tied in several braids. "Hi, Harper, I'm back. Guess what Heaven wants me to do for my new assignment?"

I poked her in the cheek.

"Ouch! That's hurts, Harper."

I sputtered. "You're flesh and blood."

"Yeah, sucks, doesn't it? But Big G in Heaven decided that this is the next best thing for me."

She strolled past me without waiting for an invite. A bright pink suitcase on wheels trailed behind her. I closed the door and she turned to me.

"As of now, I am your cousin, Cresil. I've come to stay with you and Aunt Clara for good, as my parents have passed away." A big grin flashed upon her face. "Because you see, I'm your guardian angel."

Epilogue –Harper

Halloween arrived with the scent of burning pumpkin, sticky candies, and a gentle autumn breeze hinting of winter not far away. Most of Moon Ridge was a ghost town, but those who survived had come back.

To keep it all normal for the children, they decided Halloween needed to happen. Mrs. Hewitt and Jake were finally living in the trailer FEMA gave her until their house was rebuilt, but Jake promised to drop by for a late dinner and to watch a DVD after he finished his training with Sotuknang.

Yes, it appeared Heaven brought Sotuknang back and he had resumed training Jake. Heaven seemed to have also fixed it, so no one noticed that the world had skipped six weeks in time.

I convinced my parents to go out to dinner, and that Cresil and I would manage quite well, giving out candy to the trick-or-treaters. After much reluctance on Mom's part (I sensed this had more to do with my archangel father than leaving Cresil and me alone with costumed children), Mom finally left the house, Dad's hand pressed against her back as they headed to the car in the driveway. Minutes later, I watched them speed down the street, the last light of the late afternoon shifting to dusk, heading for Charlottesville and that diner Mom and Mrs. Hewitt stopped at when they escaped from the town.

Dad really likes their apple pie.

About eight, the candy ran out, and just as I laid my hand at the light switch ready to turn the porch light off, a shadow darker than the night bounded up the steps. For a minute, my breath caught, but the porch light was still on, and I saw it was Jake. He carried a pizza box that exuded a delicious odor.

"That smells good. Pepperoni?"

Jake's grin grew broader. "Yep, it has that, plus sausage, roasted chicken, mushrooms, and anchovies."

"Anchovies?"

His smile grew sheepish. "I like anchovies."

I stepped aside to let him enter, clicked off the porch light, and shut the door before locking it. I followed him into the living room.

He deposited the box on the coffee table just as Cresil walked out of the kitchen. With a flick of his hand, the box's lid flipped up, and inviting odors grew heavier from the pizza reveal.

Jake shrugged off his jacket and tossed it to the nearby chair, clicked his fingers, and a DVD appeared out of thin air. "This is science fiction with scary aliens as the bad guys. I figured aliens might be all we could handle after our supernatural adventures."

Cresil snatched it from him and peered at the green egg glowing on the cover. "After living in Hell most of my immortal life, these creatures will have to be worse than demons if you want to scare me."

Later, halfway through the film that Cresil watched intently, Jake and I snuck outdoors for a few minutes. An almost-round moon rode the dark sky, with what looked like a trillion stars lending their light along with it.

"Jake, how lovely!"

"Yes, lovely."

I tore my eyes away from the sky and looked at him. Though dark, I knew he stared at me and hadn't meant the night's beauty. My breath hitched.

He stepped closer.

My breath hitched again. My heart pounded.

He whispered, "Happy Halloween, Harper." His breath heated my lips as he kissed me. He tasted of pepperoni, sausage, chicken, and cheese, even the saltiness of anchovies, but it wasn't the flavor of those I cared about, only him.

He withdrew. "If you don't want me to kiss you, I understand." I heard the uncertainty in his voice.

I placed both hands at each side of his head and brought his lips back to mine. "Just kiss me, Jake Hewitt."

And he did just that.

The End